KEL

Diandra Daulton

DORRANCE
PUBLISHING CO
EST. 1920
PITTSBURGH, PENNSYLVANIA 15238

Dorrance Publishing Co
585 Alpha Drive
Suite 103
Pittsburgh, PA 15238
Visit our website at *www. dorrancebookstore.com*

ISBN: 979-8-88812-061-3
eISBN: 979-8-8881-2561-8

I sat up in bed, my heart racing and breath coming in gasps. I'd had another dream, a dream of him. I rolled over quickly, turning on the light and scrambling for my journal and pen. I wrote furiously trying to save every detail. The more I thought about the dream, the more it faded. I wrote until I had lost everything I had remembered. It was a race between the pen and the dream world.

My breathing slowly returned to normal and my heart settled into its quiet, steady rhythm. The dream was gone, but the warmth of his memory haunted me still. It was security and love, a comfort I had never felt and yet felt I had always known.

I closed my journal and turned the light off. I told myself I would read it in the morning. I always told myself this. It was late and I was desperately in need of more sleep. I would have to ponder the dream later.

I lay back down and closed my eyes. The memory of a stranger who never felt like a stranger, twisting in my head. As I drifted back off, I wondered who this man was that felt so close and familiar and, but was a perfect stranger. I did not know this man, had never seen him but for my dreams.

And yet it seemed my soul yearned for him, and my heart mourned his absence.

I sipped my coffee as I tried to get ready for work. Normally I waited for my coffee until after I was dressed and ready to go. But today, with the dream haunting me once again... I needed all the extra help I could get just to get dressed. I really needed to go into the office today, despite my wish to stay home.

Struggling into my pants, and not tipping over with the fuzzy sleep weight that was my legs proved only slightly easier with the assistance of my coffee. How disappointing the coffee didn't work quickly enough. After only tipping over once to unceremoniously sit on the bed, I managed to get my pants pulled up and buttoned. *First win for the day*, I smiled at myself.

It was a very busy time for work, and since the company had expanded I was relegated to straight office time to try and keep up with the paperwork load. I worked construction, or at least, that's what I still told people. I used to be out on the job sites working with the crew, but now with the big expansion and larger contracts, there was too much office work for me to go out on the jobs anymore.

I put my belt through the loops on my jeggings, once upon a time I had sworn to never wear leggings of any sort. I wouldn't be part of that trend, yea I'm a convert. The thing is I'm too practical, and these pants are stupid comfortable for the cheap price I pay.

I turned around and opened the sliding doors on the closet, and just stared at my clothes while I took another sip of coffee. Slowly I sorted through the pretty blouses and chose a blue number with multiple layers. The bottom layer fit snug against me, ending just above my hips. The following layers rippled and fluttered as I moved each slightly shorter until the very top layer ended just below my breasts.

Wistfully, I looked at my carpenter pants and the blue company T-shirts. I missed the days of wearing those to work, but even my boss didn't wear the company T-shirts anymore. "We are the face of the company," he would say, "We need to look clean and professional."

I grabbed a pair of knee-high boots and walked back into the kitchen. It's a large kitchen for a small house. The house is an old eighties era trailer, cheap thin walls that are terrible for heat and air conditioning. It's a three-bedroom two bath, but the living room, dining room, and kitchen are mostly open floor and take up half the house.

I plopped down in a chair and began to pull on my boots. I was really not motivated to go to work today. I just wanted to stay home and be lazy. I looked around the empty house, so much space for just me.

That strange loneliness I sometimes felt stole over me, and I had the thought of 'my girls' again. I wanted my girls. But the problem was I didn't even know who they were. I didn't really even know what I meant by 'my girls', I didn't really have any friends and certainly not any girlfriends.

About three years ago was the first time this had happened to me; I had a memory of my two close friends that I called cousin and sister. But the problem is, I was never that close to anyone. Except they felt like lifelong friends who had just been ripped from my memory. I had asked my family about them, well my mom when I could be convinced to talk to her on the phone anyway, and got the "you are losing it" answer so I passed it off as a dream.

I really felt like something was missing though and every time that loneliness hit me, I felt that even more fully. I was starting to not feel like myself, like I was living a lie. A story someone had made from an old life, but they had forgotten to completely rid the old life. And now it was bleeding through, I shook my head. That sounded completely crazy. How could my life be a lie? I mean it's my life and I am living it.

Six months ago, there was another interruption in my life. I started to dream of Him. I don't know who He is, or where He is. I don't even usually remember the dream. I had started in the last two months keeping a journal when I dreamed of any of them and trying to remember more. But even as I would write in my journal the dream would slip from my mind.

It was like an invisible force was trying to pull it away without my noticing. But I did notice, and I was getting frustrated. I felt like he needed me. And I desperately needed him, and that really bothered me. I don't need anyone and I don't want to need anyone. Needing people leads to bad roads, and I've been there once before so I refuse to go there again.

I looked at the clock and sighed. Memory row would have to wait, it was time for work. I zipped up my boots, rinsed my coffee cup and walked out the door. I probably should lock my house, but I live way out in the middle of nowhere with no neighbors for miles and felt safe in my little corner of the world. I didn't even have friends who came out this way, so no one really knew where I lived.

The drive to work every day was tiresome, an hour drive into New Orleans on a good day, with all the terrible rotten drivers. I couldn't believe how many people lived here after I started driving into the city. Seems like they should all be dead from stupid driving. Must be a divine intervention keeping them alive.

After the grueling drive to my office, with a lot of road rage and some swearing, though I tried hard not to give in to that urge and it was not all on my part, I was finally settling in behind my desk. I sometimes did work at home so I took my computer with me daily, just in case of ever having a day where I didn't feel well enough to go to the office I could still get my hours in.

I got my computer out of my bag and set it up, opening my email and turning the phone to answer instead of just voicemail. I checked my messages and opened my folder of work stuff. Then I got up and started more coffee in the pot. I would need all the help I could get today.

As I settled into work and got my rhythm going, I let my mind wander again. Unlike my usual spells of loneliness, this one stuck around and I was beginning to feel rather sorry for myself. I wasn't much for pity, so self-pity was about the worst thing I could think of feeling.

I needed a vacation, that was all. As lunch time approached, I decided I would go out to eat. I changed my mind daily, sometimes I brought lunch or ordered lunch in or went out. On my lonely days, I went out. I wanted to be around people when I felt lonely.

I closed my laptop and locked the office door. I glanced around, considering local restaurants. I just wanted to walk. I already had my parking spot and was not willing to give that up. I started walking at random, not really thinking about where to just calculating mentally the distance to walk.

Boss, as I referred to my boss all the time, wasn't coming in today so it would just be me for lunch. The work crews all took their lunches to work with them, it was hard to make time to leave a job site. I remembered the days of sandwiches and chips or just snacks for lunch. It was a good diet plan. Office work is not a good diet plan. I chuckled quietly to myself at that thought.

As I approached the restaurant, I smiled. I always seemed to end up at the Italian place when I wasn't really thinking. I do really love Italian food. I love all food truthfully, but Italian in my books is the best. I have a love fest with pastas and bread and butter and garlic. There really was no way that those foods couldn't make any meal better as far as I was concerned.

I entered the restaurant and found a lunch crowd and inwardly groaned. One thing I haven't mentioned, I don't like people much and hate to be jostled in a crowd. I know it's a contradiction with loneliness and wanting to be surrounded by people. It's a fight I have with myself constantly. I don't want to be crowded by people, but I feel the need for people to be around. Or rather with people life wasn't so bereft, even if the press of a crowd was like a physical torture being visited upon me.

I quickly stepped around the waiting patrons and asked for a table for one. On a stroke of luck there was one immediately available, and it was even the seat I usually preferred and tried to always sit in. So I took my seat, ordered an unsweet tea like any good northerner and read the menu. I didn't really need to read the menu; I almost had it memorized and still usually ordered the same thing. But reading a menu in a restaurant was a normal thing to do, so I did it.

The door opened and closed as people came and went with the bell ringing constantly, the waitress came and took my order and I sat quietly observing the people around me. There was the man who should practically own this place since he ate here so often. I had the idea he was here at least once daily. He knew all the staff by first name, and a lot of their families.

The woman with the bad A-frame haircut who likes to order the staff and patrons around like she owned the place. She had once tried to tell me I couldn't sit where I was and needed to move to the other side of my table because my shadow cast over her table and she didn't appreciate me blocking her sunshine. Inside, away from the window, she was upset that I blocked the sunshine. I had kindly told her I was happy where I was, then in my passive way turned my chair so I couldn't see her anymore.

The restaurant was full and busy, people everywhere. Some faces I knew, some that I did not. I saw people together laughing and joking and the ache in my chest grew. I needed something, something I couldn't get here. Something it felt like I had once had, but somehow lost. I hated that need, it felt like the itch in the middle of your back that no matter what you can never reach.

I sat there reflecting on that, that I could mourn what had never been. The man I dreamed of isn't someone I know or knew in my past; I didn't even know if he was a real person. The two girls I missed were never people that I had met. But the ache of their absence felt real. The loneliness that could be unbearably overwhelming was real and I didn't understand it. I felt a tear track down my cheek, and wiped it away.

I must present a sad sight, sitting alone in a crowded restaurant and crying for no reason, thankfully a quick glance told me no one had noticed so I didn't receive any pitying looks. I locked away the lonely sad thoughts, and straightened in my chair just as my lunch was set in front of me. I didn't like pity, not pity from others or self-pity. It always seemed a waste of time and energy. Lately though, I have been feeling a lot of self-pity for my self-imposed loneliness, I'd have to do something about that.

I had ordered spaghetti and meatballs. An old favorite of mine, a perfect fallback for a miserable feeling day. After adding cheese to my spaghetti, I picked up my fork and wound the noodles in for my first bite. I've seen people who cut their noodles to eat spaghetti, I think that's an abominable way to eat it. You have to wind the noodles around your fork, and when you get the trailing noodle that always happens you suck it in. Like *Lady and Tramp* shows. Cutting pasta into little pieces is weird.

The door to the restaurant opened, and I glanced up. A man with broad shoulders came in the door and walked to the hostess. When he looked over towards my end of the restaurant, my hand froze, my bite of lunch almost to my mouth. I probably looked like a caricature of myself, cartoonish maybe with my mouth open to receive my bite but frozen in place staring at someone.

He had sparkling deep blue green eyes, a chiseled slightly pointed chin, full round lips and a smile that could knock a girl over. A quick glance around told me that the other women in the restaurant had noticed him too. I snapped my eyes back to the man and watched the hostess almost trip over herself to get his name and find him a table. Like me, it appeared he was alone.

But his looks weren't why I was frozen looking at him, I recognized him and felt like I knew him, beyond just that recognition. My heart had skipped a beat when he walked in. It was as if an old friend had come back after years apart. It was impossible for this man to be here; I had been dreaming of him for months. Dreaming of this man, who had just walked into the restaurant and was now standing before me as real as any person.

I continued to stare at him, spaghetti still poised, I wanted to rush over and throw my arms around him and squeeze the air out of him in a hug, and maybe kick him because I also felt he shouldn't be here. I had never felt such strong and conflicting urges about any person before, especially not someone I didn't know.

And then, our eyes met and his eyes widened briefly in a look I can't quite define, then narrowed in a frown. I looked down at my plate and took my bite. Forcing myself to focus on my food and not look at him. Even without looking up I knew when he sat, and that he indeed sat alone. I also knew that he was still watching me. I ate quickly, paid my bill, and hurried to leave the restaurant.

As I walked by his table, I glanced at him from the corner of my eye. He still had a frown fixed on his face and was openly watching me walk by. His frown caught my attention fully, I didn't understand it at all, and I stumbled and bumped into a waitress nearly causing her to lose the tray of lunch dishes she was carrying to a table. I mumbled embarrassed apologies and fled the restaurant, all but running back to my office. I felt out of breath and out of sorts.

I sat down behind my desk again, determined to put the man out of my mind. But I couldn't, all afternoon while I worked he was in the back of my mind. His frown had broken a piece of my heart, where I had felt elated and excited when I saw him; he had frowned and looked... well I wasn't sure what the frown had been, but it still tore at my heart.

That had hurt me in a way I couldn't understand and didn't want to even think about right now. I worked hard to focus on my job and before I knew it, it was four o'clock and time to go home. I packed up my computer, cleaned the coffee pot, it still had the full pot of coffee I had made that morning and packed up shop.

I got in my work truck and began the drive home. Thoughts of the man and the loneliness that had vanished when I saw him, only to come back full force when I left the restaurant, had me distracted on the way home. I didn't even care about how bad traffic was. I pulled into the driveway, and walked into my house.

As I turned on the lights I felt again that something was missing, no one greeted me when I got home and that, today of all days felt wrong. Where were my friends or pets, why didn't I even have a fish? Just something to make coming home less empty. But I wouldn't get a pet, I couldn't justify asking someone to help care for it, besides I didn't have anyone to ask, and I don't do well with fish, they were too fragile and my best efforts had never been enough growing up.

I sighed and set my purse on the side table near the door and set about making a drink and dinner. I was too lazy for anything fancy so I got a burger from the freezer and some fries. As my dinner cooked I sipped my drink, a whiskey coke this evening, and looked around the sad little house again.

There was nothing personal or special here. I had a basic couch, ugly and gray but it served the purpose. A T.V. that I rarely turned on. But no pictures or knickknacks. I didn't even have posters on the walls. I had once decided to decorate the house, but then when the day came to go shopping, I found other things to do instead, and I never did try to decorate again. It took too much planning and time.

I growled and kicked out at nothing. "Stop this, you're being stupid. You have work, and a house. You can pay your bills and still afford to eat. There is no reason to be a silly twit." I often chastised myself aloud, it was sometimes just nice to hear a voice in the house.

I took a moment to remember what it was like to hear other people in a house, loud voices clashing together trying to be heard first. Laughter, jokes and maybe a little music. Not that my own house had ever had that, but I did when I was growing up.

I didn't live close to any family; I had moved away years before stating I needed something different. Well I had definitely gotten different. My family is loud and boisterous, and very 'in your face' and my life here was quiet and boring. I guess I just didn't fit in with them anymore, when I left, things had changed. I had changed, and no one knew the real reason behind why I had left.

The sound of the smoke alarm going off dragged me from my melancholic thoughts, and I growled in sheer frustration. Yanking the pan off the stove, I twisted the knob and turned off the burner. Quickly, I scooped my burger patty out onto a plate and examined it. A little crispy, but still edible. I got the fries before they too became burnt crispy critters and moved to my couch to eat. I made it three bites into my burger before I decided I just didn't want to eat. I was too emotionally raw, and the food was upsetting my stomach. I hated days like this, when I couldn't get the emotions under control, it happened most often after a dream of the man. But the dream, and then seeing him in person had twisted everything inside me into tight knots of pain. Pain I didn't understand, and the harder I tried to untwist the knots the tighter they wound.

I sighed and took the food back to the kitchen, I guess I had lunch for tomorrow. I packed up the food and spun around to place my plate on the floor. It was as if I expected a dog to be there to lick it clean. I didn't have a dog. I hadn't had a dog in years, not since I had moved to the south.

Sometimes weird little habits like that hit me, I would turn to tell a friend a joke but there was no friend. I would set a plate on the floor and realize there was no dog to lick it. I even once called for a dog as I was leaving the house. I always brushed these off as weird misfires in my brain. I had grown up with pets and friends, so I just blamed old memories for the instances.

I always talked myself out of getting a dog though, and tonight with everything not having one when I had expected it to be there was the hardest. I worked too long hours to justify it. And what would be the point of a dog if I had to pay for 'Doggy Day Care', might as well just have kids at that point.

"Stop! Just stop!" I said loudly and forcefully into the empty kitchen. I took the plate to the sink, and rinsed it before placing it in the dishwasher. "You are a grown woman, Kel, you have a life and house and your bills are paid. Stop moping and wishing for something else." Sometimes like pep talks out loud like that would help, not today. If anything it made me feel worse.

I stalked out my kitchen and practically threw myself down on the couch, angry at myself. I took small sips of my whiskey and coke drink and stared at the wall willing my mind to go blank. It was a trick I had taught myself, to be blank and only exist. I hadn't practiced in years, not since.

I stopped that thought, that would not help with the blank mind. I closed my eyes and titled my back against the couch. I needed the bliss of quiet empty thoughts; I needed the images and feelings to fade away. I thought of the sky at midnight. Dark and open and quiet. No beginning, no end, just empty.

I jolted upright with a start at the cold liquid slosh into my lap. I groaned and dropped my head back; I had fallen asleep and spilled my drink. Nothing like the cherry topping to a crap day. Sometimes I felt sure this world was out to punish me. I couldn't explain why it felt that way, except that, like today, sometimes there was just no end to bad.

I heaved a bone-weary sigh and got up to clean my mess. No sense letting it stain the couch. I collected the cleaning spray and some paper towels and began to mop at the droplets, thankfully most of the drink had soaked into my clothes first. I finished and placed my now empty glass on the counter. I needed a shower and some real sleep.

I wandered down the hall to the master bedroom, carefully averting my gaze as I passed by the empty other two rooms. I didn't even use them for storage, I could never bring myself to open those doors and stare into that void. Heaven knows why I bothered to live in a three-bedroom home with it being just myself.

It always felt like the rooms should be full, like there would be people or things. I used to imagine one as a guest room with a spare bed, and a pillow and cheery comforter. And the other could be an office, I could set up a desk and my computer. Then on days when I stayed home to work, I could do it not from the couch.

But I couldn't open the doors, not since the first time I had looked in those rooms and seen the empty bareness of them. I had cried for hours; an uncontrollable depression had swept through me and my chest had ached from the heaving sobs for days after. That was enough that I never looked into those rooms again, and had developed the habit of looking away from them whenever I walked down the hallway.

I took off the day's clothes and threw them lazily at my laundry basket, missing entirely and finding that I couldn't even dredge up annoyance at that fact. I would usually pick them up and put them in the basket, but I was feeling too tired to care. I would be annoyed about the clothes in the morning. I couldn't spare the energy today.

I drug my feet into the bathroom and flipped the water on, waiting only a couple minutes before hopping in. A couple minutes was enough though, the water was scalding! Biting my lip and trying not to slip in the tub I adjusted the temperature. I like hot showers, but even I don't want to boil.

I did my routine scrub down and conditioned my hair. I have very curly hair, naturally so. And it's a fickle beast about the care it receives. I had finally figured that out in my mid-twenties, and now in my early thirties I had hair almost to my lower back. It was soft, and could make the most perfect curls. That is until the humidity spiked and I would look like a sheep who touched a light socket.

Finishing in the shower I toweled off and braided my hair for bed. I looked at myself in the mirror, narrow oval face, thick dark brows, bright blue eyes. I didn't see much in my reflection, there was a sadness tucked behind the eyes and a tightness to the set of my mouth. I searched my face, looking for something. Or anything to explain why I hated to look at myself.

I didn't think I was ugly; I was pretty enough. I love my hair and my eyes; they are my favorite parts of me. I had a good body shape, curves in the right places and I wasn't overweight. I had long legs, so what was it that made me hate to look at myself? It was like I was looking at a copy, and the copy was wrong somehow.

There was something missing in me, and though I couldn't say what, it was like the missing thing was a neon sign pointing at me. Like it said "Incomplete!" in flashing letters.

I bared my teeth at the mirror, how could my own reflection be such a betrayal to me. Shouldn't your reflection be in good favor?

No wonder I was single, I couldn't even convince myself I wasn't a head case. And no guy would want a girl who looks like a second's notice would have her crying and that she didn't know how to smile. I glared at the mirror and angrily slapped the wall, turning the light off. This melancholy was starting to become a problem.

Yawning hugely I climbed into my empty king-sized bed, I really should downgrade to a twin this was more than I needed. I closed my eyes and promised myself that tomorrow would be better. I wouldn't see the man; I wouldn't be depressed, and I wouldn't miss people and animals I had never had.

I snorted even though I knew that was a lie, but I could try. Tomorrow I will make an effort to branch out and make a friend. Someone other than Boss who, though I liked, didn't count as a friend since he wrote me paychecks.

Tomorrow would be better, tomorrow would be brighter. The problem with Tomorrow, is that it never comes to be. Tomorrow is always Tomorrow. Tomorrow never comes, and promises made of tomorrow are bound to disappoint.

CHAPTER 2

"Oh, come on!" The woman next to me laughed. "We'll be late and it's your fault! How come us girls are ready to go and waiting on men?!" The exasperation in her tone made me laugh. We were standing in a living room staring down a hallway waiting for the boys to finish prettying up.

"No kidding boys, let's go! I am starving!" I shouted, and right on cue my stomach growled adding its complaints to my statement. I patted my belly.

The woman next to me laughed, "That's not exactly a reason to rush Kel, you're always starving." She grinned at me in a conspiratorial way and I couldn't help it. I grinned back, she was right. I was either starving or not interested in food at all.

"Yea yea yea," he said before rounding the corner, an exasperated face mocking us. "You're always starving, Kel." He winked at me, and smirked. That smirk of his was a weapon. While he used it to mock you, it would also create havoc with your insides.

I stuck my tongue out at him and then took in his appearance. No man should be allowed to look as good as he did, especially not all the time. I wouldn't complain though, I sure enjoyed the view, and I loved watching other women when they realized he wasn't up for grabs. It was a game he and I would play together.

My heart glowed at the sight of him, my height of about five foot ten inches he had an easy gait and an almost swagger that said he knew he looked good. And he was not wrong, though I don't think he can ever not look good so I am probably biased.

I trailed my eyes over him, dark curly hair with touches of silver. Bright blue green and always smiling eyes. A full mouth, the perfect shape to kiss. He was sporting a scruffy beard currently, but I liked that too.

He had the epitome of perfect Greek God form, broad muscled shoulders down to a tight narrow waist. The jeans he wore accented the waist, and when he moved the muscles in his legs bunched and flexed. His arms swung loosely at his sides and his button shirt stretched the broad muscled chest, hugging in all the perfect places. He had rolled the sleeves up to just above his elbows and it drew the eyes to powerful muscles there.

A pinch on my arm made me spin to the woman. "What was that for?" I demanded with a scowl, facing her. I crossed my arms, and rubbed the spot she had pinched. It stung a good amount. I could already see the red angry welt that meant she had gotten me hard enough I would have a bruise in the morning.

"I want to leave... for food," she replied, drawing out the o's in the word. "The way you were looking at him... well, we'd have never made it to dinner." She grinned at me, and then started to laugh.

I glared at her and turned to stomp out the door...

I sat up in bed and tasted salt on my dry lips. I was crying! I hated to cry! The dream had been so real though, those people felt real and to wake up only to find it had been a dream and all made up in my head... It began to make me feel like this world, the real physical world, was the dream and my dreams were real. It twisted my head around.

I imagine Alice felt this way when she went down the rabbit hole, everything seemed so real that the real seemed wrong. Or maybe Neo in the Matrix movies would better fit the bill. He was in the real world, and then they said 'SURPRISE!' you've been lied to and this world is a fake. I shook my head, trying to clear the fog of sleep and dispel the dream.

I looked at the clock, 5:30 AM. It was close enough to time to get out of bed anyway. I grabbed my dream journal and walked slowly to the kitchen. I was going over everything I could remember so I would be able to write it down. I held a small hope I might keep it all this time.

That was the most vivid dream I had had yet, but the details were already starting to fade. I could still see them though, the man and the woman. She had been significantly shorter than me, with rail straight dirty blonde hair and a mischievous smile that said she got up to no good often and enjoyed every minute of it. Her hair was short, but framed her face nicely. She had dark eyebrows and blue eyes, her left eyebrow seemed permanently raised in silent laughing sarcasm. There was a hidden fierceness that said she would fight to protect the people she loved, but she had a softness of care and compassion too.

I poured myself a cup of coffee and began to write the dream down. I wrote furiously because as I wrote it seemed to be fading faster, like always happened. It's like the longer I tried to remember it the faster it fled my consciousness. I hated that about these dreams, every dream was the same every time.

The man in my dream was a dead ringer for the one in the restaurant yesterday. I thought I had never seen him before yesterday, but that was just the shock speaking. I must've seen him around and somehow my dreams had grabbed his face. That was why I had reacted the way I did. I nodded to myself, justifying the man and yesterday's embarrassing display.

This stranger had become my subconsciousness' outlet for the dream, nothing more. And he probably frowned at me because I made calf eyes and stared open mouthed over my food. I would've frowned at me; I should be thankful he didn't call me out for drooling. Had I drooled? Probably, that man was gorgeous.

I grew slowly more mortified the longer I thought about him and I realized what had made him scowl at me, I could never go eat out again! I wouldn't be able to face him if I did. Looked like I was packing my own lunch for the foreseeable future.

I sipped my coffee and packed my lunch stuff, then headed back to my room to dress for work. It was Friday, and I was feeling down still from the day before and the most recent dream. Two nights in a row dreaming was like slow self-torture. Never before had that happened, I guess seeing and recognizing the man yesterday had thrown my dream self into overdrive.

I grabbed my brightest colored sweater and tossed it on the bed. I decided on my comfy blue jeans today and sent those out the closet door as well. I chose a black tank top to wear under the sweater, it is designed to be loose and comfortable but that means I really need an undershirt with it.

I quickly pulled on my outfit and went to brush my teeth. The sweater is such a vibrant pink that fluorescent lights make it blinding, and I love the silly thing. Just wearing it had lifted my mood already. I grinned at the face in the mirror, careful not to make the mistake of last night and look too closely.

With clean teeth, and a brighter outlook on the day I grabbed my lunch and headed out the door. I could make it through today, then this weekend I would go dancing or something. Go be around people, and purge the loneliness. I chuckled to myself, I probably wouldn't my house but I always thought about it. And they say it's the thought that counts, right?

I hopped inside the work truck and fired it up. I pulled out my rarely used cellphone from the glove box to see if the Boss had sent anything. He knew I never took it in my house. It lived in the glovebox of the truck, or sometimes I would take it into my office to charge. Never ever into my house though.

I couldn't explain my aversion to the cellphone. Everyone had cellphones and ninety-nine percent of the world had smartphones. They were a fact of life, even my mother had a smartphone. But, I hated that I had one at all. It was a necessary evil in today's time and world. But that didn't mean I had to like it.

I had a missed call from my mom, she would be annoyed that I left the phone in my truck again. She was always harassing me about not having it. "What if something happened?" She would say. So what if something did happen? Did she think that her being fifteen hundred miles away and me having a cellphone would help?

Even if something happened, like a break-in and I called my mom she could call the cops. But no one would be here in time, so having the cellphone in my home wouldn't make any difference. And the idea of it inside my house made me feel less secure. I could never get my mom to just accept that I would not take it inside so it was a constant lecture, I had long stopped arguing about it.

Sighing I decided I should just call her back now and get it over with. It wasn't that I didn't like my mom, I did. We got along well; we were just two different kinds of people. We had been close once, she was one of my best friends. I don't really know what happened and why we weren't that way anymore. I guess part of it was that I moved so far away and didn't tell anyone about my plan before I was gone.

"Hello?" She answered with sleep still present in her words.

"Ah, crap. Sorry I forgot again; I was calling you back." I cringed, the time difference between home and where my mom lived always got me. It was only 6 AM for her, whereas it was 7 AM for me and I was headed to work.

"Ugh, let me call you back at a reasonable hour. Will you have the cell or should I ring the office?" she said and I heard the yawn punctuate the end.

"Just call the office. Love you." I hung up and pulled out of my driveway.

I flipped on the radio, and let the music calm me. Most people don't think of hard rock as calming, but something about it could just soothe my rough places. It was like a balm on open wounds to me, the beat could always cheer me up. I could go from ready to hide in a ditch to bouncing and head banging with the right song. I almost always had a song playing in the back of my head too. Sometimes I woke up singing songs.

The drive seemed to take longer than usual today, though the traffic was rather light and slowdowns minimal. I kept circling back to the dream. I had never read what I wrote down, though I always said I would. It was another of those aversions I couldn't explain. Like the phone and decorating my house.

I would try to read it, and then my head would start to hurt and I would find other things that needed my attention more. So I only ever wrote in the journal, but this time I felt like I needed to read it. I needed to see what else my mind had conjured for me. Especially if I was now projecting that onto strangers in the street. The thought was already giving me a headache and making my stomach turn. Maybe I wasn't ready yet then.

I sighed, I almost felt like a coward for not reading it. Like I was taking the easy way out, but really they were just dreams. Sure I had dreamed of the man from the restaurant, but it was just dreams. Why did I feel like reading them would make a difference? And why did I feel scared of that difference? I decided not to ponder those two questions any longer and began to loudly sing to the radio to drown my thoughts.

I got to work and saw no one had yet claimed my spot. I say my spot, really in the city it's free for all but when I drive to the same place every day I try to park in the same spot. I'm always annoyed when someone else is there. Usually it's just some tourist and that makes it worse.

They take the best parking and ALWAYS clog the streets and sidewalks. They gawk at the world like they've just never seen anything like it before. And the worst crime of all, they feed scraps to the seagulls and pigeons.

You can always tell when someone has committed this transgression, there's a noise the birds make then all hell breaks loose and people are screaming while the birds are dive bombing pedestrians, and fighting for the food. I swear they crawl out of the cracks in the sidewalk and buildings.

I get it tourists bring money and yada yada. They just need to do the touristing away from me. Illogical, sure, but I don't care. Plenty of people feel the same. I imagine the same tourists who annoy me feel the same about tourists near their home. It's a fault in the mind, I suppose.

I got the truck parked, and paid the parking for the day on my cellphone before tossing it in the glove box. Grabbing my lunch and computer bag, I locked the truck and headed inside. It was a nice little building. Like all things New Orleans old, and so it has its quirks and issues. But I still liked it.

I sat at my desk, pulled the laptop from my bag and got it booting up while I went to the coffee pot. I wasn't as bone deep tired today, but I still wanted more coffee. I got the coffee going and leaned against the counter looking around.

There were classy business decorations all over, we were a combined office and the Boss rented both his and my desks. Every business had added a little flare, and touch to the decor. Someone's advertising sign here, a company party picture there.

It was more homey than my own home, I liked to look at all the little things. The coffee finished brewing and I poured myself a mug and headed to my desk. I didn't have pictures on my desk at work either, like my home it was bare. But I could look around and see everyone else's desk and personalizations and smile.

My computer had fully come up and ready for me to login in and start my day. Hoping the day would go by fast I dove into my work. There was a lot to do today, payroll needed to be entered. Invoices created and sent out. Estimates sent to the Boss for final approval before they went to the client. I missed the days of swinging hammers and being one of the builders, but this was still busy paid work.

I looked up when someone entered the office and smiled, "Hey Boss." I greeted the man who came rushing in. Boss was always rushing, even when there was nothing to rush about. But for all his rushing he still took forever to travel between jobs. We used to make jokes about it, he'd say "I'll be there in five minutes" and he might make it in forty-five. No one ever did figure out how that math worked.

"Morning, Queen Kel!" He said in his brightest cheer voice.

I don't know when the Queen started but it always made me smile. Boss, his first name is Bob but I prefer Boss, was an average height man with a pot belly. He often went on diets, and would lose weight but like everyone he was cursed to plane out. Then he'd fall off the wagon.

"I have payroll entered and was going to start invoices, unless you want to do estimates first," I said, taking another sip of coffee. I rocked slightly back and forth in my chair as I watched Boss.

"Change of plan!" He practically chirped, obviously he was in a good mood. "You are going to drive, and I'll do computer work while we check on jobs. Like we used to. You need to get out of this office!"

I sighed; I didn't mind the arrangement. But it goes back to my weirdness about other people. I need them to stave off the loneliness but I still didn't like to be around very many people. And I was always uncomfortable meeting new people. I closed my computer and grabbed my mug.

Heading back to the office kitchen I poured the rest of coffee in my to-go cup and emptied the pot into it all well. Then I filled my bottle and turned back, heading to the office space and stopping to smile at Boss. "Ready when you are Bossman."

"Lead the way!" He said pointing out the door. I shook my head and started in the direction of his truck. I paused outside on the sidewalk, looking up at the sky while Boss locked the door. It was a cloudless day and warm and wet. It should be a crime to be that wet with no clouds in the sky. I hated the south, but here I stayed.

We headed down the block to where he had had to park, tourists are a menace I tell you. Boss had just gotten a new truck and was super proud of it. It was his off roading truck though I doubted he ever did much off-road. He liked to camp a lot in his big camper though, so maybe I was wrong.

Boss climbed in and set the GPS on his phone to give directions. "We're going to a new job today, just started it. Got a new hire out there, I want to see how things are going." He fluttered and fussed, setting the phone and computer up just so and I pulled out onto the road.

Boss doesn't like my kind of music, and I find his tastes to be even weirder than he thinks me, so most times we just rode in silence or talked. According to the GPS it would be a forty-five-minute drive to the new job site, which was only about fifteen miles away.

I groaned at the GPS screen. "I guess the good traffic from this morning is gone." I grumbled. I hated to drive in traffic, people were stupid and accidental death was always one idiot away from fact. I swear most of the people in the south wanted to die in a fiery crash. They were insane.

"Yes," Boss agreed. Already deep into the computer works. Looks like a silent trip then. We drove in silence and I had a weird feeling of dread that got worse the closer we got to the jobsite. I was uncomfortable and kept shifting in my seat. I didn't want to go there, something felt wrong, off. And I didn't understand what or why.

I internally scolded myself, this was a new job. What could possibly be wrong? Other than meeting new people this job should be just fine. There wouldn't be the nostalgia of running into old work friends from my time in the field, so really nothing should be wrong. Still the feeling worsened and I started getting cold sweats.

Boss, bless all, didn't seem to notice. I said silent thanks into the universe, I didn't want to try to explain why I was fidgeting and sweating. I was glad I wasn't hyperventilating too. It's strange really, I don't remember ever having panic attacks so much before I moved. But I could send myself into a spiraling mess of panic and hyperventilate at the drop of a hat.

With a sense of extreme foreboding, I parked at the new jobsite. I took a deep breath and turned off the truck. I got out before Boss and stretched, trying to ease the knots in my stomach. I felt like ants were crawling on my skin. I wanted to rub my arms, I wanted to run away. This was ridiculous, I couldn't explain any of it and yet I was terrified to be here.

I heard the other truck door close, and turned around walking over to stand by Boss. "So, we've got a complete interior remodel going here. New owners are basically remaking the whole thing! This is good money for us." He was still in a good mood, and it showed in the way his words seemed to bounce off his tongue.

I nodded, rubbing a hand over my stomach. "Well let's go see what's what then," I said, hoping that moving around would distract me. I couldn't shake the feeling that something was wrong, and it was here at this job. Maybe not wrong, but some part of me seemed to warn me that staying here would turn my quiet little existence upside down and inside out.

I gritted my teeth and stepped through the open front door. It was pure chaos. Workers were everywhere, power tools running, hammers swinging, sheetrock being smashed. I grinned; I really did miss this. I love to work with my hands, while I was glad the company had expanded and I was good at the office job. This was where I preferred to be.

I turned in a slow circle surveying the work, Boss was right they were basically changing everything. There were temp walls in place to support the ceiling so old walls could be removed and redone. It was complete madness! I missed this madness; the office work was fine, and I wasn't beating my body up or smashing my hands anymore. But this, the building and the making…I craved this. There is something so self-satisfying about creating and building something with your hands.

I froze mid-way through my observations, Boss was talking to a man I recognized. The antsy feeling got worse and the dread heightened. It was him. The man from the restaurant, and the one haunting my dreams. He stood near Boss not having seen me enter and seemed to be explaining things at the job. He kept gesturing around.

I knew somehow that my foreboding and dread to be here was tied to him. The universe for once being on my side had tried to warn me about it. I felt the blood leave my face, and my heart started racing. How was that possible? Why did he suddenly start appearing everywhere?!

Boss glanced back and waved me over without really looking to see if I was coming to them or not. I felt like I was walking through molasses, my legs were stiff and heavy. My hands felt tingly, and there was a buzzing in my head. I licked my lips as I walked over, and thought about the fact I had just resolved to never go out and risk running into him again. Now here he was.

The universe may have warned me, but that didn't stop it from dropping him here to torment me either. It's like "Hey this will suck, but here you go." I had stopped believing in fate and a plan a long time ago, but this was eerily like someone interfering in my life.

"Kel!" Boss said cheerily when I approached. "Dear lord, are you okay?" He peered at my face with concern. I knew I was pale; my nose was probably pinched too. I scrambled through my brain to find an explanation; I was not going to admit this stranger had me in a panic attack.

"Must've had a bad breakfast," I answered hoarsely and like I was out of breath. "I'll be okay. Just need to push through it." I tried to force a grin to my face for Boss, thankfully Boss seemed to accept this.

He shook his head and appeared mollified with my answer, and continued on. I tried to look at the man but couldn't bring my eyes past his shoulders. I battled dueling urges to hug him and run away. It's a miracle I was still standing there.

"Kel, this is Jack. My new hire foreman," Boss said, trying to make introductions. He in his usual way did not seem to notice that the air could be sliced with a knife between Jack and I. Boss turned away from us and looked around.

I forced my eyes up and promptly stared past his ear, no matter what I tried I couldn't force eye contact. But I stuck my hand out to shake his. I mentally berated myself, I wanted to look at him but between the feeling of dread, my dreams, and yesterday I wanted to sink into the earth more.

The contact of his hand in mine was like someone throwing ice water over my head. His grip was firm, and strong and surprisingly warm for the ice water feeling I now had. Calloused hands told a story of manual labor. His fingers curled over my hand like it was a natural place for them to be, and the warmth of his skin raised goosebumps across my arm.

I almost yanked my hand free, remembering at the last moment not to offend this man. He cleared his throat, and for the first time I forced my eyes to his face. He had that small frown again, though it wasn't visible on his face in the way you would think. His mouth smiled, but it didn't touch his eyes and his brows were almost imperceptibly drawn in.

I felt disapproval from him, judgement. Immediately, my spine stiffened, who was this man to judge me? Something of the new defiance I was feeling must have registered on my face because an eyebrow quirked up and a challenge flashed in those blue green eyes.

"Pleased to meet you, Ms. Kel," Jack said, and I realized that only a couple seconds had passed between the introduction and his words. Ms. Kel? This man would stand here and judge me then call me Ms.? Like it was respectful to do so?

"Oh, I'm sure the pleasure is mine. You can drop Ms. I am just Kel," I added with a hint of a sarcastic drawl, I had already forgotten about being pleasant. He had the nerve to frown in disapproval and then challenge me? Well, I just wouldn't put up with that.

My hostile reaction shocked me a little, I could be completely misjudging this man. I might actually be the only one passing judgement and shoving that off on him. I thought about that, and dismissed the idea entirely. I saw his judgement and I would respond in kind.

Boss, seemed to miss the whole exchange and captured Jack's attention again. They started to walk around the job discussing priorities and timelines. I stopped listening. Boss could ramble on for hours given the opportunity.

I followed quietly along feeling like a hole inside me had been filled only to be emptied when Jack looked away from me. I wanted him to look at me again, and I also wanted him to never look at me again. I felt like I was splitting in half. I wanted to yell at him, and demand he leave. Tell him he couldn't be here and I wouldn't tolerate it a second longer! I would never do that though, I didn't fight. And I didn't know why I wanted him here and gone simultaneously.

If I thought I was a mess before Jack entering my life had added a whole new layer of disaster. I groaned internally cursing the universe, the world, God who or whatever had decided my life needed to be so hard to handle.

But Jack never did look back, and when he and Boss finished their tour he left without another word. I bit my tongue hard enough I worried about it bleeding and spun on my heel heading to the truck. I didn't know if in doing so I stopped myself saying something about the brush off or stopped myself crying at the hurt I felt.

The rest of the day passed in a blur as we went from one job to the next. I couldn't stop the stinging rejection and pure sadness that felt like it would crush me. It was irrational, completely I just met the man and I didn't even know if I liked him. But the sight of him walking away without a word made my chest ache. It was like a break-up had occurred. I couldn't fathom it. I couldn't understand why I felt this way. I was so lost in thought, it took a moment to realize we were at the office again and Boss was getting out.

I hurried to follow so I could pack my stuff and leave. I needed to get home, to get away from him. I started to feel like a coward running away, so be it. I could be a coward, because thinking or confronting this new complication was not my idea of a good time.

"Okay, Kel, have a good weekend. I'll probably see you Monday!" Boss said as I left to finish gathering my things. Boss had not brought anything in the office so he had just switched the driver's seat and headed home.

I waved too busy in my own head for words, and packed up my stuff. I cleaned my desk of the coffee mug I had used and did a quick wipe down. I hated a messy looking desk, and coffee or food leftovers would drive me mad. I washed the mug, and set it in its place on the shelf. I opened the fridge, grabbed my lunch that I had not eaten today being in the truck with Boss, and my computer bag and headed out the door. I set the lock and alarm on the building and got in the truck.

I fired it up, and let it idle for a bit. This was the original work truck and I wanted to make sure it got time to warm up. If this truck died I'd have to drive my own vehicle and I didn't want to do that. It was just more convenient to continue to use this truck, and so I babied it.

I leaned forward and rested my head on the steering wheel, closing my eyes and hating my luck. I muttered every swear word I knew and even made some up while I sat there, shaking my head side to side. I tried really hard not to swear anymore, especially out loud and around people. It seemed too aggressive to me. But right now, swearing felt good. Like a release of a sort.

A knock on my window had me air lifting out of my seat in panicked terror and swearing louder as I looked out the window. I froze for the second time today when those blue green eyes clashed with mine. *Damnit, Damnit, Damnit!*

I cracked the window. "You're like some kind of stalker aren't you? Serial murderer maybe? Do you enjoy running over my world with a bulldozer?" I asked, adrenaline and anger grinding my teeth together. "It is absolutely rude to sneak up on people and upset their lives! Why are you here?" I seethed and almost shouted that last question.

He took a step back from the truck and arched a brow at me. "I'm looking for Bob," he said simply. He looked at me like I was overreacting, like he hadn't just taken years off my life by scaring me.

"Well, he's not here and won't be back until Monday." I started to roll up the window and he stepped forward placing his hand on the glass to stop me. "I will keep rolling the window up," I growled through clenched teeth.

Why did I say that? Would I really roll his hand up in the window? As I looked at the hand there I decided I would and pushed the button again, he yanked his away and a look of shock and indignation crossed his face.

"Are you always this rude to your co-workers?" He asked, and anger clipped the end of each word. His scowl just sparked my own anger and temper.

I stopped rolling up the window with about two inches to go at the top so I could reply to him, but if he stuck his hand in again I would close it before he could move.

"Rude?!" I asked him incredulously. He scares me and calls me rude? This man really had some nerve. I realized in some small distant part of me that I was reacting completely irrationally towards this stranger. That I was letting him get to me. I realized this, and dismissed it in half thought.

"Yes, rude," he stated with an obnoxious air of superiority. "You've been rude since the first words you spoke to me." He did a little head nod that people sometimes do when they feel justified in what they have just said.

I got out of the truck and stepped in front of him. "I'm not the one who dismissed you like the trash on the street. I'm not the one frowned in disapproval at the first meeting. And I'm definitely not the one going around scaring people!" I ended that last with a jab in his chest.

The action seemed to startle him as much as me. I never did things like that. I am not a confrontational person, I moved here in part to get away from confrontation. We both gaped at my finger as if it had acted of its own accord.

"Ummm… I… uhhh…" I trailed off lamely and felt the blush bruise across my cheeks. "I'm sorry, I uhh I haven't been sleeping well. It… uhhh seems to have umm made me testy." I stumbled over my words in a way I hadn't ever done.

He looked at my face, then back at my hand which I still held between us. I quickly dropped it, and tucked it behind my back, stepping back and away and running into the truck. I went from ready to go to blows with this man, to stumbling and stuttering like a girl with her first crush. He stepped closer and I felt boxed in. "I don't think testy covers it, Kel, and I did not dismiss you like trash. In case your pampered office self failed to notice I was on a jobsite and not only that I was in charge of the running of said job site."

I glared at him, realizing that the way we were standing he was taller than me and I had to look up at him. I opened my mouth, but he pressed on before I could speak. I thought about kicking him, that would make him shut up and I would feel better too.

"I did not frown in disapproval; your shirt could literally glow in the fucking dark, and I wondered why such a soft little creature was on my jobsite." He fingered the hem of my pink sweater and wrinkled his nose at it. "What is even the point of this color? To blind everyone?"

I felt indignation rise and more blood stained my cheeks, this time in fury. Soft *little* creature? He didn't know the first thing about me, but he assumed wearing a pink sweater made me a soft *little* creature? I was angrier about being called little than I was about being called soft, but they were close in my priorities to be mad about. I opened my mouth again.

"AND..." he said that word loudly, cutting off the words I hadn't yet said. "I was going to apologize for scaring you, but then, you went off the deep end like some kind of crazy woman!" He tossed his arms in the air and then crossed them over his chest. His eyes glittered challenges at me.

"How... What... I did not..." I stuttered and stumbled as everything I wanted to say tried to come out all at once. "How dare you insult my favorite shirt!" I finally managed. The words jumbled and tumbling out in a rush.

I cringed inwardly, *that was smooth Kel. Of all things to finally say you sound most angry about the neon pink shirt, not the insults to your person. You could have at least told him you're not soft, that you started on the job sites. But, no, the sweater was definitely the most important insult.* My internal monologue was a critical cow, I hated that voice. So superior like it was just another part of me, but like that was a better part of me.

He leaned forward and placed a hand on either side of my head against the truck, he was close enough I could see the staining of gray in his curly beard. I had the sudden desire to kiss this man. A desire strong enough I almost closed my eyes and leaned into him.

Wait?! Kiss this man? I hadn't kissed a man in years, and I had sworn to never let another man close enough to kiss me, and here I was wanting to kiss him. I fought that urge with figurative tooth and nail. I clamped my mouth tightly shut and let all my venom pour out in the glare I gave him.

"In case you didn't notice, *sweetheart*," the added inflection on sweetheart gave every sign of meaning anything but the nicety of the word. "This is construction, and soft little girls have no place here." He plucked the hem of my sweater again, "either get tough or stop wearing the pink." He turned on his heel and walked away from me without another word.

My mouth fell open as he turned and stalked away. I was speechless, I couldn't even defend myself by saying I started on the job sites and recently moved to office work. I was left speechless, and fuming. What gave him the right to pass judgement on me?

I watched as he left and despite everything I admired him. He was as perfectly shaped in real life as he was in my dream. Why did he have to be so awful though? Why did I have to want him to come back? But also needed him gone?

CHAPTER 3

I gave myself a mental shake, managing to bang head against the window. I guess it was not as mental as I thought and got back in the truck. I think I hate that man, but when I tried to focus on that feeling it wasn't the true viciousness of hate I felt. I didn't actually know how I felt right now. I was again a mass of tangled emotion.

The more I tried to unwind the feelings the more they twisted into knots and looped around. I was back to where I had been last night, with a web of emotions rolling around. I ground my teeth, called him every name I could think of and started to drive home. I didn't look around as I passed him while still walking, I didn't want to look and see if I noticed the way he had unbalanced me.

I gave only the slightest thought to why he was still walking when there was so much open parking around. Maybe he was just one of those types that said he was healthier because he would park far away. He could look down his nose at everyone who parked close because he was superior to them.

That would certainly fit his "Mightier Than Thou" personality. I stewed over what he said the whole way home, and by the time I got in my driveway I was angry at myself for not having refuted his claims of being a soft girl. I had never been a soft girl.

I grew up ranching and throwing hay! I started by working in the field with this company! Who did he think he was to judge me? I slammed the door to the truck and stomped up the steps to my front door. I saw the mail sitting there on top of a box that wouldn't have fit in the mail box.

The box was from my mom. I groaned, I probably missed her call and I didn't check the office phone before I left. I opened the door and all but threw everything inside on the couch before stomping back to the truck to grab the cellphone that I also hadn't checked.

Sure enough, missed calls and a text from my mother. I sighed in resignation and called her back, going up to sit on the porch while we talked. I felt heavy and tired with every ring, praying Mom wouldn't answer. She picked up on the third ring.

"It's about time!" She answered without even a hello. I felt even worse now, my mom meant well but the upset in her tone brushed the raw edges of myself wrong.

"Gee, Mom, hello to you too," I said, a groan slipping into my voice. Couldn't my mom just be happy I called; did she always have to be so... abrupt? With the encounter today with Jack I just wanted my mom for once to sound happy I had called her back.

"Don't give me attitude, young lady!" Her voice snapped through the phone, sometimes it seemed my mom forgot I was an adult and she would talk to me like I was still a kid and living at home.

"Mom!" I said in exasperation. "I'm thirty years old and I can do what I want. Including giving attitude to whomever I want!" My heartbeat kicked up in an adrenaline rush, like it did when I would get into confrontations.

There was a long pause on the other end of the phone, and I realized I had just argued back to my mother. I couldn't remember the last time that had happened. What had that man done to me!? Now I was arguing again? Next thing you know, I'd start swearing and punching people.

I needed to purge Jack from my life, first thing Monday I would tell Boss he had to go. That was it, Jack had to go. He was slowly making my world a mess. He was making me a mess! I had a quiet existence until he started barging into my dreams and now he had to impose in my reality too!

"I'm sorry Mom, it was a long day at work. Boss showed up and had me drive today, and I forgot to check the office phone before I left." I used my best placating tone, trying to steer away from a fight. I took long calming breaths and willed my heart to a normal pace again.

Sighing in exasperation my mom started to talk. She told me about things at home, the horses and dogs and cows. I felt nostalgia start again as she spoke of the things I had left behind when I moved. "Anyways, the reason I called though is to say I'm getting married in June."

I sat up straight and did some calculations. "MOM!" I almost screeched at the phone, "That's only four months away!" I didn't even realize she had been seriously dating, and now married in four months?!

"Oh, stop. That's plenty of time for you to plan to be here," she said with her motherly edge in her tone. It was the motherly voice that said you were a naughty child and just needed to do as you were told. It would bring toddlers into line, and send teenagers off the deep end. As an adult it just made me exhausted.

"MoooOOOOooooom," I groaned, drawing out the word. "You know I don't like that short notice. Four months? That's not doable Mom!" I don't like to not have a lot of time to plan, too much can happen if you don't plan for long enough. There's too much left to chance.

"You know, you used to do things spur of the moment!" She snapped over the phone. "It's four months away Kel, even you can manage that!" My mom sounded angry now, she rarely got angry and when she did I always just gave in. Because the fight was not worth it.

I couldn't remember a time I had ever been spur of the moment, despite common opinion even my move here had been agonized over for a year. I sighed, there was no point arguing we both knew I would be there anyway.

"Okay, Mom," I said feeling defeated and with a suddenness I couldn't explain I felt all the loneliness crash in. "I gotta go make some dinner, Mom. I'll talk to you later and we'll work out the details. I love you."

"Love you too baby," she replied and hung up the phone.

I walked back to the truck and put the phone in the glovebox then went inside. It was a beautiful evening; the tree frogs had just begun to chirp. The sky was getting dark, and stars were starting to appear. If I were in a better mood I would stay out and enjoy it, but I just wanted to get inside and pretend the world didn't exist anymore.

I grabbed the box my mom had mailed me, and took it inside. I opened it and threw it away without taking out the contents. She had sent me pictures, pictures of him and me. I growled in disgust; she was not subtle at all. Why did she have to butt in and be nosy like that, she never could just leave my decision alone.

I took a long hot shower, even sitting on the floor under the stream in an attempt to drown the day away. I would do this every time I wished for a long bath. It was the closest I could get. I wished almost daily for a real bath tub that I just sink into and soak in.

I didn't understand the volatile and violent reactions I had towards Jack. I am a pretty passive person; I often get left behind or pushed aside. I just was that easy to forget, quiet and passed over person. I was okay with that, I wanted that. I didn't like to be noticed.

Past boyfriends, or one past boyfriend, had accused me of not fighting enough, whatever that even meant. I just never saw the point of fighting. What did yelling and losing your temper ever accomplish? I could never discern any benefits to fighting. It seemed to just be a circle. One yell sparked another yell and things would spiral out of control.

Then my mom's sudden marriage had really caught me off guard. Had I truly been missing that much? How did I not know she was even serious about someone? I dropped my head to my knees, my hair veiling my face as the water ran down my head and spine.

I wasn't ready to go back, I hadn't been back in the five years since I left. I was sure my mother had planned this now. That she was forcing me home in an attempt to make me stay. She had never approved of my leaving, but then she didn't know the whole story either.

I shuddered in the shower; I would not go there tonight. Bad enough the pictures had awoken that dark beast in my mind, I would not bring that memory to life, it was done and gone. I felt chills and knew that the shower could do nothing more to quell them, so I turned the water off and got out.

After drying and putting on some comfortable lounge clothes I decided I would eat last night's dinner, drink some whiskey and go to bed. As the previous night's dinner reheated I looked again at my empty cold house. Not cold in a physical sense, but in an un-lived-in sense. There was nothing warm and welcoming here. I snorted to myself as I looked at it.

No wonder Jack had been awful to me, he must've seen right to the cold empty inner depths of me and been repulsed by it. I was repulsed by it. I could never look long in a mirror because those depths would start trying to come to the surface. I feared that one day they would finally crack me open and everyone would see me for what I was. Cold, broken, bitter, sad and lonely. That was the truth of it. The self-righteous voice in my head reminded me at least once a day that I was cold and bitter.

I took a moment to reflect that I hadn't been much better than a bitter angry woman to Jack, but he had judged me before I had said anything. So I would not take too much of that blame. I mean really he had started to judge me in the restaurant. Okay, so maybe I had stared at him like a weirdo. But I wasn't the only girl who stared at him, and then he judged me at work because I liked bright colors.

I smacked my forehead trying to force those thoughts back into my box at the back of my mind. As long as I smiled no one would look too closely. I was one of the "blessed" girls, I had wide hips and plenty of chest. People tended not to look any closer than that. It was the way of the world; the surface was it. No one dug deeper anymore. I had to read romance novels for that kind of thing.

Except, that Jack had, or he had seemed to anyway. He certainly didn't react to me the way most men did. Maybe it was the way I had responded to him that had gotten him an in-depth view into my mind. I resolved to act like he was just another rat in the sewer from here out. I would not let him see in again.

I pictured a rat with Jack's face scurrying around and made myself chuckle. I would not let him get to me anymore, he had rattled me today that was all. I will be better prepared tomorrow. The microwave dinged, and it felt like the world was righted again. I would ignore Jack when I could and tolerate him when needed. I would plan for and go to my mom's wedding in four months and then come back and life would continue as it had for the last five years.

I decided I needed a distraction tonight so I found a comedy movie to play in the background while I ate and planned my weekend. I had thought about going out but meeting Jack, and my general dislike to ever actually go be around people, had probably maxed out my people quota until the wedding.

I did need to mow the grass though, and I could play with my plants. Some of those needed repotted, others needed fruits harvested. I mindlessly stared at the movie while I thought about the weekend spent outside. If the weather was nice enough I might even sleep on the hammock on the back porch.

The back porch is screened in for such occasions, otherwise the bugs would drain me dry of blood. I finished dinner, took care of the dishes and poured another drink. I still had no idea what was on T.V. but I didn't care.

I drank the second drink, and had a third before the movie was over. Feeling a little tingly and fuzzy all over and knowing I had a stupid grin on my face I turned off the T.V. and lights and headed to bed. I walked slowly, thinking about my mom and Jack. I had been pretty short with them both and should probably apologize when next I spoke to them.

I flopped face down on the bed and was asleep before I could even get under my blankets.

"KEL!" *The man shouted, panic in his voice.* "Dammit woman! Where are you?"

I couldn't reply, if I answered he would know and they would get him too. It had to be this way, I had to protect them. All of them, they would never understand but it had to happen this way.

A cold hand closed around my throat and I was pushed backwards away from the voices calling my name. "Move, he's waiting" the equally cold voice demanded, turning me and shoving me forward. "Or do you want me to go get him instead."

I shook my head and turned to walk away. I felt the tears start to flow. It was for the best. They could be safe, I had set the guards in place to protect them, and I would go. It was the deal I made. I was the necessary sacrifice.

I woke up with my hand pressed to my mouth as if to hold in the scream that was pressing up my vocal cords. My head pounded, my heart raced and I was shivering. What had that been? I swear that voice had been Jack's. But that was so different from the other dreams. The other dreams were like glimpses of someone's life and they were happy and good.

But this dream held fear and sorrow, and it felt more like me than any of the other dreams had. I tried and tried to figure out why this one was so different, why it felt so important that I not forget this dream. I held as tightly to the images as I could. Gripping them with mental iron fists. Trying to commit every part to memory, even as with all the dreams they were starting to fade, slowly tantalizingly.

What or who was the *they* of my dream, I hadn't seen any faces. I just felt a primal fear, like they were the things of nightmares. My thoughts spun in maddening circles in my head. As full wakefulness crept in the dream faded faster and my thoughts became less frantic and sad and more focused on why I was so cold. I stopped thinking of the cold voice, and of Jack and the woman calling me. My toes were like icicles, and goosebumps raised along my arms.

I looked at the clock and saw it was barely midnight, and I was on top of the blankets. No wonder I was so cold. I crawled under the blankets refusing to give the dream any more thought and let myself fall back to sleep. I would not let this continue to rule my life.

I woke up feeling like a dump truck had crashed into me and dumped a bed full of gravel on top of me. Everything hurts, everywhere. My head was pounding like I had drunk the whole fifth of whiskey. My jaw hurt as if I had clenched it all night. Every muscle pulled and ached and knotted at the slightest movement.

I lay in my bed wanting to cry from discomfort, but terrified of the pain that action might cause. I closed my eyes and tried my breathing exercises to loosen muscles and relax the body. *In*, slowly curl the toes. *Out*, slowly uncurl the toes. *In*, point your feet at the wall. *Out*, point your feet back to yourself. And so on up through my legs. Then I started on my hands. When I got to shrugging my shoulders I was feeling like I could actually get out of bed.

Still I completed the exercise tensing and relaxing my abdomen, rolling my neck from side to side and finishing with sitting up and stretching to reach my toes. I still hurt, but it wasn't so all consuming that I couldn't get up.

Gingerly, I turned on the bed and slowly lowered my legs over the edge. I was moving like someone put through the medieval torture of stretching. My feet touched the ground and I hissed angrily. How does a dream affect the bottoms of my feet?!

I crammed that thought away in the back of my mind before the dream could come back. I was not ready to even try to think about that. I carefully tip-toed down the hall, staring at the wall opposite the other two bedrooms and headed for my kitchen. I needed coffee, lots of coffee.

I walked into the kitchen and pushed the start button, a habit I had formed so long before I don't remember when it started was to have the coffee prepped the night before and either have the auto brew set or just ready for the start button. Preparing the coffee in the morning half awake and bleary eyed just never sounded like a good idea. And on work days, it takes forever to be ready.

I turned and walked out of the kitchen as the pot started to heat and sizzle and got a soft fuzzy blanket from the couch. I love soft fuzzy things; I cannot walk down the aisle in a store and see a soft fuzzy blanket without touching it.

I wrapped the blanket tight around myself, thanking any God anywhere that cared to hear for the relief from pain. I would have sat on the floor and cried if my blanket made me hurt the same way walking did. I was raw and felt like my skin had been flayed open leaving nothing but exposed nerves.

Blissfully though my blanket was soothing and comforting. Like a soft touch of love, the blanket seemed to wrap around me and the world was a little bit better. I can't explain why I always felt like that with my fuzzy blankets.

It was like they were the most precious gift from a person very dear to me. But that was silly because I had bought them for myself. I like myself plenty enough, probably as much as the average person is wont to self liking, but to feel as if the blankets were precious gifts was a bafflement I had never sorted out.

As I stood there cocooned in the soft blanket the sounds and smells of brewing coffee added another layer of comfort to me. It was the sound and smell of normalcy, of a world that made sense. A world without crazy dreams and men I knew but didn't know. A world without the women I missed without ever having met. I prayed silently they were like Jack and actually people I would someday run into on the street or at work.

My quiet little house, my bare walls, the coffee, and the blanket, that was what I knew. That was comfortable, lonely, but comfortable. I don't branch out often, I don't like sudden changes and new things. New things could lead to heartaches and change was always a thing to be approached with caution.

I didn't want change. I realized with a start I was even a little miffed at my mom for getting married, though it was a minimal change to me it was still change. I was a touch mad at Boss too when I really thought about it. He had brought that Jack on, and that was a huge change. My life wasn't full and complete, sure, and I had bouts of pure lonely misery. But I was settled, content. Change would ruin all of that.

I clenched my jaw then flinched, that still hurt. I really need to learn to let go of things I couldn't stop. My mom would get married, and that would be that. I would show up and show a happy face, then I could escape back to my quiet corner of the world.

Jack was here for at least the duration of the project, but I had the feeling Boss was going to keep him on. Personal disgruntlement aside it really seemed like he had a good handle on things, and he and Boss got on great. So, I would deal with that too.

I came to my internal resolution just as the coffee finished and with more determination in my steps, though still soft stepping, I went back into the kitchen. I grabbed my mug and set it on the counter, I had a cabinet of dishes and multiple coffee mugs but I generally only used one.

I made a face at the dishes; I had full sets completely unused. I would ever have company for meals. I had to have friends and people who wanted to be around me and me around them for that to happen. I should sell everything and buy some plastic plates, bowls and cups. That's all I needed anyway. Sell them and find something better to put in the cupboards in their place. Maybe more Tupperware for my packed lunches.

I closed the cabinet door with a huff, I wouldn't get rid of dishes and I knew it. I had that thought every couple of weeks and never acted on it. I don't know why I never did. I just couldn't bring myself to actually get rid of them.

I poured the coffee and added a little of my weekend cream, that is what I called the stuff I had recently discovered at the liquor store when getting whiskey. I would never add this to my coffee during the week when I needed to work. But on a weekend morning when I planned to be home all day it was a nice touch.

I gathered my coffee in my hands, cradling it like it was a small fragile animal and went back to the living room to sit on the couch. I gingerly sat down, grabbing a second blanket to now wrap around my legs as I tucked them into my chest on the couch.

I wrapped my arms around my knees and settled the coffee mug on top. I love sitting like this, a blanket wrapped around me back to front, and one around my knees with warm coffee in my mug. I don't like scalding your mouth to cinders coffee, I want drinkable coffee. But for unflavored coffee, there was also a subtle balance between drinkable and grossly cold.

I smiled to myself and took the first sip, almost sighing as I felt the heat going from my throat to my stomach. I felt the hot liquid settle and it was a balm to my tired being. I sat there like that staring at the wall and determinedly not thinking of anything while sipping my coffee.

I now knew that the man in my dream had a real face, Jack's face. And Jack's voice. I allowed myself some thought on this. Jack and I must've crossed paths briefly before, maybe at that same restaurant where I saw him the other day. That's where I got his face and voice from, it had to be. There just couldn't be another explanation.

I didn't believe in coincidence, or fate, or anything supernatural. You lived, you died and whoever you were just faded. Some people got lucky, and lived on in memories of loved ones or in the work they did. Most people just faded though.

My mom believes spiritually, karma, consequences and reincarnation. She believes a soul lives over and over and over until that soul is a perfect being, born of human life experiences, and could then rejoin the ultimate perfect being, God.

I believed that too, once. Then my eyes opened… NOPE. Stopping there, I won't think about that. About what happened, about *him*. I shuddered, closing my eyes and shutting down my thoughts until the memories stopped trying to surface. He had ruined any belief I had had in a God.

Sighing I sipped more coffee and with the memories firmly buried again I went back to contemplating Jack. I was slightly unnerved by how well my dreams had shown him. By how exact his voice had always been. I wondered if I had ever seen the women I dreamed about too. If my subconscious had decided I was too lonely and chose these random faces and voices from people in the crowd.

I let my mind drift from Jack to the women. I had seen the shorter woman in a recent dream, she was the one that I had first thought to call cousin. Though like the other one being called sister, I didn't know why. We laughed and smiled like we'd always known each other. In my dream it really felt that way, but I reminded myself I didn't have any friends like that. No one that I had remained close to for a long time, and especially no one from before my move.

The other woman, the one I thought of as sister, was a mystery to me, she wasn't as clear as the 'cousin' woman was. She was slightly taller than my five foot ten inches, I figured her to be about six feet. She had blonde hair ending just past her shoulder blades and green eyes.

I knew that in my dreams I missed her too, but it was with less heartache than I missed the other woman. Like something had happened, strange as it felt to consider it was like her and I had had a falling out. I reminded myself again I didn't know her, I had had plenty of falling outs with the people I left behind. But she wasn't one of them.

I wished I had names for them, that my dreams had given me names. At least now I could call the dream man Jack. I thought about it a moment longer and decided I would name them myself. It was my dream after all, so therefore I could do what I wanted too. Knowing the man to have Jack's face and voice and thereby calling him Jack had made me want to name the women too.

I closed my eyes and pictured the shorter woman, tilting my head side to side as I contemplated her mental image and thought about everything I had seen and heard. Well, everything I could remember. I could read my journal and probably find more details, but I still shied away from that idea.

I sat there holding an empty coffee mug while I considered. She needed an M name. I ran through every M I could come up but nothing felt right. Frustrated, I decided it wouldn't matter if it felt right, she would be called Mary. I nodded sharply to myself as if that decision was majorly important and I had accomplished a great deal by naming her. Though the name felt wrong, I was sticking to it.

I opened my eyes and stared woefully at my empty coffee mug. I needed more brain juice before I tackled the task of naming the other woman from my dreams. But I was so comfortable and warm that I didn't want to get up. I figured this is where a partner in life and home could come in handy. I could smile sweetly and convince some man to refill my coffee for me.

I made myself laugh aloud at that thought and mental image. We would both be on the couch and I would ask so sweetly using all the nicest names I could come up with to try and get him to refill my mug. And he in loving exasperation would roll his eyes at me, but still get up to do it.

I felt a pinch of regret and sorrow that that would never be a thing in my life. I was a happy single woman, so I always told myself. Relationships of any kind added complications to life. If you have friends, they want things from you. Things like hanging out, or going out together or talking consistently.

If you had a romantic partner they were even more demanding. They wanted time, and to be the most important. Even if that particular demand was one sided. That thought left a bitter taste in my mouth and sighing in disgust I got up to refill my own coffee mug.

I placed my mug on the counter and poured my coffee. Then opening the fridge I pondered with a little head bob side to side whether to use plain milk or have another special cream coffee. I thought about what needed to be done today. Cut the grass, maybe repot plants... Nothing that would mean I couldn't indulge a little more. Besides, it was Saturday! I will be good tomorrow.

I added the cream, butter pecan flavored that went amazing with my pecan flavored coffee, and went back to my couch. I would finish this mug, name the woman and get to doing daily chores. I rarely ate breakfast and after last night's dream I wasn't sure I wanted too.

I cocooned myself again in my blankets and took a sip of coffee before settling it on my knees and closing my eyes to picture her. I turned her image over and over in my mind, there were fewer dreams of her and the ones that left memories were fuzzy but I still focused on what I could remember. C, I decided, she had a C name. Carmen... no. Carolyn... definitely no. I went through the Cs like I had Ms and again, it just never felt right.

I sighed in annoyance and decided I would just call her Carly. I would have Jack, Mary, and Carly. I would write those in the journal later, it was again at my bedside and I didn't want to move until the important business of coffee drinking was concluded. Again the name didn't feel quite right, like with Mary but I wasn't changing them now.

I laughed at my inner monologue of name choosing, I often amused myself and had to be careful not to laugh out loud in public. People give you looks like they think you need to be committed if you just randomly laugh when you are alone, and trying to explain that you laughed at your own thoughts does not help. It's dumb really, I bet everyone laughs at their owns thoughts, but do so in a public setting and the judgements rain down.

I continued to nurse my coffee, loathe to actually do any of the outside work I had assigned myself, and thought about Mary and Carly and Jack. I thought about what it would be like if my dreams were real and we were all close friends. The dreams definitely emphasized Jack and Mary as more predominant in my life. But I knew Carly had a part too.

I thought about dating Jack and almost choked on my coffee. We would surely kill each other. We hadn't even managed a truly civil conversation and we had just met. I laughed harder thinking about it. No that would not work, obviously my subconscious needed a lesson on compatibility.

I thought about Mary, short and quick to laugh. We weren't a good fit either, I was too quiet and serious. She would soon be bored of me and I would be without a friend. But the dreams showed Mary and I as close friends, the parts I could remember. And the impression was we were inseparable, not that she was tired of who I was.

Now Carly, I think she and I could actually make a friendship of things. She left the impression of bitter sadness and loneliness. She felt like me, like who I am. That stung a little the more I thought of it, because I didn't want to be the way I was.

As I thought about them I wondered if they weren't just reflections of myself. I had once laughed like Mary did, open and often. I did have a quick temper like Jack. I just hid it behind walls of indifference. I had already drawn the similarities to Carly and didn't want to look too closely there. I didn't want to dig that deep in myself, not today.

I tried to take another sip of coffee and realized despite my nursing efforts the mug was empty and it was time to go about my day. I could contemplate fictional characters and their likenesses to myself later. Now it was time to be productive.

In a spur of the moment silly and rather dramatic gesture I flung the blanket off my legs and bounced to feet, very quickly recalling how my feet hurt. I glared at the blanket as if it had been its fault that I had done such a foolish thing.

I carefully walked to my bedroom thankful that the mower I had was a riding mower or I wouldn't be doing the grass today. I chose a pair of ragged blue jeans and an old threadbare t-shirt. They would be perfect for outside yard work. I looked through my shoes and found some that had memory foam insoles, those should help with my feet. I was fast becoming annoyed that my feet still hurt so much, everything else had pretty much faded.

Finishing dressing I was relieved to find that the shoes did actually seem to relieve some of the discomfort. I rocked from toes to heels a couple times just to make sure all was well enough. And smiled in satisfaction.

I turned to leave my bedroom but the laundry basket caught my eye, might as well get that started too I thought. I scooped it up and headed down the hall to the laundry room. It was in the same hall as all the bedrooms. I quickly dumped all my clothes in the wash, moving things around to balance the load, and added the soap.

I know some people actually find the way I do laundry to be appalling. I don't sort by color or type I just throw it all in. I do have some sweaters or dresses that get washed separately but they are so rarely worn that they don't really count.

I closed the lid with a flourish and it made a sound like a gong. I grinned, stabbed the start button and continued on to the outside. I made an internal joke that the lid sound was the gong of one task done and the next to be started.

I stepped out on the front porch and stretched. It was a beautiful day, warm temperatures with mild humidity. I didn't immediately feel like I would drown if I took too deep a breath. The sun was warming and soothing. I paused in the full sun and let it soak into my back rolling my shoulders forward and sighing.

The warmth seeped through my clothes and into my muscles and bones. I felt more tension leave my body and took a deep, relieved breath. By the end of the day I should be so relaxed that this morning's pain will be a long distant memory.

I walked to the garage and punched in the code to open it. I had a large garage consisting of a single riding mower, a weed eater and planting stuff. Soil, pots etc. I didn't even keep the work tools in here, they stayed in the truck on the off-chance Boss sent me to a jobsite to actually work there.

It was a sad sight, a garage like this should be full of things. Cars or tools or something. But the garage like the house echoed how empty my life was of things and people. I stared into the garage and my mind wandered back to Jack, that man was starting to become a nuisance.

If Jack were here, and in this house what would the garage look like? I pictured tools and workbenches and pure chaos. The idea made me chuckle, Jack seemed so uptight that picturing a chaotic garage belonging to him was just too far-fetched. I bet that even specifically set his dresser the same every time laundry was done.

Folding things in a particular way and setting them in nice neat lines. As opposed to me, I folded things, but I rejected neat lines. It was just impossible to maintain. Open the drawer once and things moved, close it and you would know they moved again. Neat lines were overdone, and only truly obsessive people bothered with them.

I startled myself by laughing out loud, I bet Jack was that kind of really obsessive. I bet things had to be a certain way or he would get all twisted in knots. Maybe I should figure that out, and find ways to upset that. I think I will enjoy seeing Jack get bent out of shape and flustered.

I walked to the mower and set it in neutral gear pushing it out of the garage to start it and let it idle a bit. I was very particular about engines. They needed a chance to warm up. I had read or someone had taught me at one point that it was important for motors to get a chance to run at idle before being put under load, or rather put to work. When or where that knowledge came from I didn't remember. It was just a lesson that stuck, and so I stuck to it.

I got the mower going and because it has a safety switch in the seat I had to stay sitting so it would run. I suppose it made sense to have the safety switch, it would save mowing companies from lawsuits when someone got drunk and fell off their mower and was run over by it. Perhaps that was why the switch was there. Because that happened once, it certainly wouldn't surprise me.

I turned on the little radio I kept on the mower, and got the volume up to be heard while I cut the grass. It was just better to cut the grass to music. It didn't feel so monotonous that way. Mowing the grass was a terrible chore, and even on a riding mower I never wanted to do it. I had to have the distraction.

After about five minutes of idle time I put the mower in gear and got to work. I had a large yard and even with the riding mower it still took about an hour to cut the grass. Then because I was lazy I would go back over the trails of cut grass a few times. This would cut the grass clippings more finely and disperse them better. It was a far better idea than raking the grass after it was cut.

I hummed and sang along to the music focusing on my work and avoiding any thoughts of the dreams or the three people who haunted me. I especially made sure to avoid Jack, if he came to mind I started picturing butterflies all around.

I finished the mowing and set to weed eating, thankfully my shoes were doing the trick and I had minimal discomfort in my feet. Weed eating always took two to three hours depending on how particular I felt that day.

Today I decided to take the extra time and hit every spot. All in all my yard took about four hours to do, but I felt very accomplished when I finished. I looked down at the basic black plastic watch I always wore and with a start realized it was past noon. My stomach growled then and decided lunch would happen before dealing with my plants.

I put the mower and weed eater away, closed my garage and went back inside to make some lunch. Grilled cheese was the first option readily available and so I set about to make it. I put butter on the bread, got the Colby jack cheese (I don't use the cheap American cheese, that's for dogs and teenagers) and warmed the pan.

With the pan hot, I dropped the first two pieces of bread butter side down and listened to the sizzle. As the sizzles got quieter I added the cheese and the top layer of bread. When the sizzling stopped completely I flipped the sandwich over. They were a perfect golden brown color, and passed the touch test for crispiness.

When the sizzling faded on the other side I turned the stove off, moved the pan to a cold eye and served my sandwiches to a paper plate. I use paper most often because it's less dishes to do. And yes, I have been chastised about environmental effects. In my defense I save the plates and burn them.

I took my lunch to the couch and glanced at the little side table that was small enough it was almost unnoticeable. I had left a book there and while I ate my sandwiches decided to read. I love to read; I love to get lost in another world and become immersed in someone else's life.

I often pictured myself as the brave heroine in my adventure fantasy action novels. Or the most desired woman in my romance novels. I would be the detective in a mystery. I could be happy and care-free or serious and earthly.

The current novel I was reading was a romance, the lead female a serious booky type and the lead male charismatic and arrogant with a careless air. They were drawn together by her need to escape and hate that they have to work together. Honestly the end will be they are in love and live happily ever after, all romances end that way. But I love the in-between more than the ending.

I picked up the book and began to read, losing myself to fights and laughs and adventures of the book while I ate. Unfortunately, I got too lost in my book and suddenly the book was over and it was dark outside.

I sighed. I knew better than to read in the middle of the day. I can get so lost in my books that the world could almost end and I wouldn't know. I checked the time and let out a soft chuckle. It was eight PM. I hadn't just read until dark, I had lost half of my night too.

I stretched and slithered down on the couch laying fully across the seat. I hate this couch, it's rough and uncomfortable and short. I want a sectional, big and soft and fluffy with a reclining chair. I don't know why a sectional couch instead of just a recliner. I really only need a recliner, it's always just me. But whenever I go to the furniture stores I always admire them.

I suppose it fit into my wish for friends, with a sectional we could all sit on the same couch but in our spots if we wished or cuddle up to watch movies. I think it would be nice to have friends you could cuddle up with and watch movies. Not in my cards though.

I stretched again, yawned and got off the couch. I put my finished book on the shelf for finished novels, selected a detective mystery and took my plate to the burn box. Every couple of months I would take my burn box outside and burn the plates and whatever mail I had gotten. I could sit and watch the fire for hours, that's why I didn't do it all the time.

I set the book on the counter and washed the pan, drying it and putting it away before pouring a glass of wine and taking the wine and book to my room. If I started reading I might read all night, at least I wouldn't have dreams then.

I turned all the lights off in the house and shut my bedroom door. I flipped on the bedside light and set the wine and book down so I could dress down for bed. Climbing under the blankets I adjusted the pillows for the proper amount of propping up and gathered my book.

I hadn't read this one yet, but I liked the author and had read previous novels of hers. I opened the book, grabbed the wine and started to read. At some point I put my empty glass down on the bedside table, at a later point I fell asleep with the book in hand and the light still on.

I heard Mary join Jack's frantic calling and walked faster forcing him to walk faster with me. If we could just get away everyone would be safe. I would have done it and protected them all. I walked faster forcing him to follow. I couldn't let them catch up, we needed to be gone before they figured it out.

I felt the weirdness that was the door in the world to another place. It was like walking through Jell-o made of clouds. Sticky and thick, but cold and light as well. I cursed the day I first felt that feeling. And I cursed them. All of this came down to them.

"Stop." That cold voice demanded squeezing the back of my neck. With a pop that was felt rather than heard I knew that the door was sealed and I knew Jack and Mary wouldn't find me. I felt immense relief and sadness that I could never see them again.

The hand on my neck shoved me forward, and we walked down a long hall to a door at the end. The hall just ended at this door. I looked around, this was nothing like the other doors I had been through. I wondered if they could manipulate these places. We hadn't really learned much about them and the pockets yet.

The hand squeezed sharply on my neck and I stopped looking around. The door opened and I shoved inside. I turned around to protest, or yell or something but the door was gone. Like it had never been there. I swore at the blank wall, what was the point of this? Why was I here?

I turned in a circle and looked at where I was. It was a round room, no doors or windows. Just a desk in the middle with a chair on either side. What was the point of that? What was the point of not just killing me? I growled in frustration and glared at the table and chairs.

"Sit, Kel" a voice from behind me. A voice I knew. A voice that could sew terror into my being, a voice often promising pain. It was a voice from my nightmares, and my past. One that shouldn't be here now. I felt off balance and like a rat in a trap.

Horror sank to my bones; it couldn't be him. I was frozen in place, too afraid to even turn around and assure myself of the impossibility. My knees felt weak, and I had stopped breathing properly. I couldn't move even as every instinct screamed that I had to move now. That I had to run.

"I said sit!" The voice hissed in my ear and I flinched. Why was he so close? How did I not hear him move? Ice ran through my veins in place of blood, and I was cold and afraid.

I was roughly shoved forward and I sank down into a chair, my mind whirled at what this meant as He walked to the other side of the desk and sat down. I knew I had been right when I heard the voice. It was Him.

I woke up with a scream building in my throat, I turned my head and released it into my pillow. I wasn't sure why I was screaming. The dream didn't make any sense, it was like a follow on from the one the night before. Why would that happen? How does that even happen? And *WHY* was I having so many dreams all of a sudden?

I had woken up before I saw whoever it was in my dream sit in the chair, I never saw his face. But even awake, the memory of the voice made me ill and gave me chills. I don't know how a dream managed to have that effect in the waking world. I could think about that issue later. That I heard the voice before I felt sure, but I wasn't sure about when and where? And the longer I tried to figure it out, the harder it was to remember anything but the fear, and the more my stomach tried to revolt. I couldn't remember that voice without wanting to throw up. So I shoved the voice aside.

The scream burned itself out and I felt raw. Not just my throat from screaming, but my emotions and my head. I still felt the sorrow of leaving Jack and Mary, or rather the dream interpretations of them. But also the certainty that leaving them was right. That doing so protected them in some way. My dreams were really starting to mess with my reality.

I felt like we had loved each other deeply and I couldn't figure out why that was. Why would my own mind plant feelings like that. Why would it pick random faces from the street and make dreams of them being so important to me that without them I felt like there was no real life.

It was maddening, I had had a peaceful life until six months ago. That must've been when I first saw Jack in a crowd. It was his fault my life was miserable! I felt tears pool in my eyes and angrily I swiped them away. I had cried more in the last few days than I could remember crying in a long time. Damn that Jack for walking in and ruining my quiet if somewhat miserable existence.

I sighed and got out of bed to splash water on my face. I knew logically it wasn't Jack's fault, I couldn't really blame him for being the face that was chosen by myself to torment myself. Logically I understood, but emotionally? Emotionally and irrationally I wanted to find him and punch him. A lot. I don't think I would be satisfied with just one punch.

I wanted to punch him right in his smug perfectly shaped face. I wanted to scream at him and tell him everything was his fault, I wanted to ask him why he had to make my life so hard and couldn't just leave me alone. Why couldn't he just go away? Irrationally I wanted to hate him.

I went back to bed, turned my light off and stared into the dark until I fell asleep again. Miserable and angry I prayed with every fiber of my being not to dream again tonight. The cracks inside myself felt near to the surface and I worried one more dream tonight would truly break me apart.

When I woke up to the day I was eternally grateful to have not dreamed again for the last couple of hours that I had been asleep. I was still angry though and wrote down both dreams in my journal, also writing their names. Jack, Mary and Carly, three people a part of me desperately wanted to know more of and about, and a larger part wished I'd never seen their faces.

It seemed that seeing their faces in the dreams had caused my life to spiral out of my control, and I wasn't handling that well. I'm not a control freak, but some consistency and the regular normalcy of my life didn't seem to be too much to ask.

Sunday passed in a similar ritual to Saturday. I didn't read during my lunch so I managed to re-pot and take care of my plants. I harvested the vegetables that were ready, pruned the branches on every plant that wasn't glowing healthy and kept my hands and mind too busy to think.

I finished just as the sun was setting and went inside, too tired to eat dinner. I poured whiskey and coke in a glass and sat on the couch. The work of the day had left me feeling tired, I kept finding small tasks I could do to stay busy.

But now it was dark, and there was nothing to stop the thoughts. I wished they would just go away. I wanted a redo starting back to the first dream of Jack. Just erase it all and try again. I was dreading work in the morning because I might run into Jack.

Worse than that I feared meeting the woman Mary was formed after. Would she be just like Mary in my dreams? Or would she be completely different? I wasn't sure I even wanted the answer.

I finished the drink and took myself off to shower and go to bed. I will deal with tomorrow when tomorrow happens. I just wish it didn't upset my normal so much.

CHAPTER 4

Monday dawned bright and hot; it would be one of those days I was glad to work in the office. The heat and humidity would just leach the life out of a person. I got out of bed when my alarm sounded, got dressed without much thought to my outfit and headed to the kitchen.

I poured my coffee, packed a lunch and breezed out the door. I never took long getting ready in the morning, it always allowed me to sleep a little later than most people. I started the truck, and checked my cellphone while it warmed up.

My mom had called yesterday, she would be mad that I hadn't answered. Oh well, she should know better by now. I was never going to keep this phone on my person, and it was never going in my house.

There was a text from Boss, "We have a lunch meeting today, I will see you at the office." I smiled. I liked lunch meetings, free food and Boss was always good company. We weren't close, but he had kind of tried to be a fatherly like figure to me and I would appreciate that. I had never had a father; he had died before I was born, and my mother would never speak about him.

I pulled out of my driveway feeling like it would be a good day, and smiled while the radio blasted. I immediately started singing and held a tiny hope that this would be a good day. I should've known better honestly, it's Monday nothing good ever comes on

Mondays. Take me for example. My mother had the bad timing to have me on a Monday and my life was like a soup sandwich. An uncontainable mess.

I got to just outside the city with ten miles to go to the office and traffic came to a standstill. It took an hour to get to the office. ONE hour to drive TEN miles! That was beyond ridiculous, these people literally drove these routes every day and STILL they would get in wrecks or cause traffic jams... This city was a nightmare.

When I got to the office and I tried to open the door, I dropped everything. My computer bag, my lunch, even the truck keys. I stomped my foot and stared up at the sky, "Come on! Can you at least give me a little break?" I asked aloud, I heard the whine in my tone and was glad no one was there to hear it too.

"Do you often talk to yourself?" Jack's voice came from behind me.

It had a sarcastic lilt to it that said he was laughing at me. I wanted to punch him again, but I didn't want to turn around and face him. Facing him and seeing the laugh would be worse than just hearing it in his voice.

Apparently I had been wrong about no one being there. The universe must truly despise my very existence. I groaned and dropped my head leaning forward and bouncing it off the door in frustration. Of course he had witnessed that. Why wouldn't the universe who let this man torment me also allow him to witness my failings?

"What do you want?" I asked somewhat muffled since I was still leaning my head on the door. I couldn't bring myself to look at him, I hoped silently that if I didn't he would just go away and leave me to my misery.

I saw my bags lift up from the corner of my eye and realized Jack had picked them up for me. "I was about to ask if you needed help, when you asked the sky for a break. Should the sky answer you? I'm curious now." His voice was teasing and low, it at once made my insides melt and my temper fire white hot.

I heard the laughter in his voice and growled. Kicking the door I spun around to face him. "Do you have to mock me?" I asked him, my back against the door and my hands fisting at my sides. I had decided to fuel the temper, I wouldn't even give thought to melted insides. Not when it was Jack causing the reaction.

His face did this twitching motion then a look of innocence stole over it. "I wouldn't mock such a wonderful woman as yourself," he said with a tone to match the look. The urge to punch him was becoming almost overwhelming. My fists twitched like a muscle had jumped in anticipation.

Why did this man make me so violent? I swore, and yelled and now I wanted to punch him? I really needed to find the inner me that was calm and passive again. I couldn't keep letting Jack get to me. But I also couldn't help it. It was like he had a Kel booklet of instructions and knew just exactly where to dig.

I glared at him, and turned to unlock the door. I snatched my bags from him and stormed through the door trying to slam it in his face. Trying and failing because he had seemed to guess I would do that and had stuck his foot out.

"What do you want, Jack?" I asked furiously, setting my bags on my desk and turning to face him and crossing my arms. That was a mistake, I had enjoyed the office job because I could dress like a pretty girl. However, sometimes my shirts were a little flashy.

His eyes did a brief dip, and in horror I realized that with the shirt I wore crossing my arms displayed my chest like I was purposefully trying to flaunt it. I dropped my arms, grabbed the jacket I always kept on the back of my chair and put it on, zipping it to my chin.

One second Jack was staring at me, the next he was bent double laughing so hard he was gasping and holding onto the desk next to him for support. He laughed so hard I wondered how he managed to breathe.

I contemplated kicking him, in the position he was now I could literally kick that smug stupid face. He'd probably even stop laughing at me. If I broke his nose his face wouldn't be so perfect either. But I didn't kick him.

I stomped my foot. "Jack!" I almost yelled at him. "It is beyond rude to laugh at someone! Especially that much!" I knew I shouldn't let him get to me, shouldn't let the hurt and indignation bleed into my voice. I knew it, and I still did it.

Jack straightened as if someone had hit him with a cattle prod, and all amusement was gone from his face as he then scrutinized my own. He looked at me with such intensity, it was like he peeled away parts of me. Like he was searching for something inside me and he had almost found it when I stomped my foot and yelled at him.

I turned away from him, uncomfortable with the level of intensity in his stare. I slumped into my desk chair and asked again. "What do you want Jack?" I let the tiredness of the weekend, the exhaustion of the dreams and the emotional overload of him slide through my voice.

"Bob asked me to come here and help with some estimates. Then we are supposed to have lunch, before I go check the progress at the jobsite," he answered me and for once there was no mockery in his tone, just a calm statement.

I groaned, dropped my hands to my lap and pressed my forehead to my desk. "The universe hates me, if I believed in reincarnation I'd say I must've been an awful person in my former life." I grumbled at my desk.

"What did you say?" Jack asked, and I heard him walk closer. There was more than pure curiosity in his tone, he had sounded excited like what I said meant something to him. It was a strange tone, and I decided to ignore it.

I hadn't meant to say that aloud, and I flinched mentally chastising myself. I sat up and pointed at a desk with multiple monitors. "If you're here for estimates, pull a chair over there. Boss should be here soon, and that is the collaborative estimate desk." I wanted him to go to the desk and leave me alone for a while.

I didn't look up at him, just continued to point. I didn't want to see pity or disgust in his face. I started to get my computer set up and determined to ignore him. I could make this work, if I just stayed busy Jack would fade away into the world.

It worked. Boss arrived about ten minutes after we did, he greeted me but was a man on a mission and went straight to the computer. He and Jack buried themselves in estimates for new jobs that Boss wanted Jack to oversee, I guess I was right when I thought jack would be around awhile.

I busied myself with creating and sending off invoices. The morning passed quickly like this and before I could prepare myself it was lunch time. I considered telling Boss I didn't want to go, but it would be rude to stay behind when he had offered.

"Kel, lunch!" Boss said in a cheery tone. Boss was usually a cheery man. I liked that, even when I was feeling down Boss could be cheerful enough to add some happiness to my attitude. I smiled at him. I really did like my boss. My smile faded somewhat when I saw Jack and knew he would be joining us.

I glanced at Jack and saw him studying me intently again, that frown back in place. I have no idea why but I was so irked by his look that I stuck my tongue out at him. Again I surprised us both, I don't do that kind of thing, it's so childish and impulsive. And far more aggressive than my usual behavior.

Yet, here I was jabbing strangers in the chest and sticking my tongue out. Jack would be the bane of my existence at this rate. I glared at him, sure that my behavior was solely his fault. He still had a look of surprise on his face, but it faded to amusement as he took in my glare.

"Alright! Let's go, I'm driving!" Boss said, apparently unaware still of the tension between Jack and myself. That was probably for the best, Boss would want to fix it and probably make the whole thing worse.

I sighed inwardly. Normally, Boss driving wouldn't be an issue. But it meant that he wanted to go somewhere not within walking distance, and Jack would be with us. If he was unbearable I wouldn't be able to just walk back to my office.

Feeling like a petulant child for being upset by this fact, I closed my computer and walked out the door ahead of the men. I still had my jacket on and the heat outside was brutal, but as long as Jack was around I would not take it off.

Boss walked by and before I could take a step to follow Jack was there. "Careful sweetheart, you'll melt that delectable chest right off," he murmured as he passed me and I saw the grin of wicked amusement on his face.

I stared after him, my jaw hanging open, lost for words. He turned his head and looked over his shoulder. "Well come on, the working men are hungry." Again he had that grin, and the urge to hit him was becoming harder to ignore. It would take me more self-control than I thought I could manage to survive lunch with Jack.

I snapped my jaw shut and stomped after him. How dare he suggest I didn't work. I had been busy all morning, just like him. I had been on the computer and been very productive, every job had been invoiced and this afternoon I would finalize the estimates Boss and Jack had done and prep them to send out. I worked hard! And why did he have to comment on my chest? What kind of person did that?!

I growled at his back, this obnoxious, arrogant, egotistical man had me defending myself against him in my OWN head! How did he even manage that?! I felt like two parts of me were arguing, it was the most uncomfortable my head had felt in longer than I remembered.

Insufferable pig that he was, he had gotten in the front seat without a word or even glance in my direction. What made him so special that he as the new guy got the front seat? And what had I done to deserve such treatment from him? I spent the ride to the restaurant glaring holes into his head imagining a conversation where I was brave enough to call him out and tell him he was insufferable.

My temper simmered the whole way to the restaurant, and I hoped for some patience to make it through lunch. However it seems the universe is punishing me and patience through lunch would not be granted.

We were seated at a table in the back and somewhat isolated. The server took our drink orders and we all quietly studied the menu. Boss asked me to order his usual salad with grilled chicken and avocado. Then he went to the bathroom. That left me alone with Jack.

I gritted my teeth and raised my menu higher, trying to hide him from sight. I prayed that he wouldn't say anything, that he really didn't love to torment me as much as it seemed. That it had all just been a misunderstanding. I lucked out again.

I know I promised to apologize for being so abrasive to Jack, but that was before he had laughed at me this morning. Before he had confronted me and set my temper to soaring heights. No all thoughts of apology were gone as if they had never been.

"So," Jack began. He turned slightly in his seat, and tilted his menu down to look at me. I slammed my menu down. "No," I said flatly, staring him in the eye.

"No?" He parroted. Shock evident on his face.

"No," I repeated. Forcing my face to remain neutral though I wanted to laugh.

"What do you mean no?" He asked with an incredulous look appearing on his face.

"What do you mean, what do I mean? No. Just no. It's a simple word and surely even your brain can process the meaning of the word no," I responded, my temper again heating.

He gritted his jaw and said through clenched teeth, "I know what no means, woman. I don't know what you mean by it." He was practically hissing by the end of his sentence. Apparently insulting him was a good ticket to his temper too. I filed that information away for later usage.

"I mean, no," I said angrily. "No talking, no questions. No. No. NO!" I whisper shouted the last word at him leaning across the table. I was glad I still had the jacket on, having refused to take it off. The way I leaned over the table would have been worse than crossing my arms.

"I was trying to make conversation! Like polite people do," he replied. His tone was annoyed and edgy, but his eyes sparkled with amusement like he was enjoying a private joke. A joke that was most likely at my expense.

I snorted, "you'd have to be a polite person to make polite conversation. I am pretty sure you lack that qualification." I threw my accusation of politeness at him with as much ferocity as I could. With any luck he'd stop talking now.

"Did you get the job because you're so blessed in the chest area?" He asked me with spite in his voice. Completely shifting gears and catching me off guard. Instead of deciding not to talk to me, Jack had decided to insult me.

"How dare you?" I snarled. I was angered, he wasn't the first man to accuse me of such things. Before I had 'earned' my spot on the job sites the men on the crew were less than welcoming. Using my bodily assets as the reason I was there.

"How dare I, what? Did you see the shirt you are wearing? I did, it doesn't leave much to the imagination. And I'm sure Bob has seen it before. Maybe you wore it during your interview, because I can't imagine your dazzling personality won him over." The look of annoyance he had been wearing vanished with a look of self-satisfied glee. He looked like a toddler taken to a candy shop and told he could as much as he wanted.

"That doesn't mean you have to comment on it! What gives the right? It's not like I knew you were here and thought to myself I would wear this shirt specifically for that purpose." I was fuming, I liked my shirts. I felt like a pretty girl, I didn't get to be a pretty girl on the job sites. Out there I was just another set of hands. As much as I missed not being in office, I also really like dressing like a pretty girl.

"Oh, honey, if you didn't want them to get attention you'd wear that jacket all day every day." His lips started to quirk up in a smirk. I was learning to hate that smirk, at the same time that it made me want to just smile and forgive him, it could send my temper white hot.

"Maybe I just don't want them to have your attention!" I snapped, then realizing what I said I felt the immediate stain of a blush on my face. I really didn't want my chest getting any attention, but Jack had again gotten under my skin. I sat back in my chair and pressed my lips in a thin line, repeating silently to myself that I would not say another word to Jack.

"It doesn't appear they get any attention, maybe you should be glad for some." There was a nasty edge to his, as if he knew about me. In one of my novels I would qualify for the title of spinster, a woman not married and never to be married. It was like Jack knew that and saw it written all over me. As I had thought earlier, he must have a Kel booklet of instructions. Not only could he get completely under my skin, but he knew where to hit that would hurt the most.

I felt the sting of pain that he had noticed how lonely I obviously was, and I looked down at the table. He didn't need to see that he had struck the mark. I didn't want him to have more to hold over me. I was settled, dammit, the lonely feeling was only a sometimes thing!

"Don't talk to me like you know anything about me. You don't know me. You don't know my life," I said and to my own horror, I heard the hurt in my voice and I knew he did too but it didn't seem to bother him. My promise to not say another was thrown out the window by my need to... to... I don't even know why I needed to reply to that comment.

"I know enough. Cute girl, big boobs, office job at a construction company. It's easy to figure out," he said it with an easy tone, like that was all he saw of me. For some reason that hurt more than anything else did. I was more than what he had said.

I picked my head up and gaped at him, what was wrong with this guy? "Why are you so awful?"

I asked him before I could stop the words. I snapped my mouth shut again, dammit Kel! I thought *stop letting him bait you!*

"If you think I'm awful, don't enter the real-world sweetheart," he said with that smirk coming back. Equal parts of me wanted to punch his smirking face and kiss it. I again felt like I was being torn in half. A feeling I hated more than I could rationally explain.

"Tell me," I said with a pondering tone, using the feeling of being torn apart to spark some temper. "Has the stick in your nether regions been there since birth, or was it placed there by a scorned lover."

The look of appalled shock on his face was enough to make me laugh and forget my own shock over what I had said. I dropped my head to the table, the laughter shaking my shoulders as I tried to contain it and not laugh too loudly.

"Ass," he said flatly. Even his eyes had gone flat. His face was void of emotion; it was an impressive look. It really gave the impression of one dimension flatness. I committed that to memory to maybe study over in private later.

"Excuse me? Are you calling me that?" I really tried not to swear, especially around people. I had once flaunted the swearing, and then one day decided that I didn't want to anymore. At least not where there were listening witnesses.

"No. I am correcting you. It's commonly stated as 'stick up your ass," he replied mildly. He arched an eyebrow at me then, and one side of his mouth curled up. That smirk was a weapon, and Jack knew how to use it.

I stared at him, losing myself for a minute as I studied his face. I forgot I was angry and why. He had the most perfect eyebrows, and eyelashes. This man's face was designed by a Goddess to make women the world over jealous. His lips had the perfect curve and fullness, and even when he was pressing them flat in anger that fullness was obvious.

Kissable lips, I thought. With a start I realized where my mind had gone, and quickly did a mental scramble to find the anger and push away thoughts of his face and lips. It didn't take much when I remembered he had called me soft, and accused me of using my body to get my job.

"That's what I said," I growled, getting back to where we were in the conversation. I really needed to get a handle on myself. If I wasn't envisioning myself punching him I was day-dreaming about kissing him. It was like the worst case of schizophrenia.

"No, you said nether regions." He grinned. I saw the triumph in his face, he knew he was getting to me. He crossed his arms casually leaning back in his chair. He tilted his head slightly and watched me waiting for my temper to explode.

"Well, you got the point," I sniped, crossing my arms. I had to stop; I couldn't keep reacting to him. I was letting him win and I knew it. I couldn't stop myself though, I tried and I told myself over and over after I would open my mouth that I wouldn't give the satisfaction of responding again. And over and over I broke that and responded.

"You don't swear, do you? Are you always goody-two-shoes?" He had a sweet almost forced innocence tone when he asked that.

I bit off my answer when I saw Boss approaching the table. I was not a goody-two-shoes, I just chose to speak differently. I chose not to be so abrasive, swearing could be extremely abrasive. I had used to swear often, I knew what a well-placed swear word could do and now I chose not to. But that didn't seem to register with Jack, he just found it as an amusing way to mock me.

"They haven't come for our orders back Boss," I said as he sat, so grateful for the distraction of his appearance I could have hugged him. As if that statement were a magic signal, the waiter appeared to take our order.

I ordered first, choosing a cheeseburger with everything and adding bacon. Boss got the salad he wanted, and Jack went for a Rueben sandwich. I handed my menu to the waitress and determinedly looked away from Jack.

"You're not shy about food," Jack commented mildly. Though his tone was mild and conversational the eyebrow and comment were designed to rile me again. I threw a nasty glare his way before grabbing my glass.

I took a long drink of my unsweet tea and looked back up to narrow my eyes at him again. Did he have a special power or something? It was like he knew exactly where to prod to instantly flare my temper. I ate fast, and I ate often. I LOVE food, there cannot be enough inflection on that word to describe my relations with food.

Food, unlike humans, is constant and so rarely let's you down. If food let's you down you can almost always trace it to the human who prepared it. I will admit there is some stuff that nothing can make edible, like olives and eggplant. Just thinking of those disgraces to food could make me shudder, and it was an effort not to.

I opened my mouth to say something back, but before I could reply Boss answered him, "No, Kel, here is a woman who admits to liking food. That's a hard trait to find in any woman these days, and still sometimes catches me off guard." He grinned at me.

I smiled at Boss, deciding to ignore Jack. "You know me Boss, I always say 'Feed me and tell me I'm pretty'. Do that and we'll get along just fine." I used my best chipper silly tone, I have no idea where the phrase came from, but it just suited.

Jack choked on his water, and I turned towards him in time to catch a strange look. Like he wasn't sure what he was seeing, but that look disappeared so fast I began to wonder if it was imagined. He smirked at me.

"Careful, too much eating will detract from your pretty," he said in a voice that sounded teasing but the glint in his eyes disproved that. He was being malicious and cruel, and he knew it. I don't know why he was doing that, and it took everything in me not to throw my drink in his face.

He was insulting me! And he said so charmingly that Boss thought he was joking and laughed! I stared at him, completely lost for a comeback. He was insinuating I would get fat! No one had done that in years! I snarled under my breath, "How dare he try to food shame me."

Boss started to talk shop then, and I turned to stare at a wall studying Jack in my periphery. He was intentionally baiting me, I realized. He was trying to flare my temper, like he was looking for a fight with me. But why?

I pondered over the why until our food came, then it was time to ponder over the delicious burger. But when I was done eating, the questions came back. Why did he antagonize me? Why did I rise to the bait? Why was he so familiar? Those thoughts and flashes of my dreams clashed around like Roman warriors in my head. Images from mostly forgotten dreams sliced through.

Jack and I together, intimately. Or just sitting on a couch and talking. Walking along a beach. Always happy and comfortable with each other. And always I wanted to be near him, in my dreams I felt different than reality. In reality I didn't want to be near anyone, but in the dreams I wanted to be near him. Him and Mary and Carly.

As the thoughts roiled around inside my head like a hurricane at sea, Boss and Jack finished eating. Boss paid the bill and we all left. The ride back was filled with more chatter from the front seat, I again was sitting in the back. This time I wasn't as angry about it. I was still trying to figure Jack out. He was like a puzzle with the key piece missing, and if I could just figure out where that piece was it would make sense.

We arrived back at the office, and I almost ran for the safety of my desk. I slumped in my chair and willed my thoughts to quieten, I had made no progress on Jack and I needed to work. I didn't need this, for him to rule over my attention and life. He was just a man working for my boss. Not even really a co-worker.

Sometime later after I had settled and gotten to work on finalizing the estimates, Boss came in. He was grinning and cheerful, and it was hard not to return his smile. Jack I noticed was not with him, he must've left immediately after lunch for the job site visits.

"I really like Jack, Kel. He's funny, really on top of things and man knows his stuff. I think he'll be good for us," Boss said cheerfully. "I'm going to head home, Kel; the wife needs me to get some stuff on the way and you know how it is the wife gets what the wife wants." He grinned at me, and I laughed.

"Have a good evening Boss. Are you coming in tomorrow?" I spun in my chair to face him. I spun a little hard and had to correct direction, causing myself to tilt over the arm slightly. Boss chuckled at the movement.

"No, not tomorrow. I have to go look at job sites, and meet with potential clients. Maybe Wednesday though," he said, turning away to collect his computer bag and various other items he always carried.

"Okay, see you then," I said with a smile and he went out the door, I smiled at the door for a minute after he left. I wished lunch had been a better experience, but I had still enjoyed Boss's company.

I worked on the estimates until four, I didn't realize how many Boss and Jack had accomplished. I might not even finish them all tomorrow, that was a good thought. It meant we would have a good chance at a lot of work flowing in.

I packed up my work stuff, left my lunch there. It was just snack things anyway and headed to my truck locking the office on the way out. I paused just outside and looked around, I realized I was looking for Jack and mentally kicked myself.

I did not want to see him, that was all. I went to the truck and started it. I hadn't called my mom back yet, so I decided I would now while the truck warmed up. It gave me an excuse to get off the phone since I wouldn't drive and talk on the phone.

"One of these days you'll just keep that phone with you!" My mother greeted me on the second ring. Great, she was in a nice mood, I thought wryly. I wished just once she would say hello and be cheerful about it.

"And one of these days you'll just give it a rest!" I snapped into my phone. "No Mom, I won't. I hate this thing, if it wasn't essential to work, I would throw it in the ocean," I sighed; I really shouldn't have snapped at her. It never did any good, and I didn't like to or want to fight. "What's going on Mom? You never call this often."

I heard her huff on the other end of the line. I had just snapped at her again but I wouldn't apologize this time. "I just wanted to say I saw Alex yesterday and he asked about you."

I felt my face pale and my hands went cold. "Mom, tell me you didn't tell him anything," I said with some desperation. Why would she tell me that? I felt the buzz of fear start to turn my stomach to ants.

"Yes, yes. I kept your secret and didn't tell him where you were, I don't understand why you just left him. He asks about you often," she said, sounding annoyed at me. She always sounded annoyed about Alex, but I couldn't tell her what had happened. Besides I didn't even think she would believe me. She adored Alex.

"Mom, it's my business! Butt out!" I snapped. Then I dropped my head to the steering wheel, Jack was ruining my life! I never snapped at my mom like this before him. "I don't care if he asks about me. I'm not his business either."

"Don't talk to me like that, it's not my fault you ran away and you're too embarrassed to admit it!" She snapped back. "I don't even know why you ran away! If you weren't going to tell poor Alex, the least you could've done was tell me, I'm your mother!" The hurt in her voice made my heart ache. She wouldn't understand, and she never would've believed me.

"Mom, please just don't, not right now. Okay? I'm sorry I snapped, work is stressful and I'm tired. I just don't like talking about him, so can we just not? I need to drive home anyway." I let some pleading into my voice.

"Fine, just fine. Drive safe. I love you." I heard the beep and then the line was quiet, she had hung up. That was the thing about my mom though she always ended calls even the angry ones with 'I love you', she might then hang up on you but she always said those three words... She said that if anything were to happen those would always be the last words, I liked that.

"Love you too, Mom." I was annoyed that she had hung up before I could say it. I put the phone in the glovebox and put my seatbelt on. I missed talking to my mom like I had before moving away, we had been close once and our conversations were nice. I sighed heavily.

There were no cars coming so I pulled onto the road and headed home. I swear I saw Jack standing a couple blocks from my office watching me but when I looked again no one was there. I really must be losing it.

I didn't see Jack for the next three weeks and life settled back down. I hadn't had any more dreams of him or the women and all the estimates were accepted and work began immediately. It was a hiring frenzy.

I conducted interviews, and got new hires in the system and Boss ran around like a crazy man. Time flew past in a blurry haze, for three weeks it felt like I lived on the phone or in the interview room. My life was new faces, and paperwork. Thankfully when hiring new people it didn't feel quite the same as meeting them. I had the upper hand because I chose whether they got the job or not.

Finally one afternoon work settled. All the new hires were on jobs, and everything was started and going smoothly. I leaned back in my chair silently congratulating myself on how well everything had happened.

Before I came to work in the office nothing worked this well. I settled in for a moment of self-indulgent pride, closing my eyes and leaning farther back in my chair. I heard the office door open and assumed Boss had come back from his latest meeting.

"Hey Boss," I said without turning around or opening my eyes. I was comfortable and feeling good. We had accomplished a lot in the last three weeks.

"Well now, that sure is nice of you," Jack drawled. "Didn't know you thought so highly of me Kel." I heard the mockery in his tone again. It must be a permanent sound.

I shot forward in my chair and spun around. Dammit, it really was him. He was like a bad rash, or the plague! Why was he here again? Couldn't he just stay at the job sites and leave the office to me!?

"Ugh," I said, throwing myself back in my chair. "Why can't you just stay in my night-mares? Do you have to haunt my waking life too?"

"Aw, sweetheart, you dream about me?" He asked in a lazy tone. But there was an edge that caught my attention. Was he angry? It didn't sound angry, but nothing else made sense. Even anger didn't make sense. Surely even Jack knew no one could control their dreams.

I swore, and sat up in horror realizing I said that out loud and he had replied to it. This man was a nightmare, the words I didn't mean to say just always fell out around him. I apparently couldn't control my mouth any better than my dreams.

He laughed. "OH! You do swear. I'm impressed," he said in a tone that said he actually wasn't. "Do you have a swear jar? You'll need to put a fifty in for that language." He smirked at me and cocked a hip to rest against the wall.

"Just go away Jack!" I moaned in defeat. I slumped forward in my chair and placed my head in my hands. "Just leave me alone. Why do you have to enjoy tormenting me?"

"Truthfully, I love that spark of fire when you're angry," he said nonchalantly. I heard his footsteps approach but stop a few feet away. As if he were taunting me to finish closing the distance.

I sat up and gaped at him. "What?" He tormented me, and harassed me and fought with me because he liked my temper? Was the man crazy?!

"You're so boring, so plain in general. But when you get riled and that temper flares… " He trailed off on a sound like a groan. "You sparkle, and it's like there really is life there." He finished. He insulted me with such grace that it sounded complimentary.

I stared at him; did he just call me boring?! And plain?! I surged to my feet and stomped over until I was almost nose to nose with him. "I am not boring or plain." I growled in his face, my own flushing hot with the indignation of his insults.

He reached up and tweaked my nose. Tweaked my nose like I was a child. Then he grinned, "there's that spark" he said staring into my eyes. He really was crazy. And just a few weeks ago he accused me of being the crazy one.

I swallowed, but I couldn't look away or step back. I felt like prey caught in the predator's grip, one movement and I'd be dead. My breathing got ragged and short, and in a desperate move I shoved him away. Proud that I had found the strength to do so.

"Don't do that!" I almost yelled at him, feeling my heart race and adrenaline course through my veins. That was too much, too intense. He was too much. Jack had a way of filling a space so completely I couldn't breathe. When he was close the world felt out of control. And even a touch so simple as tweaking my nose set my nerves on fire, my body reacted to him as violently as my temper.

"Do what? I was standing here. You are the one who got in my face, remember?" He asked. His none was nonchalant, but I heard a hidden depth. He wanted me to answer him, he knew he had affected me and the reaction was not wholly in anger. I wouldn't give him the satisfaction of hearing me admit that aloud though.

I looked around the office for an escape, I had to get away from him. I realized then that I was the only office staff from every company still here. That meant I was again alone with Jack. I turned and hurried to the kitchen area, hoping he would realize Boss wasn't here and he would leave.

I poured some water into a glass and began to swallow it in great gulps. I left the sink running, that was a mistake because I didn't hear him approach. I didn't know he was there until I felt his body radiate heat down my spine. He reached past me and turned the faucet off, then casually rested his hand on the counter to my right.

On the left side of the sink, the counter came up to a bar and spun in a quarter circle. The sink itself was almost in a corner between the back counter and the bar, with his hand there I was effectively blocked in. I glanced around, and considered even climbing up on the counter to escape him.

I gulped and set the glass down, realizing my hands were shaking. He was so close, why did he always have to get so close? I swear I can feel his body heat warming mine from my shoulders to my toes. I shuddered, and I know he felt it because our bodies brushed with the movement.

"Not brave enough to go face to face with me now?" He asked softly, his breath sliding over my neck. A caress of air that raised goosebumps across my arms, and made my stomach twist and roll uncomfortably. Another tease of his breath across my neck as he waited for my answer had me closing my eyes.

Unbidden images from lunch three weeks ago came to mind how he had smirked at me and talked about my breasts. I remembered too how he had frowned at me. And memories of dreams of intimacy with him caused my insides to flutter. Every other memory alternated. Nice Jack, cruel Jack, intimate Jack, and crude Jack as if my whole life had only ever revolved around Jack.

My face heated and I clenched my hands, the conflicting sides of him were so confusing. One of him frowning and looking disapproving, one of him with hands and mouth and body... Blood rushed to my head, and poured into my cheeks, I tried to shut out the intimate images of Jack.

I refused to turn around. I couldn't face him, not for the world. I just knew he would see the thoughts in my eyes, he would know what some of those dreams I had admitted to held. I was sure he would see the intimacy, and I needed him only to see fire and anger. I had vowed six years ago no man would ever again see intimacy in me.

"I see your blush staining the back of your neck, Kel. Face me." The last was said so low it was almost a growl. His voice vibrated my neck, and his breath caressed my ear. I shuddered again. I couldn't focus anymore on anything but the way I felt in this moment, the way he felt.

I shook my head, "No," I whispered. Then clearing my throat I said louder, "no." I struggled to focus on my breathing, forcing myself to slow down and not hyperventilate. That would be an embarrassment I didn't want to deal with. Jack would never let me live it down if I fainted at his feet like that.

His free hand landed on my shoulder and spun me around before I could process what had happened. "I said, face me." He growled out when we were standing almost chest to chest. A deep breath and our bodies would touch like they did when I had shuddered.

I pushed back against the counter, willing myself to pass through it like a ghost. My hands clenched at my sides and I glared at him. It didn't make a difference the distance between us remained the same close proximity.

"You are not my boss. You don't own me, and you don't tell me what to do," I said, finding that temper again. It gave me the steel I needed to slow my breathing and stop focusing on his nearness, on his heat that seemed to warm every part of me.

He grinned at me lazily, and his free hand reached up to touch my braid. He wrapped the braid around his hand and locked eyes with me again. "Like I said," he murmured. "I like the spark." He had leaned in to say those words, and was just a breath away from my lips.

He gave a sharp tug and my head hit his shoulder. Then he dropped my hair, spun on his heel and left. Just like that. I watched incredulously as he rounded the wall and disappeared from sight. I heard the door open and close, and I could feel I was completely alone.

The air rushed out of me and I slumped to the floor. What was that? For a moment after he had grabbed my braid I had been sure he would kiss me. And even though at the time I was ready to hit him if he did, I now felt disappointed.

I huffed in disgust at myself, I couldn't believe I was disappointed. But there it was, I had wanted Jack to kiss me. And I was let down that he hadn't. I was feeling bereft and cold that he was no longer so close to me.

I pulled my knees to chest and dropped my head on them, "stupid, stupid, stupid" I berated myself. "He just did that to get a rise and see if he could affect you. And like a doe eyed fawning teenage girl you did exactly what he wanted." I sighed; I don't know how I will ever face Jack again.

I think I could easily hate him, and yet I was drawn to him. I wanted to be near him, and I didn't want it either. I smacked my head back against the cupboards calling myself stupid over and over. Every time I said stupid, I smacked my head against the cupboard behind me.

I just wanted to feel in control of my life again. Jack had walked in and all control had fled. I couldn't even control my emotions and reactions to him!

CHAPTER 5

When I got to work, I realized Jack would now be a semi-permanent fixture at the office, he even beat me there. He had been casually leaning against the door of the office building when I pulled up.

I pulled up and parked, and got my bags together. As I stepped out of the truck I was looking down, then turned to shut and lock the door. I never saw him approach the truck, and I was in my head enough I didn't hear anything either.

"You're late," he said from right behind me. His voice rumbled through the inches between us, inches I had not known were there. I had not known he was there.

I screeched in terror; I had seen him at the door and now he was behind me! I slammed the door of the truck and spun around so fast I managed to catch him in the side with my computer bag. The air whooshed from him and my bags were again on the ground in front of this man.

"What is wrong with you!?" I screeched at him, not yet having gotten my voice under control. "Why do you always have to sneak up on me? Why do you always have to take so much enjoyment in scaring me? Why are you ALWAYS around!?" I was practically shouting at this point, not a care for the fact we were standing on the sidewalk and anyone could witness.

"If... you... Ooof. If you would just pay attention... ugh... To your surroundings you wouldn't be so... owww... scared." He groaned and huffed as if every word caused him pain. "Dammit woman, did you have to try to break my ribs?!"

I'm sure he was trying to sound indignant and angry, but with the wheezing breaths he sounded anything but. I felt the laughter start to bubble inside and I tried to hold it in. I failed, before I could get a grip on the sound it had expelled from my lungs.

I grabbed a hold of the mirror on the door of the truck, laughing so hard I could barely stand straight. I should probably apologize, and feel sorry. But I didn't. I felt justified, even for a minute felt a little karmic comeuppance had finally come around to Jack.

Slowly, I pulled myself together and got my laughter under control. "Why are you even out here, Jack?" I asked him as I picked up my bags and brushed past him to the door.

"I don't have the code." He grumbled. He looked like a cranky teenager who had been told he couldn't watch T.V.

I turned around and grinned. "Ahh, poor Jack. Not yet good enough to be trusted with the code?" I smirked at him and then proceeded to unlock the door. I took immense pleasure in the fact Jack didn't have a code to the office. It was a small victory that I couldn't quite explain.

I didn't hear what he said, but I caught the tone and figured I probably better off not knowing. I felt better after laughing at him, finally something was in my favor. I walked into the office building feeling almost justified, and my smile grew with every groaning breath I heard behind me.

I set my bags down on my desk, and turned a triumphant smile spreading across my face. "Maybe now, you will stop sneaking up on me." I used my best tone of superiority as if I had intentionally hit him, like it was part of a grand plan.

Jack slowly pulled himself upright and walked until he was standing inches from me. "Don't act like you intended to hit me, I heard your little scream. It was all chance and accident." He sneered at me, and crossed his arms. "You should learn to be nice to me Kel. I have a desk here now." He gestured behind him to what had been an empty desk yesterday.

He stood so close that the motion had him brushing against me ever so slightly. I clenched my jaw and stepped back until I was almost sitting on my desk. Jack matched my movements, and even seemed to be taller.

"Maybe it was an accident. But I can still use it as a lesson on manners." I returned his sneer, and casually pressed closer to the desk. But I misjudged and wound up sitting on it. My feet kicked forward as I ungracefully sat, I managed to just not kick Jack in both shins and was mildly disappointed about that.

Jack didn't hesitate, he stepped in closer so I could not slide off my desk without being pressed right to him. Now he truly was taller than me and took the opportunity to look down his nose at me. The beard he kept was curly like his hair, and the curls gave it a scruffy wild look. I had the urge to run my hands over it. Instead I sat on them.

"I have manners enough that I don't need lessons from you." He leaned down and pressed his hands to either side of my hips on the top of the desk. "Especially since you've not said one nice word to me since our first meeting."

I had leaned away when he bent over, and he straightened so suddenly that I felt off balance and almost wound-up laying on the desk, that would have been mortifying. Jack spun on his heel and walked the ten feet from my desk to his and sat down. I smirked when he huffed a pained breath.

I slid off my desk and decided not to say anything back to him, it was like he'd been nice to me either. I grabbed my coffee cup and tried to take a sip, I came up empty and peered through the lid. I must've finished it driving in, I really needed to sort my head out.

Sighing heavily I walked to the kitchenette and started a pot for the work space. I told myself I wasn't avoiding Jack, it wasn't being cowardly to wait for the coffee to finish. I was simply saving energy by staying in the kitchen until I had my mug filled.

The coffee finished, and I poured my mug. Then I wiped the counters down, washed dishes left in the sink by some other office person. Took the trash out the back door to the dumpsters and looked for something else that needed to be done.

I caught myself then, I was avoiding him. "Coward," I hissed quietly at myself. "It's your office, now go own the space." I stood up straighter and lifted my chin. I could do this.

I grabbed my mug and walked back to my desk. I turned my desk ever so slightly that I was able to see Jack out of the corner of my eye. I was determined he wouldn't get the chance to sneak up on me again.

As nonchalantly as possible I said, "I made coffee. If you want it. Empty the pot, you have to remake it, office rules." I peeked out of the corner of my eye at him, but before he could reply the door opened and the other company's office people walked in.

I watched the flow of human traffic; it must be a required office day. Usually there was only one or two other people besides me and maybe Boss. Today every desk was full. I let loose a small breath of relief, I would not be alone with Jack today.

The day went into full swing and I got lost in my work. I never noticed that Boss had come in until I heard him say to Jack that they needed to visit a job. I watched as they left and said a quiet hope that they stayed gone the rest of the day.

The universe was listening to me for the first time ever. My day finished out and I hadn't seen Jack again, with a light step and smile I left the office and headed home. Tomorrow was Friday, and then I could have a Jack free weekend.

The drive home flew by, traffic was light and mostly free flowing. I got home still with a bounce to my step and went inside. My bubble deflated slightly when I realized I wanted a bath and I was too tall for the cheap shower and tub units in the house.

I sighed, I would just turn the water to hot and sit in the tub while the shower ran over me then. I could make it work. I dreamed of someday having a place with a big bathtub I could soak in for hours. I would have wine and a book and just hide away.

Dinner was easy tonight, I didn't want to put much effort in so I grabbed a lasagna, got the oven going and put it in. It would be fine there while the oven preheated. And it gave me time to shower and not overcook the lasagna.

I set a timer in the kitchen and headed to my room to shower. I sat in the tub while the hot water ran over me and felt like it was cleansing something. I didn't know what, but it just started to feel like I was lighter. Like somehow the hot water was unknotting the mess inside me. It wasn't really, everything still jumbled and turned over but the water gave me some temporary relief.

Covering my mouth and nose I tilted my head up to let the hot water spray onto my face. With my eyes closed I could almost imagine I was out in the rain. I love rain, it's like a cleansing of the world. However, rain in the south sucks, it's hot rain for thirty seconds then the sun comes back and it's so humid you could almost swim through the air.

I kept my mind blank as the water poured over me and just enjoyed the sensation. The trails of water running over my skin felt like they were pulling the bad out and running it down the drain. I eventually washed my hair and body, and just as I was finishing my water ran cold. I grinned to myself at the perfect timing and got out.

I dried myself, braided my hair and put on my loose sweats and baggy t-shirt. I could smell the lasagna and followed my nose to the kitchen, in another bout of perfect timing the timer had thirty seconds left.

I pulled the lasagna out, removed the top and set it back in the oven changing the setting to broil to crisp the top. I bounced on my toes for a couple beats excited for dinner. I really love Italian food. Pasta and bread and butter and garlic. Someday I wanted to visit Italy. I wanted to travel a lot actually.

I wished to see Ireland, Scotland, Rome, and Greece. I wanted to be able to go anywhere without the concerns that kept me here. Like money and bills, and just generally being responsible. It also costs a lot of money to travel, and while not completely broke I couldn't afford to not work either.

I made myself a salad and poured some water in a cup. I decided to forgo a drink tonight. I wanted a clear head tomorrow. The timer dinged again and I pulled the lasagna out. It smelled delicious and my mouth watered in anticipation.

I carefully walked it to my T.V. tray, I don't have a table. I never needed one so it was never worth the purchase. I set the lasagna down and collected my water and salad. Truthfully the small two serving lasagnas were the best idea ever. I could eat half for dinner and take the rest to lunch and have no wasted leftovers.

I stared at the dark T.V. screen while eating my dinner, I had no interest in turning it on tonight. Finishing dinner, I cleaned up and prepped the lasagna for tomorrow's lunch and decided to head to bed early.

I was asleep as soon as the light was off and my head touched the pillow. A full belly and long day can have that effect.

"You don't look surprised or pleased to see me, Kel. And we have such history together, I thought you might at least be pleased." The nightmare in front of me smiled lazily at me, he knew I wouldn't be pleased. He was still as arrogant and self-assured as he had always been, that had not changed in the ten years since we parted ways.

"What are you doing here?" I asked, trepidation tainting the sound of my voice. The doorways were a secret, and not many people ever knew and most who found one never came back. We had been trying to find and destroy them among other things. Like rescue those who were lost here.

But we had been found out, our entire operation and the people I loved had been threatened. They had given me an ultimatum, come with them through the door or watch as they killed the ones I loved. The answer was obvious I left, nothing in the world was worth the lives of even one of my loved ones.

"You haven't figured it out?" he asked, a superior note in his voice. *"Come now, Kel, you used to be so smart. Don't tell me that man has dumbed your wits."* The tone he used when saying man was equal parts disgust and hatred.

"That MAN," I gritted out, *"Is one hundred times anything you could ever be."* I sneered at him. I was terrified and deflecting that into anger. I didn't quite understand everything going on yet but the ideas I was getting made the situation that much worse and dangerous. *"You're one of them aren't you?"* I spat out. The realization had hit me suddenly, it was the only thing that made sense of him being here. He was one of those creatures.

Faster than I could track, he had left his seat, grabbed my shoulders, and shoved me against a wall. *"Don't push me Kel,"* he snarled in my face. *"I'm the reason you are alive. We don't tolerate trespassers. And if I hadn't given the order they would've killed you on the spot when we found out. Count your blessings we have… history," He grinned in a way that chilled me to the core.*

I took short sharp breaths, my back hurt from the connection with the wall and expanding my lungs was difficult. "I knew you were never right, never human," I spat at him. "Just end it and get it done with."

One of his hands curled around my throat just tight enough to be a threatening gesture and he leaned closer. "I've only just begun, darling. This is not an end it scenario, you are now mine forever. You should have never left me. You will pay that, and more. You will beg my forgiveness for leaving" His tone had a dangerous quality and the words he spoke held promise.

I didn't doubt anything he said and the cold leaden ball of fear in my stomach had my body trembling. I would never escape him again, I realized. Fear so tangible I thought I could taste it took over my senses. My only relief was that my loved ones would be safe. Whatever happened to me here in this place, they were safe…

I groaned and rolled over. Was I dreaming about aliens now? I had said not human, and creatures. As if dreams of Jack weren't enough, now my subconscious was throwing aliens into the mix. Even if there were aliens on Earth, there was no way that they would take notice of me.

I tried to focus on the face of the man (creature?) from my dream. I felt deep inside that I knew that face and if I could just remember it in my waking moments the dreams might make sense. But the harder I tried the faster the face faded.

Heaving a sigh of defeat I got out of bed and followed the morning routine of readying for work. I just wanted my life to be normal again. My morning routine seemed to be the only normal I had anymore. I didn't like that. I didn't like that one bit.

I hadn't looked at the time when I left my house, and the traffic was minimal again so I wound up getting to the office very early. I grabbed my bags, looked around for Jack and seeing that he wasn't here I took a step forward towards the office.

A shadow I hadn't seen pulled away from a tree and moved towards me. It was early enough that I couldn't distinguish much more than a male form. The sun shining at eight AM off city buildings and reflecting every which way always made it hard to distinguish much.

"You didn't scare me today, Jack. I was watching," I said as the figure approached, grinning like I had won some great accomplishment. Not getting scared by Jack felt equivalent to winning the Olympics.

My smile faded as the man came into view, I took the two steps back until I pressed against my work truck and my bags slid to the ground. I felt the blood leave my face and limbs, and I suddenly grew bone deep cold.

He stopped a step in front of me, and smiled. I hated that smile. He was six feet tall, athletic body from always working out. Muscles cut sharp lines in the tight pants and shirt he wore. He had a square jaw and thin lips. His eyes were so brown they were almost black, a fact that had fascinated me for a long time. Before I learned that eyes that were that dark, were because of a very dark inner person.

"Who's Jack, Kel? Don't tell me you've tried to replace me." He sneered his lip curling up. "You know you can't replace me Kel." Alex was a good-looking man, and once I had looked past the sneers he gave others and only saw the good looks. Then the sneers turned to me and things went wrong from there.

"Alex…" I breathed softly. "You're not supposed to be here." I swallowed thickly and my mouth dried out. Why was here? How was he here? I thought I was rid of him years ago, when I moved away.

He stepped another step forward and pressed a finger to my lips. If Jack had that I would have bitten the offending appendage. But with Alex, the touch made me feel fragile and breakable.

"Hush, darling. I came for you, I have missed you, Kel. I'm sure you missed me." His voice was deep and gravelly, a rumble so low it was like the earth itself was speaking.

I shuddered. That voice had overridden my common sense often in the past, a soft word in my ear and I would forgive and forget. Now that voice brought primal fear and paralyzing terror to my body. I felt incapable of escape and he only had a finger to my lips.

"Tell me you missed me too, Kel. We both know you did. You really shouldn't have run away; it's taken so long to find you." He moved his hand to my cheek and stroked it, there was an odd glint in his eyes. Like Jack had had the other day, as if there was some big secret I was missing and it was eternally amusing to everyone around me.

"Why did you run away Kel? I told you you weren't allowed to leave. I specifically said you were mine forever. Why did you disobey me?" He finished with mock disappointment in his voice. I knew the sounds of real disappointment. I shuddered, he was teasing me and I didn't know if that was good or bad.

I took a quavering breath, "You know why I left."

The words were barely audible as they left my mouth. Memories of what he had done began to flood my mind, I couldn't shut them out. I was bombarded with the images that had led to my leaving. I felt my stomach start to turn sour, if I couldn't stop the memories I would be sick right here.

"Oh, come now. You know better than to try that with me, you know it all happened because you made it. But everything will be fine now. I'm back with you, and we will make it right as rain." He smiled as if the world could be perfect purely because he was here, instead of the world suddenly being an inescapable hell.

"You can't be back," I whispered. "You have to leave, Alex. Please?" My voice shook and broke on that last word. Maybe if I said it, he would leave. Maybe he really was here on the misguided notion I missed him and if I made it clear I didn't he would leave.

"Oh no darling," He purred a wicked light in his eyes. He leaned forward and whispered in my ear, "I'm here to stay. And don't you mention again my leaving or yours. You know how I hate that. We wouldn't want to start our reunion with any..." he trailed off and winked at me. "Unpleasantness."

Footsteps approached from the right and I saw a frown crease his brow as he pulled back. Jack came into view, and for the first time I was relieved to see him. I could have wept with relief that he was here.

"Kel," Jack said, taking in the scene. "Everything good here?" He raised an eyebrow at Alex, before sliding his eyes back to me. Alex caught the glance and I saw him tense and ball his fists.

"Jack." I greeted in what I hoped sounded like a normal voice. "Just fine." My voice squeaked on fine and I forced a cough like that was the reason for the break. "Just completely fine. We were just talking. It's fine." I forcibly stopped myself before I could ramble on further.

"Alex," Alex said, stretching his hand out to Jack. The two men clasped hands and it appeared they were trying to break the other's fist. Pure hatred seemed to leak from Alex, while distaste radiated from Jack. "Kel did mention your name. Who are you?"

I took a deep breath and using the distraction that Jack had created I collected my bags and ran to the door before either man noticed. I hurriedly punched in my code and pushed through the door. I could hear muffled sounds of them talking, but I didn't stay close enough to understand.

I dropped my bags on my desk and raced to the bathroom. I barely made it inside before my stomach revolted. I don't know for how long I was sick, or how long I stayed with my head on the rim of the toilet. All I knew was fear and hatred, and the cold comfort of the porcelain. I was overwhelmed with thoughts, emotions, and memories I thought long buried. Never dealt with, I knew enough of myself to know I never dealt with them. But they were buried, and hadn't surfaced in six years.

I got up and went to the sink, splashing water on my face and rinsing my mouth. Now that Alex had found me I had no doubt I wouldn't be rid of him for a long time. I'd barely managed to escape years ago. And that had taken a long time of planning and preparations. I'd just have to work harder to find a way.

I squeezed my eyes shut, blocking the memories that threatened to overwhelm me again. I couldn't do that today for a second time, I couldn't think about him and what had happened. I needed those memories to go back to their box. With figurative hands and feet I stamped the memories down and shoved them deep, slamming an imaginative lid over them.

I looked at my reflection in the mirror and slowly took ten deep breaths. I patted my face dry and walked out of the bathroom, right into the solid and warm chest of Jack. His smell was masculine and fresh, it soothed me in a way I couldn't comprehend. It was unsettling, being soothed by Jack. I hardly knew him. He shouldn't be able to soothe my rough places.

His arms wrapped around me as we collided, I had been moving faster than I realized and the force of it had knocked him back into the hallway wall and taken me with him. We hit the wall and Jack managed to keep us upright. I'm not sure how we didn't just slide to the floor in a heap, the man was a miracle worker too apparently.

When I realized his arms were holding me snug to him I had to fight the urge to relax into him. It felt natural to be here against him with his arms holding me. It felt comforting and good. It felt right and natural, like I was made to be here in his arms always. I don't believe in soul mates anymore, and so the feeling of belonging with a stranger pushed the rest of my fear away and left blazing hatred. I used the hatred to push myself back together.

I ground my teeth together and pushed away from him, feeling like that was a trap. It had once been comfortable and good with him too.

"Why are you hiding out outside the ladies' restroom?" I snapped, using my anger to hide any other emotion that might try to show through my cracks.

I shouldn't have snapped, but I couldn't handle him and Alex on the same day. I felt like I was drowning and the anger and hatred burned some that away, it gave me some room to breathe. I was starting to hate that I needed to use anger as a functionality tool. What did that say about me as a person?

To my surprise Jack didn't respond in anger, instead there was worry and something else in his eyes. Something I didn't care to examine closer, so I looked away as he said "I was coming to check on you, you've been in there for twenty minutes and I thought someone else might notice something was wrong." There was a softness to his voice that bothered me. What right did Jack have to worry about me?

"Oh what?" I snapped, turning my head back to him. "You wanted to save the gloating over my misery all for yourself? Well here I am gloat away!" I tossed my arms to the sides and stood there staring at him. I felt tears burn my eyes and harshly blinked them away

"That's not what I meant. I don't want to gloat about your misery," he said, and I could see frustration building in his face. Good that was better than pity, frustration and anger I could handle but not pity. A tiny voice inside tried to be reasonable saying it was worry and not pity, and that they were different things. I snuffed that voice out, I didn't want to hear what it was saying.

"No? You mean you don't enjoy seeing me miserable? You sure have fooled me." I gritted my teeth and my breaths became shorter and harder with anger. "Go ahead and say what you think. I'm a silly, soft girl who's scared of her ex and ran inside to throw up. That's what you think isn't it?"

He looked at me saying nothing. But something like remorse crossed his face, remorse or… or… pity. I hate pity! I couldn't stand to think he pitied me, the cracks inside me started to swell, if I didn't get away soon I would break. I was barely holding myself together, already emotions were leaking, I needed Jack to leave me alone. Then if I broke no one saw it.

"Say it!" I snarled. Desperate to make him angry, to wipe the look off his face. He couldn't care, he didn't know me enough to care. I wouldn't let him know me enough to care, because the care of men had never been good for me.

"No," he said softly. "Because that's not what I think or…"

I cut him off with a wave of my hand. "I don't want your pity," I spat the words at him, sounding like an angry hissing cat. I was starting to become desperate to make him leave. I was going to break apart any minute.

"Dammit, woman!" He snarled and finally all traces of concern and softness left his face. "I don't pity you; we work together, and you look as if you might need a friend." His voice was trying to sound reasonable, but there was an edge of anger and still that other emotion. That one that seemed to be a pity for the mess that I was.

I snorted, "What do you know of my needs?" I folded my arms defensively, and squeezed them tight across my chest. Maybe that would help me hold the pieces together.

He sighed heavily, "Everyone needs a friend sometimes." His voice was back to being soft. His eyes shuttered and for a second something like sorrow showed there.

"I don't need anyone!" I spat. "Especially not you!" I shoved past him and hurried to my desk. Out of the corner of my eye I swear I saw his face fall in utter grief and sorrow. As if I had truly hurt him.

I shook my head. It must've been a trick of the light. There was no way what I said had hurt him. I had to get through today, that was all just today and I could go home and make my next move. I could figure out how to get away. Away from Jack and Alex, away from a life determined to see me break. And away from the feelings inside myself.

I dove into work with a furious determination to not deal with Jack. I did the payroll, and invoices. I reviewed estimates. I was so deeply buried in work that the hand on my shoulder had me jumping from my chair.

Boss stood there with a kind smile on his face. "Rough day?" He asked me. Boss didn't show me pity he never had, there had been only kindness between us always. Kindness and a fatherly affection that he showed me.

I nodded, "I just needed to be busy. I'm sorry I didn't notice you were here." I looked around the office. There was only Boss and I inside, even Jack's desk was empty.

"I just got here, Jack called and said he was concerned you would work straight through to Monday." Boss tried to sound flippant and light.

"Jack should mind his business," I growled, trying to keep the words low enough that Boss wouldn't hear them. Then smiling I looked at Boss. "Thank you. I'm going to go home now."

"Kel?" There was a cautious quality to Boss's voice, he didn't use that tone with me often and it caused me to look up at him. Why would Boss feel the need to be cautious with me?

"Yes, Boss?" I asked him and my tone was equally cautious. Jack had sent him here, what had that nosy busy body said?

"You'd let me know if you were in trouble, right?" His tone and face almost broke me, I almost told him right then that things were wrong. But I didn't, instead feeling angry that Jack had called him.

I bit back an angry retort. It seemed Jack was reporting on me as well. Instead I forced a bubbly smile on my face and said "Of course, Boss. Always." Or never was the truth, but he needed reassurance.

He nodded thoughtfully, but worry still crinkled the corners of his eyes so I packed my stuff quickly and we left the office building. The sidewalk was thankfully free of either Jack or Alex. I hurried to the truck, waving over my shoulder and Boss.

I climbed inside and without giving the truck time to warm up I left. I needed to get away before Alex came back. I needed to leave.

CHAPTER 6

I realized I was being followed when I got on the interstate, I had had my suspicions driving out of the city, but now I was sure. In the same way I knew that car really was following me, I knew who was driving it. A dozen scenarios ran through my head about driving the wrong direction or trying to drive until I ran out of fuel.

I dismissed them all, he would follow me and if I didn't go to my house it would just add sparks to a volatile temper. I felt a weight settle in my stomach, and dread made my hands go numb. Somehow I managed to get home and into the driveway. I don't remember the drive.

I sat in the truck, hands clenched on the steering wheel, my foot on the brake and the engine still running. I couldn't make myself let go of the steering wheel long enough to turn the truck off. I couldn't make my body do anything. I had frozen, whether in fear or numbness I wasn't yet sure.

The door opened, and a hand slid into the truck putting it in park and turning the key off. My seatbelt was unfastened and he pried my hands from the steering wheel. I was pulled from the truck and led by my hands like a child to my front door. Every step felt like a drum beat of death, and yet none of it touched the hollowness inside me.

It was unlocked, I never locked the door. I had felt safe here. I knew now that safety had been an illusion. I had never been safe, just temporarily out of sight. The reality of that crashed through me like a wave breaking on rocks. Never been safe.

Roughly he pushed me through the door then followed and shut the door sliding the lock into place. I flinched as the deadbolt clicked. That was what finally broke through the click of the lock. It was the sound of doom, and fear broke my hollow insides.

I spun around backing away from him. "Why, Alex?" I asked backing through the entryway, it opened into the dining room, and I didn't stop until I backed into the wall. "Why?" I asked, a sob trying to escape.

I didn't even know what I was asking. Why had he come here? Why would he not leave? Why couldn't he move on? Why had he done what he had in the past? There were so many why's and I didn't' know what I wanted answered.

He watched me back up until I couldn't anymore and then like a predator he stalked forward. "I told you once, you were mine," he said. "I told you that we would be together forever." He stopped a foot in front of me.

"And you thought," one hand came up to the wall beside my head hitting hard enough I felt the reverberations and flinched. "You thought you could just leave me?" The other hand landed on the other side, I was boxed in.

I stared at him in terror, "I had to leave," I whispered. Again those memories start to rush through my head, angry words and flying fists making me flinch. I knew well the pain of the words and the fists. Like the blood from a raw wound that had had the scab ripped from it, they flooded into my mind.

His face started to get red and his jaw clenched, I recognized the signs of his temper. Recognized that if I didn't say the right thing next that he would lose control again. I never knew what losing control held in store for me. So, I did the only thing I could think of.

I timidly rested my hand on his chest. "Forgive me," I said, bile rising in my throat at the words. I just needed to placate him; I would work on getting away later. If I could just get him to not be angry it would be okay.

Alex has a temper, a temper I had been on the receiving end of. A temper that had left me bruised or sometimes broken, a temper I knew intimately even if I never sorted out triggers for it. He always knew where to hit me, there was rarely an outward sign.

A broken toe could be explained away by my tendency to stub my feet on walls. No one need know I had been late getting his drink and he had stomped on my foot, accusing me of walking slowly on purpose,

The one broken arm, witnesses saw me fall off a horse. I had planned carefully for a year to get away and hide. I had stashed money, researched places to go and when he had been on a work trip I had left.

My mom had always believed I had just spur of the moment left, she always thought the best of Alex. No one knew what happened at home. I never could bring myself to tell anyone. How do you admit to being the woman that let herself get hit?

I rested my other hand on his chest, and dropped my gaze to the floor. Maybe if I didn't look at him it would help. "Please," I said quietly, and closed my eyes. Every instinct inside railed against what I was doing. I should be fighting back! Bile rose in my throat at my next words. "I'm sorry, Alex."

I couldn't fight back. Alex out muscled me and even if I got away right now I had nowhere to go. I had chosen to live somewhere where there were no neighbors. And I had never made friends, always avoiding making close bonds. Alex had taught me that. He had been my closest bond once.

The sound registered first, a ringing sound. Then my face was on fire. I had had my eyes closed and so I had not seen his hand move. I concentrated on not reacting, I made no sounds and didn't move. I squeezed my eyes tighter shut. Most of the time not reacting would cool his temper, there were sometimes though that he kept going until I did cry. I prayed this was the first and not the latter.

His hands closed around my wrists and he used them to tilt my chin up. I opened my eyes and found his full of fury staring back at me. "Don't leave me again," he said. The tone in his voice promised without words the consequences if I did. I suppressed a shudder.

I swallowed and nodded. "I won't," I said the words tasting like acid. But if I could lull him into believing me then I would leave and this time I would find a way to leave the country. I wasn't the same girl of six years ago. I wouldn't be cowed this time, at least not internally.

I would give him the outward appearance he wished. Alex wanted me compliant and I would give him that, until he let his guard down enough for me to get away again. This time I'd make sure he never found me.

He released my wrists and stepped back, and like a practiced actor his victory smile appeared. It wiped away all traces of fury and temper as if they hadn't existed. But I knew better, and I still felt the sting on my cheek. I wasn't in a hurry for more pain.

My weekend passed in a blur. Alex wouldn't let me out of the house. And every time I tried to go outside, he reminded me he was in charge. I wasn't allowed to eat all weekend. Alex said I had gotten lax in my body pride and a couple missed meals wouldn't hurt. I tried to stay on his good side, but I had learned years before he didn't have one. Sometimes all it took was a look. He said I had grown defiant and forgotten the rules. He reminded me of them. Every one, every time. Some he made up on the spot because he felt spiteful. But he was clever, there was never a mark that could possibly be visible. And Alex knew I wouldn't willingly tell anyone, it was why I had run. He knew that, and I knew that. I could never bear the thought of someone pitying me for the bruises and so I kept my mouth shut. Maybe it was just my pride taking over common sense.

I barely slept all weekend, and when I did sleep there was no rest in it. I was on alert for the next swing, the next snide comment. I felt like a caged cat that had been declawed and didn't have any canines. All my defenses were useless, and I was helpless. I felt the years we had been apart slip away. I was back to being the small beaten and cowed woman who had run, my earlier affirmations about staying strong inside lost in a whirl of fists. I started to lose my grip on the me that I have been since moving away.

I prayed silently every chance I got for the weekend to end. I didn't even know who I prayed to, anyone who would listen I supposed. The weekend did end, like it always does, but it was the longest weekend of my life.

On Monday morning when my alarm went off a fight ensued. I demanded to be allowed to go to work. Alex told me I couldn't. So I told him if I didn't show up my Boss would send the cops to my house. It wouldn't happen of course, not even boss knew where I lived but Alex didn't know that.

That seemed to get Alex's attention, and grudgingly he agreed I could leave for work. He followed me into the city, and said he would be waiting for me to get off work. I didn't doubt he would watch the building all day to ensure I couldn't slip away.

I entered the office as fast as I could and again dropped my bags and ran to the bathroom. As I was sick, images of the weekend flitted in front of my vision. No matter how I tried to shove them away.

I tried only once to go outside, before I could step through the door it was slammed shut and I was knocked down. I had tried to get something to eat, before I knew I was allowed, and had felt the pain of that choice. Every memory playing itself like a reel of horror, I couldn't escape them even by squeezing my eyes shut.

I finally stopped when my stomach was completely empty and sat back on the floor leaning against the wall. I closed my eyes and tried to think of ways to get away. I knew I had to, I just didn't know how. It had taken a year to plan last time. I was worried I might not get a year this time. I began to think that Alex wouldn't be lulled into complacency, he would probably watch me like a hawk. Never leaving me alone to plan and plot. I shuddered, and my stomach tried to heave again.

Except here at work, he didn't come into the office, and as long as I didn't use my work computer to plan I could use this time away to figure something out. Alex had discovered my computer over the weekend and went through it. I knew he would continue to do so. He had found the cellphone too, but determined it was nothing worth his time.

I never heard the door open, but the cool hands pressing my cheeks didn't startle me. I caught his smell first, whatever cologne he wore was fantastic. I needed a body pillow doused in it so I could feel that comfort when I slept. I half chuckled, that would probably get me killed when Alex discovered it. He was the jealous and suspicious type.

My stomach was at least temporarily settled and I moved from the toilet to lean against the wall, keeping my eyes closed. I should get up and rinse my mouth, but that would take me more energy than I had. So I stayed where I was on the floor.

"Your hands are cold Jack," I said without opening my eyes. I took a deep breath and tilted my head slightly to the left. That's the cheek Alex slapped Friday. Though worse had happened since, I felt the memory of that sting come back, and Jack's hands soothed it.

I wished I had the courage to show him the marks Alex had left, they would all fade in a day or two. But if I showed Jack now... Perhaps he could whisk me away, and I wouldn't need to be on my own. Or perhaps he'd believe I deserved it. I was afraid of the latter and so I couldn't bring myself to do it and I kept my mouth shut.

I didn't want to open my eyes. I was afraid the judgement I was sure would be on his face. I just wanted to stay like this and pretend we were friends and all was well. I sighed and pressed my face harder to his hand. I had been surprised that a bruise had not been left, not visibly. But the cool pressure of Jack's hand felt like a balm on the hidden bruise.

"Kel," He began. A tone of caution and worry that had me wanting to shrink away from him. I couldn't go anywhere with my back to the wall though, so I would just need to make him stop talking.

"Shh." I cut him off. "Please just, just don't. Just sit here quietly?" I whispered the question, still not opening my eyes. Please just sit here Jack. I thought. I don't want to be alone and I don't want to talk.

"Okay," he said, I heard him moving then felt his legs press against mine, his hand never leaving my face. I don't know why sitting like this with Jack felt so good, but I relished the comfort. I don't know how long we stayed like that. I may have even drifted off. It was so natural to sit silently with Jack. To just be casually touching. I felt a tear run down my face, and Jack's body tightened.

"He's probably going to kill me," I said barely audibly. I wasn't even sure I had spoken aloud until Jack replied to me.

"No, sweetheart, he isn't." There was a firmness in Jack's voice that had me opening my eyes. His lips had thinned and an ember of fire burned those blue green depths.

"I didn't mean to say that," I said embarrassment staining my face. "You can just pretend I didn't say that." I hoped he would, but a part of me knew he wouldn't. And that he wouldn't let it go either.

"I can't unhear it sweetheart." Jack said, and for once the kindness in his voice didn't spark my temper. I was so tired. I wasn't sure I had the energy to be angry. I was so tired, and being around Jack had caused my defenses to fall away.

As if a heavy weight had come over me I felt pulled to sleep, my eyes started to close and I felt my head nod. I had enough thought to chastise myself for passing out on the bathroom floor in front of Jack.

I felt my weight lifted, and I was moving. I couldn't open my eyes. I had never been so tired before. It felt like a lifetime later that I was placed on a soft surface and a blanket pulled over me. A soft fuzzy blanket, as if Jack knew that would be the exact thing to give me the most comfort.

A door clicked quietly shut, and in the dark room I gave in fully to sleep. Nightmares tried to invade the peace of my sleep but every time they did, a warm hand and soothing voice chased them away.

I don't know how long I slept. The sun was shining when I opened my eyes. I looked around the unfamiliar room and panicked. I flung the blankets off and tried to get out of bed, but I was tangled in the sheets and fell on the floor.

Strong hands gripped my arms and the panic took over. I clawed and kicked and tried to bite. I had to get away, I had to make him let go! I couldn't be caught and trapped! I fought and fought sure that Alex was here, that he was the reason the settings were unfamiliar.

"Kel!" The voice penetrated my panic and I realized I had squeezed my eyes shut. "Dammit, woman! That hurts, stop. I won't hurt you!" The hands gripped tighter.

Jack. That was Jack's voice. My eyes flew open and I found Jack's face. "Jack?" I asked in confusion. The haze in my head was slow to part. Why was that Jack's voice?

I looked around the room I was in. I knew this room; it was one of the upstairs Airbnb rooms in the office. Sheepishly, I turned back to look at Jack. Right, I was at work and had passed out on Jack. He had been kind enough to take to a bed for some sleep, and I repaid him by attacking him.

There was a red mark blooming on his cheek, and some scratches on his arms. He had managed to pin my legs by sitting across my lap, and I realized he held my hands behind my back.

"Um, Jack?" I asked timidly. "Um, can you let me go now?" My voice was quiet as I surveyed the marks of my struggle on his skin.

"That depends. Are you going to hit me again?" He asked, there was caution but not anger in his words.

I flinched, and dropped my head. "I'm sorry," I whispered, feeling shame for allowing the panic to take over. "I'm so sorry, Jack."

His weight shifted and he let loose my hands. I watched his feet as he stood, then a hand was outstretched and dangling in my vision. I took his hand and he pulled me to my feet. His grip was firm and warm and the help he offered gentle, as if I would shatter like glass. Maybe I would.

I was still staring at the floor and Jack took me to a chair, gently pushing me down to sit. He offered a cup of water and then another chair was pulled over. Still staring at the floor I didn't drink. My throat felt tight, and even the thought of water was making me feel ill.

"Drink Kel," he demanded a firmness in his tone that stopped all arguments. I obeyed. "Look at me," this command was gentler but no less demanding. Something in that tone made me want to obey him and I clenched my jaw to fight the urge.

I only blindly obeyed one man, and that was because I knew what would happen. I didn't think Jack was of the same mold as Alex, but that didn't mean I had to obey him too. Even on a simple command such as 'drink'.

I tried to raise my face to his, but embarrassment over my panic and the soft trickle of memory flushed my face and made eye contact impossible. Had I really said Alex would kill me? I'd never even said that to myself, why would I say it to Jack?

And then I went and passed out on him, poof fainted like a damsel in distress when the excitement of rescue overwhelms her, I didn't want to be a damsel. I wanted to be able to save myself. I had learned that was the only way, you had to save yourself.

The icing on the cake of shame was my immediate panic when I woke up. The room had been unfamiliar, and the sound of male breathing had tipped me over the edge of reason. Fight or flight kicked in, and when I hit the floor in flight it was all fight. Poor Jack.

I stared at his chin as those thoughts tumbled around. "Jack..." I started. "Look I am sorry, I am. Umm..." I hesitated. How could I make him see he just needed to go? That sticking around me would only bring him trouble. I may have had my issues with Jack but I didn't want my mistakes to mess with him.

"Kel, stop." His voice was hard-edged. "Don't you even try to find a way to push me off. Not this time. There's more than you understand at play," he said that like we were in a movie or a fairytale or something. *These aren't the drones you are looking for*, ran through my head. But this was a movie. This was my life, and Jack needed to butt out.

I snorted and finally met his eyes. "Yea, okay Chesire cat. Do I need a mushroom now? Or are you Morpheus and I need to choose a pill?" I laughed harshly and went to stand up. I didn't make it. My legs gave out and I fell back into my chair.

Jack had jumped to his feet when I did and concern flew across his features. I didn't like that. His concern was too much like pity and I don't need pity.

"Are you..." He began but I waved a hand and cut him off.

"Look it's bad enough I fainted like an idiot earlier, wait! How long did I sleep? What time is it? What day is it? Is it still Monday?" I sat up straight as I realized I didn't know the answers. What if I had slept the day and night and it was now Tuesday?

Had Alex tried to come get me because I didn't leave work? I started to truly hyperventilate, no matter how much I wanted to, I really couldn't breathe. Panic swarmed my senses, if it was Tuesday... My vision tunneled and went black around the edges, and my head buzzed loudly.

A hand smacked roughly over my nose and mouth and I was pulled from my chair to the floor. My arms were lifted over my head and draped behind me on shoulders. Shoulders attached to the chest I held firmly against, by his arm across my chest just below my own arms. One of Jack's legs crossed over mine, and he began to speak in my ear soft and quiet.

"Breathe Kel. Feel my chest expand, expand yours too. Feel mine contract, and contract your chest. In through your nose and out through your mouth. There's a good girl, just breathe," he continued to coach me on breathing and still holding me and keeping a hand pressed over my nose and mouth.

Slowly the black faded from my vision, my head stopped buzzing and I could breathe again. But with the breaths came sobs. Not the sweet pretty crying that you see in the movies, these were full body ugly sobs.

Red eyes, stuffy nose, nasally voice and whole body shudder sobs. I couldn't stop them, I tried to bring it under control but the harder I fought the tears the faster they fell. So I quit trying and sat there with my back to Jack's chest. He had removed his hand from my mouth and now had it wrapped around my stomach, his other still across my shoulders. At some point my hands had dropped and his arm had shifted so it wasn't an awkward hold.

Finally the tears stopped and I gently pulled myself away from Jack and turned to face him. I now added uncontrollable crying to my list of crimes against Jack for the day. This was just getting better and better.

I took a calming steadying breath and asked "how long did I sleep?" I was grateful that my voice only sounded a little rough. I was getting this calming thing under control.

"Just four hours," he replied gently. "It's still Monday, and it's barely lunch time." He spoke as if to a cornered animal that would chew its own leg off before letting him close. I guess I did seem like that though. If this morning's performance was any indication.

I sighed, feeling the weight that had choked me ease. It was still Monday, no way Alex knew what had happened when I got into the office. "Look Jack," I took another deep breath. "I appreciate the help, and to my own horror, the care you have given me. But this is real life Jack. We're not in the movies, there is not 'more than you understand'" I did the air quotes and used a mocking voice when I said those words. "Going on. It's just life. I'm just a girl, who chose a bad guy and instead of dealing with it and getting help, I ran away. And now he found me again, and I have to deal with it. Okay?"

He opened his mouth to speak but I held up a hand. "On my own, Jack. On my own. No one fights my battles for me, and besides you don't even like me." That last part hurt me, to say out loud he didn't like me. I didn't like him either, so why would it hurt?

"Kel," he said, and opened his mouth to say more.

"No, Jack," I cut him off again. "Just no, okay? This isn't a fairy tale. I'm not some damsel in distress that the white knight can save." I flopped back and lay down on the floor throwing an arm over my eyes. "It's just my crap lot in life."

I heard him move, but because I wasn't looking I was taken by surprise when he straddled my chest and pinned my arms over my head. Heat flooded through me, to my surprise it was not the heat of anger.

"Are you serious right now? From rescuer, to molester?" I almost screeched at him, but my voice still raw from the sobs broke and I sounded more like an angry kitten than a fierce cat. "Get off!" I hissed angrily through my teeth. I growled at him. "Jack!" I snarled when he didn't move. "Seriously!" I was almost whining now and so I bared my teeth at him.

I tried to yank my arms free and twist and throw my hips. Nothing worked. He wouldn't move or budge. He stayed there poised over me and holding me down, a tiny smirk at the corner of his mouth as I fought him. Something else sparked in his eyes at my struggle, something I was choosing to ignore because it was trying to turn my insides to liquid.

"Ugh, I guess this is what the wicked witch felt before she died. Trapped by an immovable force," I groused angrily, glaring and still trying to free my hands. I smacked my head on the floor making a face at Jack. "You make comments about my eating habits, but you literally weigh as much as a house!"

Jack's face cracked. He went from serious to collapsed on me laughing so hard I worried we would fall through the floor. "I love your randomness," he said so quietly I almost didn't hear and I wasn't sure I was supposed to. I didn't like when Jack said things like that. Familiar things, like we were still just strangers to each other. It made me uncomfortable and so I often ignored them.

Jack sat up, and grinned down at me. "You will listen to me, Kel. And if keeping you pinned is the only way to do that, so be it." His grin grew. "I'm plenty comfortable, so the arrangement doesn't bother me." To prove his point he adjusted his hips and settled more firmly across mine.

With a snarl, and strength I didn't know I had, I lurched my whole body to the side and dislodged him. He tumbled over narrowly missing a chair with his head. That was a shame. I would've liked to see if the chair was tougher than his head. Though I don't think I would've enjoyed it if he had cracked his skull open, it was only temper that made me want to see him smack his head.

He sat up, the grin still in place, "There's that fierceness!" His tone held pride, like I had done something truly fantastic. "Looks like the kitten has claws again. Good girl Kel." His eyes were bright, and full of excitement. He looked ready to tackle me to the floor again.

"Jack," I growled. "I will break your nose, and this time I won't apologize for hitting you." I was on my hands and knees facing him, my breaths heaving but this time in exertion and anger. "I'm sure you don't want that pretty face mussed. How would you ever get the girls to do your bidding then."

The grin he shot my way spoke to places inside of me I couldn't acknowledge, but I had an idea how he would get a girl to do his bidding. That smirk and those eyes were weapons. Weapons that spoke to very feminine parts of me. Maybe he did need a broken nose, it might make the smirk less attractive.

CHAPTER 7

Wisely Jack rocked back on his heels and put his hands up. He stood and offered me his hand, I took it and he pulled so hard I flew into the air and slammed into him. He had expected it, I had not and air whooshed out of my lungs. I growled knowing he had done that on purpose, there was no need to show off his strength with the memory of being pinned still so fresh in my mind.

Before I could react Jack placed me back in my chair, and took his own. Though I noticed he was out of kicking and hitting range, I guess the man did have some sense after all. I was a bit put out at that. I really did want to kick him.

"Jack, there is nothing to listen to, okay? Six years ago I decided I had to run away. I was in a bad spot and needed to escape. I planned it for a year, and then took my chance. I've been here for five years, quietly hiding until he found me. There's nothing more to it." I spoke quickly and a little loudly trying to make sure he couldn't interrupt before I finished.

He chuckled softly. "I wondered..." He murmured, then sitting he spoke normally. "That's what you think happened?" He raised an eyebrow at me and gave me a look that said I knew nothing and was completely out of my mind crazy.

I huffed. "No, Jack." I bit out. "That's 'not what I think happened'" I mocked him. "That is what happened," I stared at him angry. Angry at him, and myself. Angry at Alex. Angry at the whole world.

Why did the universe need to send Jack to punish me? Wasn't Alex enough? Was I so bad a person that I couldn't catch just a little break? The whole situation was beginning to make me rethink my take on disbelieving karma. I just didn't see how I had been such a bad person to earn or deserve this.

"Mary," Jack said. Leaning back against the chair back and crossing his arms. His face was set and jaw tight, and his eyes were like pools of liquid trying to drown me in their depths and make me see what he saw.

I stilled and blinked stupidly, the anger of seconds before fleeing like a mouse before a cat. A cold dread settled in its place, like the dread and foreboding I had felt before seeing Jack at the job site.

That lead weight settled in my stomach, that sense of foreboding had led to Jack charging into my life and causing the chaos that was him. And now he was saying names that he shouldn't know and the dread was back.

I closed my eyes, surely it was just random, maybe he just accidentally said Mary when he meant my name.

"Carly," he said and I opened my eyes to see him watching me more closely. It was like he knew those names would affect me, and he wanted to see how. He was challenging me again, and maybe even toying with me. It was like a game, where only he knew the rules and actions to take.

I felt sick, the sense that the world was wrong becoming overwhelming. Jack was making the world wrong, I just didn't know how and I couldn't seem to stop it.

"How do you know those names, Jack?" I asked in a whisper. "You really are some kind of stalker aren't you? What? Did you follow me home and read my dream journal one day?" I felt my palms start to tingle and a cold sweat roll down my back. I was going to have a panic attack again if I wasn't careful. An idle part of me wondered when panic attacks had become so commonplace for me.

He rolled his eyes, actually rolled his eyes at me and gave a heavy sigh as if I was a petulant child being obtuse about something that was so obvious. But the only thing that was obvious to me was that Jack seemed to know something about me that I didn't. I didn't like that, I didn't like that a stranger knew me better than I knew myself. I prided myself on knowing me and having control of me.

Then Jack came into my life, and suddenly I felt like I knew nothing of myself and felt like a fish out of water more often than I felt in control. Instinctually I kicked out and growled that he was too far away to reach. He winked at me.

"No, Kel. I'm not a damned stalker. And the question isn't how I know the names, it's how do you know them? What do they mean to you?" He had leaned forward now, and rested his elbows on his knees. He was back to giving me that intent stare.

"They mean nothing, it's just some names I chose for people in my dreams." I snapped my mouth shut. I didn't mean to say that. Damn this man for getting to always speak without thinking. What in the world made that reaction happen?

"Dreams, huh?" He echoed, a pondering look coming over his face. "And what about me, Kel? Am I in your dreams?" He gave me a sultry look that should be outlawed. The look sent tingles through my body and caused goosebumps to raise the hair on my arms.

"NO!" I snapped jumping to my feet. I felt panic again, not the same all-consuming panic. But the panic of foreboding, of knowing that if he kept talking the world would be ruined. If he kept trying I might fall apart and break. I didn't want to know what Jack meant, a part of me deep inside knew that understanding him meant the world would go upside down.

He was talking like this was a movie and that he held the key to fixing everything. But I didn't want to listen, because I didn't believe him. I couldn't believe him. Why did he have to toy with me like this? I had had a settled life, and now with Alex things were bad, but Jack couldn't just make that all go away. This was the real world!

A deep hidden part of me started to scream in my head that I needed to shut up and listen to Jack that I needed to understand him, I fought that part of me. Fought with every instinct I had. I could only handle one thing at a time. Right now Alex was it, I couldn't think or deal with whatever Jack was trying to tell me.

I started backing up, saying no over and over and shaking my head. I wasn't looking at him anymore. I couldn't look at him. I backed up until I hit a corner of the room then I slid to the floor and drew my knees up burying my face on my forearms.

I kept saying no, I didn't know what I was saying no to. No to him, no to the world, no to the fact he was right? That inner part of me that had been screaming at me seconds before seemed to be trying to explode out of me, it was like a separate part of me. She was mad at my denial and refusal and she would come out and force me to listen. I fought harder against her, and managed to push back down deep again, silencing her.

Knees pressed to either side of my feet and his hands so gently pulled my arms down. "Kel," he said and his voice broke on my name. As if it hurt him that I was like this. "Kel, please. Look at me. Just hear me out. I can make it make sense. Please, Kel." His voice was pleading with me to hear him and I couldn't bring myself to do it.

"Don't, Jack," I whispered. "I'm broken, can't you see that?" I don't know what I meant or why I said I was broken. I had meant to say something else. Anything else really, I never admitted to anyone that I was broken, not even myself. Jack was breaking down the barriers and walls inside me and I was close to letting him in completely.

"No," he said quietly. "No, you're not broken. Just a little lost." He rested a hand on my cheek. "I'm here to find you." His eyes had gone soft and the warmth of his hand on my cheek caused me to tilt my head into his touch.

"What if I don't want to be found?" I asked with despair in my words, I really didn't know what he meant but it felt like he couldn't do that. Couldn't "find me", that finding me would be disastrous. It would be as bad as listening to him. I was afraid, I realized.

Afraid of the feeling that Jack was right. I didn't understand what he was right about, there were too many holes. Too many gaps for me to know what, but some part of me knew Jack was right and that started to make me angry again.

He chuckled, "It's too late for that, I am not losing you again." I heard his teeth clack as his jaws snapped shut. He yanked his hand away, and the floor creaked as he shifted slightly. As if in anticipation of my reaction to those words.

My head snapped up. "What do you mean again, Jack? We've never met before you charged into my quiet life. You don't know me, you don't even really know anything about me. Why are you even here? Do you want payment for 'rescuing me'?" I was being irrational, a part of me knew. I was lashing out at him and pushing him away, but I couldn't stop myself.

"Should I be here on my knees begging to repay you for carrying me up the stairs? I could've just passed out on the bathroom floor, I'm the only woman here and no one would've bothered me! My life was fine, until you came around! And like you're a bad luck charm everything started to fall apart!"

I shoved him physically then, and he fell back landing on his back. I scrambled to my feet and kept my back in the corner, Jack had propped up on his elbows and was now looking up at me. I shoved away all the thoughts I had just had about listening to Jack, he was crazy and he was only here to…to… Well I didn't know why he was here, but his presence made my life harder.

"You're ruining everything JACK!" I put emphasis on his name, like if I could just place all the blame on him everything would be okay again. If I could shove all my anger and worry and fear onto Jack then maybe he would go and my world could make sense. I may not have been the happiest before Jack came into my life, but I was settled.

"How do I know you aren't the reason Alex found me? Tell me that! He came around after you showed up!" I heard my voice rising in hysteria. Heard it and couldn't stop. I didn't know where that accusation came from, but it seemed right. Jack had charged into my life like a wild bull, and then shortly after Alex had reappeared.

I balled my fists and pushed so hard against the wall they started to hurt. "Everything started with you Jack. Everything. Just leave me alone." I stepped over him and all but ran for the door. I raced down the stairs, and slipped into the bathroom. I need to calm down before going to my desk.

I took a breath, splashed water on my face, and put on my business face. I could do this, just a few hours then home. Home and... I slammed the mental door on that thought. Just home I told myself. Just home. I walked to my desk glad for my even step and settled in to try and work.

Two hours later I was ready to smack my head on the desk. I couldn't concentrate, I kept thinking about Alex and Jack and Mary and Carly. How had Jack known those names? How had it come to that Jack showed up and then Alex came pounding back into my life?

I didn't believe in coincidence or fate. I knew there was an explanation for everything and the only thing that made sense was somehow Jack was the cause. Maybe Alex had hired him and he was actually a Private Investigator. That would explain why Alex looked so hateful. He would have been angry at needing help.

The more I thought about it, the more sense it made, and the angrier I was at Jack. How dare he decide to play in my life like that. Who did he think he was? I fumed at my desk, my work untouched. I couldn't focus or concentrate on anything but how angry I was.

Sighing I packed up my stuff and prepared to leave, when I turned Jack had stood up as well and tried to approach me. I rushed past him and to the truck. I wasn't surprised to see Alex there; I was surprised when Jack followed me out the door.

"Kel!" He said, trying to catch up to me. There was something in his tone that almost made me turn back. But I was angry at Jack and sure that he was to blame for everything, so I kept going.

I hurried faster, better the devil I knew in front of me than the one behind me. He made a grab for my arm, but Alex had already reached me and yanked me from reach. I stumbled as he shoved me behind him and planted himself between me and Jack.

"I told you to stay away from her," Alex growled menacingly. "She's mine, and I won't allow you near her." I watched his fists ball up and the color rise in his neck, if I didn't do something he would hit Jack.

I didn't want that, even if I was mad at Jack. I put a hand on Alex's arm. "Please, just leave it Alex. I'm ready to go home." I hoped my voice was placating enough to stop the brewing violence.

Alex turned without another word to Jack and grabbed my arm. "You are riding with me," he said using the tone that brokered no arguments. I stumbled after him as he stormed away from Jack to his car, I didn't look over my shoulder.

Alex opened the passenger door and quickly got inside, not daring to look at him or say a word. The driver's door opened and slammed shut and the engine started. Alex pulled away from the curb and sped off. I didn't look to see if Jack was still standing on the sidewalk, I was still angry at Jack.

"Did you at least pay him before you threatened him, Alex? What was the going rate for finding me?" I snapped my mouth closed and covered it with my hands, eyes wide in terror. Angry at Jack or not I hadn't meant to say that. Being away for six years had not done me any favors. I used to know how to keep my thoughts to myself. I seemed to have forgotten.

Alex growled a sound low, primal, and threatening. A sound that field mice heard before the predator struck. A sound that made me wish to open my door and leave the moving vehicle. I grabbed the handle and tried to open it.

The door wouldn't budge, I hit the unlock button and tried again. All I could think was I needed to get out, that sound held pain and maybe even death and I had to get away. Still the door didn't open, I pulled and pulled on the door handle. I tried to roll down the window something, anything. Nothing worked, I was trapped.

Alex's hand slapped hard on my knee causing an instant rush of pain at the contact, and then he tightened his grip digging his fingers in. He started to laugh, cold cruel laughter. The kind the worst villains in movies have, and you just know the maliciousness is there. This is a Disney villain's laugh, this is the guy who caught some that thought they had escaped.

His fingers pressed harder and I let out a squeak of pain. "Child locks, darling, and the window locks are set too. You can't leave this car unless I allow it," he laughed again. "As for paying that man, I have no idea what you are talking about. I finally got your mom to crack and tell me where you went."

My head emptied, all thoughts drained away at his words and I stared at him blankly. I couldn't process or think or act. I was a shell of emptiness. Even the strong angry voice that had demanded I listen to Jack was silent. Where was that when I needed it?

"Oh don't look so shocked, she always loved me." He had a smug tone that broke through the empty in my head and I felt chilled to my core. I had misread the whole situation and now I probably solidified my own disaster.

Mom had told him, not Jack? But I didn't understand that, it didn't make sense. Jack seemed to know things about me, things he shouldn't since we just met. And Alex, he had reacted so violently hatefully when he saw Jack. Why would he do that unless he had had to ask for help? Why couldn't my world just make sense anymore?

"So you didn't hire a PI to find me?" I finally whispered almost inaudibly. I was still trying to process everything he had just told me, but my brain seemed to be working in reverse. Stuck on the fact that Jack wasn't the one who had brought Alex here.

Alex laughed again and pressed the gas to merge on the interstate. I hadn't realized we were already out of the city. "You really think I would spend money to find you? I knew you'd either come back to me or your mom would tell me. I just had to bide my time."

I slumped in my seat, defeated. I had been so sure it was Jack's fault that I had dismissed everything he tried to say to me. Well, I don't actually know what he was trying to say. I had just dismissed him entirely. What if he was trying to help me escape?

I felt silent tears start to trickle down my cheeks, what if Jack had been trying to help and now I had ruined everything? Just as I had accused him of doing. My life was my mess, made of my bad decisions and I had thrown that at him. Like it would make him responsible and I could just say it was someone else's fault.

"Oh, stop crying. That's pathetic you know that? Absolutely pathetic. You're upset I wouldn't pay to find you? You weren't worth the money it would cost, not when you shouldn't have left in the first place, not when you knew better. So why would I indulge your tantrum by spending money?" Alex said with a bite in his tone. "You are mine, and you know it. There was no sense wasting money. It all worked out like it should."

I wiped my face letting Alex interpret my tears the way he wanted, if he knew I was crying because of Jack... I shuddered at that thought. Alex was a loose cannon; I never knew what the outcome would be.

I stared at my hands the rest of the drive, hoping I could have the chance to speak to Jack again. Maybe he would understand and still help me. If I could just explain to Jack that I had trust issues, and that I didn't believe in coincidence so I had convinced myself he was the bad guy, maybe he wouldn't hate me.

Alex pulled into my driveway and parked his car. He came around and opened my door, then reached a hand in and yanked me out. "House," he said, as if I were some trained animal to do his bidding.

That's just it though, I was. I turned and walked to the house, watching my feet as I went. I heard the car door shut and just as I got inside Alex was there behind me. I don't remember when I had stopped questioning and just started to do as Alex said. But I had done as he commanded for a long time without fail, and the old habits were taking root again.

A shove from behind sent me tumbling to the floor, and I rolled over to look up as the door slammed and Alex stood over me. I cringed; he was angry. Anger was never good for me, and I knew I wouldn't be able to calm him down.

He knelt down, and grabbed my shirt pulling me to a sitting position. "Did you think I had forgotten you interfered with me today? You know better than to get in the middle, you should have shut up and let me deal with that nosy *man*," he said man like it was the worst swear word. Like he was speaking of a slimy creature rather than another human being.

Something reverberated in my head at his tone, like a memory just out of reach. The way he said man, it was familiar. I tried to focus on that, but the fear that he was sparking buried that memory once again.

"Someday, you will remember your lessons," he snarled, and shoved me back down. The connection of his foot to my ribs made me gasp and curl on my side. "Stay there," he snarled. "I'll let you know when I am ready to deal with you."

I closed my eyes and tried to breathe slowly and shallowly. I don't when he left, or when he came back. He may have stayed in the house or left. I don't even know how long I stayed curled up. I had learned years ago to hide inside myself. To box up what was me, and hide. I could escape the world this way, and nothing outside my box could hurt me. No physical wounds, or terrible words. I kept me hidden and what the world saw was a shell. A false me.

I hadn't gone into my internal box in years, and it took a lot of concentration to manage. It was like the mind quieting thing, but more complete. But I did get it and the world faded. I found quiet and comfort inside my inner box. Something the real world never offered. Even these last few years, I realized, though quiet was not comfortable.

"Get up!" Alex snarled, and I jumped. He was standing over me and I didn't know how long he had been there. "We're going to bed," he said and walked away.

My stomach growled in protest as if what he said had been some kind of cue. I wouldn't ask about dinner; I was just glad to go to bed. I wanted the oblivion of sleep. I actually hoped for a dream of Jack for the first, I wanted that glimpse of a happier life.

I carefully got to my, and gingerly walked down the hall. I didn't hold my ribs like I wanted, I knew if he saw me cradling the injury it would inflame him. So instead I forced my hands to stay at my sides and just walked slowly.

By the time I entered the bedroom he had undressed and was in the bathroom, his clothes a pile on the floor. Habit had me picking them up and placing them in the basket before I could stop myself.

I quietly and slowly undressed, only groaning once as I pulled the shirt over my head. I caught sight of myself in the mirror on the closet door and saw that purple was already spreading from my breasts to my hip bone, and my side to my stomach. He had kicked hard then.

I peered over my shoulder towards the bathroom and heard the water still running and didn't see Alex. I stepped closer to the mirror and gently touched the angry purple marking. I studied it, and tried to take a deep breath.

It hurt too much to do so. I was so focused I didn't notice Alex was there until I saw his reflection behind me in the mirror. I flinched when our eyes met, he was still angry.

His hand landed roughly on the bruise and I tried to pull away. His other hand came to my other side stopping me.

I watched in pained horror in the mirror as he curled his fingers inwards, digging into the bruise. I whimpered, and my knees started to shake. His head lowered beside mine and the venom in his voice could melt steel.

"I said we're going to bed. I didn't say we were going to stand in front of the mirror. I didn't say we were going to look upset at well-earned punishments." His voice was low and dangerous. "Did I, Kel?"

"No," I answered in a whisper. I dropped my eyes to the floor and tried not to flinch away from the grip he held me in. That would only anger him more. And I didn't think I could handle any more pain tonight.

"Then get in the bed before I give you another to match on the other side." He squeezed hard on the bruise and released me. Stepping back so I could move around him.

I gritted my teeth and held in the pained groan. He didn't like to hear those noises. I quickly finished undressing and got into bed. Alex followed, and the lights turned off. The dark offered its own kind of escape, I could pretend this happened to someone else if I didn't have to actually see it.

I knew the routine, and I went into my internal box as Alex had his pleasure. When he finished and rolled away I stayed awake staring at the ceiling. I wondered how my life had come to this. Not this specific moment, but this place.

I used to say women who put up with abuse of any kind were fools, they should stand up for themselves. They should grow back bones and leave. I generally had no patience or understanding for them. But here I was, now one of those women I hated so much.

With a start I realized I hated myself. That was why I wouldn't listen to Jack. He had looked at me like I was a person worth something, but I wasn't and I couldn't handle that look. I hoped he would be there tomorrow, I wanted to apologize. And maybe find out what he wanted to say.

The last time I knew what time it was the clock read two AM, then next thing I knew the alarm was going off. I groggily opened my eyes. I knew Alex would let me go to work today. He wouldn't do anything that might draw attention and I had already said my absence would draw attention.

I got out of bed and while getting dressed I observed the bruise. Careful not to look directly at it, I marked in my mind it's colors and shape. And the pain I felt with every movement. All of it was sharp and clear in my mind.

The purple had turned black, with a tennis ball sized lump over my ribs where he actually kicked. The lump itself was an angry red and yellow sore. The overall bruise was egg shaped with the wider end over my rib cage and the tip just over my belly button. The bruising color still spanned from just below my breast to my hip bone. The colors of the bruise against my pale abdomen gave my skin a sickly tint.

I dressed carefully, and was thankful for the little favor that the bruise was on my left side. I am right hand dominant and it would've been impossible to hide. Now though instead of impossible it was just improbable.

Though I knew I wouldn't actually open up and tell anyone, I hoped it was noticed. I hoped someone was nosy enough to see and question. I didn't think my luck was that good, but that small spark of hope still sat there.

Jack wasn't in the office today, and neither was Boss. I had an email from Boss saying he and Jack wouldn't be around the rest of the week, there were a bunch of new jobs that they had to get going.

My heart sank, I had told him to leave me alone and he had. And now even Boss was gone, I wouldn't allow myself to wallow in self-pity though. Instead I threw myself into work. At lunch time, I went outside and Alex walked me to a restaurant.

He ordered a side salad for me and a burger for himself. When the food arrived and the waitress left he laughed. "You got into some bad habits without me here to take care of you, got a little soft in the middle too." He looked pointedly to my stomach; I wasn't as skinny as I had been five years before. It happened with age and an actual diet of food.

I bit my tongue, holding back the retort that would not be good for me and ate in silence. After we finished he walked me back to the office and I went back to work. At four PM I packed up and left. Alex drove home, and for once he wasn't angry. In fact we ate dinner and he was almost pleasant. Bed time was the way it had always been.

I didn't sleep again until late at night, but my week continued in the same way as Tuesday had done. Work, lunch, work, home, dinner, bed. I dreaded the weekend; I would have no escape then. I would be alone with Alex for two days again. I tried not to think about it, because doing so would start cold sweat running down my spine.

On Friday afternoon Jack and Boss came back. They came in through the back door of the office and would have been unobserved by the street. I was relieved to see them, and the direction they came from I could talk to Jack, and Alex wouldn't even know he was here.

Boss caught sight of me and his brows crinkled. "Is everything okay Kel?" He asked concern and worry so thick in his voice it was amazing the emotions didn't choke him. I must look really bad if Boss was getting that caught in emotions.

Jack's eyes flew to my face and as he looked me over a frown grew. I knew he couldn't see the bruise on my ribs, now less black and purple and more green, brown and yellow except for the lump that was still red and yellow green, but it felt like he saw. Like he knew.

I faked a cheery smile. "I'm just tired Boss, not feeling so well this week and it affects my sleep. Ask poor Jack here, he had to carry me to a bed when I fainted on Monday." I added a light chuckle to my tone, trying to set Boss at ease.

It worked. He nodded. "You could've worked at home, you know," he said with fatherly chastisement in his voice. Boss had half stepped into a fatherly role after hiring me, having no family here he felt he should help fill the role.

I gave him the proper chagrined look. "I just work better here, and I'm not contagious." I couldn't admit to Boss that this was my escape. He didn't need that. He didn't need to know how sad and pathetic my life was; it would only cause him pain.

Boss nodded and he and Jack walked to the estimates computer. I stood and went to the kitchen to refill my water bottle. I needed to get away for a minute, I just knew somehow that Jack didn't believe I was only tired.

I set the water bottle on the counter, and stretched my arms over my head, the motion hurt like hell. But I had made a habit to do this when I refilled my water, as long as no one was in the kitchen. I closed my eyes holding in the whimper, the stretch felt good except where it pulled on my bruise.

The growl to my left had me dropping my hands so fast my arm slammed against the lump on my ribs and my breath expelled in a gasp. I grabbed the counter as stars danced in front of my eyes. The pain was intense, it felt almost as it had the night he kicked me.

Jack's hands grabbed for my shirt as he tried to lift the hem, he growled again. "What is that?" He snarled inches from my face. He kept looking from my ribs to my face as if he couldn't settle on where to place his focus.

I had told myself I would be nice to Jack; I would talk to Jack and apologize. I told myself this all week, but with him here face to face growling at me demanding answers, and trying to lift my shirt? All that resolved when out the window and I snarled back at him.

"It's a bruise, Jack. Have you never seen a bruise before?" I snapped, forcing my fingers to release the counter. "So sheltered you don't know what a bruise is Jack? And here you were calling me soft. Guess I'm not as soft as you thought, since I at least know what bruises are!" My nose curled, in anger and pain and disgust at myself for starting a fight.

Jack grabbed my hand and hauled towards the ladies' restroom. I was so caught off guard I didn't fight him. He opened the door, and pulled me inside after him before closing and the door then leaning against it.

"Lift your shirt," he said casually. As if this were normal conversation. As if he had asked for a condiment at lunch or something. Not at all as if he had just demanded I lift my shirt up for him.

"Excuse you?" I hissed. Why was he always bossing me around? I could only handle one overbearing, dominant, and bossy male in my life. Jack was breaking my quota.

"Lift your shirt," he repeated and folded his arms over his chest. He said each word slowly and with emphasis, and if my 'excuse you' had been because I didn't understand his words. Not because I was offended by them, arrogant man.

"Who made you the boss of my life?" I demanded in indignation. I wanted to cross my arms too, but I already knew that movement was painful so I settled for balling my fists. I should just show him I wanted to, if only to share my burden. Misery loves company and all that.

Jack slowly pushed himself off the door and stalked towards me, instinctually I took a step back. Then angry at myself I stopped. I wasn't going to let him intimidate me. I lifted my chin in defiance, and narrowed my eyes at his approach.

"Someone needs to be the boss of your life because it looks like you aren't any good for it." He growled when he was again inches from my face. This man loved to invade my personal bubble. I felt again the heat of him start to sink into me. He could be so distracting when I wanted to be angry.

I stepped back, trying to get some distance. He stepped forward, closing it. It was like a dance, a dance that ended when I was again backed up to a wall. How did I always do that to myself? I always managed to get myself cornered with him. If I didn't know any better I would say it was on purpose, except I hated to be cornered and caged.

I stared at Jack in silent challenge, all while silently berating myself. I wanted his help! So why didn't I just give in and show him the bruise?! Pride, I decided it was all about my stupid pride. Jack placed a hand on my right shoulder, and as if we were intimate lovers he trailed that hand down my arm. When he reached my fingertips he curled his hand around mine, and slowly lifted it over my head.

He pinned my hand where I could just feel the disturbance against my hair. I swallowed still looking him in the eyes. Still trying to issue the challenge of dominance. I knew I would lose. I could feel myself giving in.

His other hand went to my left shoulder and even more tenderly he trailed it down my arm. His hand curled into mine and as if already knew the extent of the bruising he moved more gently and placed my left hand in the palm of my right.

Using one hand he held my arms there, and leaned in closer. "Why don't you ever do as you are told?" He asked, a hoarseness to his voice that I didn't want to consider, it sounded too raw and emotional. Like the familiarity he often let in his voice it didn't make sense.

My brows bunched and I opened my mouth to tell him he didn't make sense. Instead I said, "You like the challenge." I snapped my jaw shut and felt more confused than ever. Why had I said that? I was trying to say his words didn't make sense, where had the challenge comment come from?

A spark flashed behind his eyes, and a lazy smile graced his full lips. Lips I realized were mere inches from my own, lips I wanted to kiss. I could almost feel his lips, and taste the kiss. Heat built in me and I barely stopped a groan.

I pressed my lips into a firm line, halting that thought. Intimacy was not good, and would not help. I really needed to learn to control myself around Jack, probably right after I figured out how he could manage to affect me in such ways.

Jack leaned a little closer, now barely a breath kept our lips apart. "You're right. I do like the challenge. I also like to win, and sweetheart," he paused and pure mischief flashed in those blue green depths. He leaned towards my left ear and said in a growl. "I always win." He pulled his head back and locked eyes with me again.

My face felt heated, and my body had reacted in ways I didn't think it could anymore to his words. This man was dangerous to my sanity. If I wasn't trying to cause him physical harm, I was reacting to him in a way I swore to never do again. I was the world's biggest yo-yo and the worst part is I did it to myself.

His face went serious then and he looked down at my abdomen. He reached for my shirt, and I tried to pull my hands away. Twisting to try and keep him from getting ahold of my shirt, suddenly I didn't want Jack to see anymore.

"No, wait. Don't look," I said, but he had already started to pull up my shirt. "Jack," I said pleading in my voice. "Don't." I was begging him, I wanted to save him the horror of the mark on my skin.

He didn't listen, and my shirt was now far enough up to expose the whole bruise. All teasing, play, and enjoyment left his face. Fury, so hot and fierce I wondered that he didn't burst into flames, exploded across his features.

He let go of my hands and shirt, and I righted the material hiding the bruise. His hands clenched and his body shook. I reached for him, and he yanked himself away as if I would hit him or something equally bad.

I dropped my hand, and stared at him. "Jack?" I asked timidly. Afraid he would hate me and blame me. I would have done so. I had done so once, looked down on women who wouldn't just leave. Who wouldn't gather their courage and go. Then I had joined their ranks, and I understood in a way only experience could teach.

He spun to face me and I shrank farther against the wall to try to not be the focus of that gaze. "Don't speak." He said to me and turned away again.

I bit my tongue literally and figuratively and watched the man in front of me. Why was he reacting so strongly? Sure no one liked to be faced with an abused woman, but it was like he was blaming me for it. I dismissed the prior thought that I would react the same, I could be irrational at times.

His shoulder bunched and loosened half a dozen times, then he slowly turned to face me. The fury had left his face but still smoldered like hot embers in his eyes. Wordlessly he put his hand out to me.

I hesitated only a second before I placed my hand in his and he led from the bathroom. We walked past the kitchen and out the back door. Jack led me quickly in silence from the office building down two blocks to where he parked his truck. It was a nondescript truck, black Toyota tundra with no personal markings.

He rushed me to the passenger side and opened the door, gently but firmly he picked me up and set me in the seat. Then he hurried to the driver's side and got in. His face was stone cold, and void of emotion.

Part of me was afraid of that face, not for myself. I just had the feeling Jack would never hurt me, but for the world at large that face meant death. I hoped we didn't see Alex wherever we were going, the thought of that confrontation made me shudder.

"Put your seatbelt on," he said before driving away.

CHAPTER 8

We drove in silence for two hours before I couldn't take it anymore.

"Jack!" I said firmly, trying to get his attention. I couldn't handle the

stone face and silence. I was antsy and needed a distraction.

"No," he said, stone faced and not looking at me.

I huffed. "Well at least put some fucking music on if you're going to sit here in moody silence." I snapped my mouth shut and looked out the window, damn the man. He had riled me enough to swear at him.

Jack's laughter was so sudden and stark I almost hit the ceiling of the truck, I whirled in my seat and stared open mouthed at him. He continued to laugh, and even wrapped one arm around his belly. I glared at him.

"WHAT?!" I snapped, yelling to be heard over his laughter. I was the tiniest bit relieved that the laughing seemed to have lightened the mood. It was as if the clouds had parted and the sun had come back.

Jack's laughter died off, but a smile remained behind. "Damn, woman, I have missed your sass." He grinned at me.

"Stop that Jack!" I said heatedly. I had wanted distraction, not his weird familiarity with me. I just wanted to pretend the world wasn't going completely crazy.

"Stop what?" He asked me. A tone of innocence in his voice. He knew exactly what I meant and was again poking my buttons. What was it he had said? He liked my fire? He tormented me so I would get angry, and he could see my fire.

"Stop talking like we've known each other forever. We just met like a month ago!" *But I've been dreaming of you for seven months and Mary and Carly for years.* I finished silently in my head. He didn't need to know that, and I wouldn't be telling him anytime soon.

He shook his head. "No you stop Kel!" He said, anger biting at his words. "You know deep down that you've known me a long time. That we mean something to each other. Stop hiding from it, and face the facts. The world you know doesn't feel right, does it?"

I snapped my teeth together and looked at the window. I didn't even know where we were, this is how murder movies happened. The rescuer would suddenly pull over and the rescued would be dead.

"Are you taking me to the woods to kill me or something?" I asked, not answering his question. I looked out my window trying to determine where we were going, I didn't know and until now hadn't been paying much attention. I also didn't want to admit he was right. So I deflected instead, I was quite good at that.

"Because it sure seems like the swamp would be a better place to dump my corpse, at least then there would be less chance of you getting caught." I grumbled the last sentence slouching in the seat. I didn't know why I was being testy with Jack. I just was.

I knew I probably looked like an angry pouting teenager, but the fact was what he said had rattled me. The world didn't feel right, I had pretended it was me that wasn't right. That I just hadn't been able to find my place in things. I never once thought that it was the world that was wrong.

"Oh, don't be so dramatic," Jack sighed. He sounded as if he was world weary and I was an obnoxious child questioning his all-knowing wisdom. That tone sounded practiced, and I wanted to punch his arm for using it on me.

"Takes a drama queen to call out a drama queen," I snapped back. Wait what? "Uhh, I have no idea why I said that," I sighed and leaned my head against the window. "What is wrong with me Jack?" I asked, feeling like a crushing weight was compressing me to nothing.

I heard him start to answer, but my eyes had closed and exhaustion sucked me into unconsciousness. I really had to stop passing out on this man.

"It's been ten years since I left. You couldn't get a new obsession during all that time?" I sneered at him using anger and sarcasm to hide the fear.

He raised his hand and slapped me, "you will learn to keep that mouth shut Kel." He growled. "Trust me on that, darling, you will learn."

I rolled my eyes, "Just try me, Alex. Or is that your true name? What are you? Alien? Bug?" I popped my lips on the word making it sound like the most disgusting insult.

He didn't take the bait. Instead, he released my throat and walked back to the chairs and desk. "Sit down," he ordered.

It was like all choice had been ripped from my body, I wanted to stay where I was but I found my legs moving in jerky motions and then I was sitting again. He raised an eyebrow at me.

"How did you do that?" I asked, too curious to be mad. I should have been terrified, and a small part of me probably was. But if I focused on that I would crumble, and I needed to be alert and strong.

"I am old Kel, older than your race of men." Again, he said men like it was an insult. "I watched your kind crawl from the mud. I watched you grow arms and legs, and eventually brains." "We used to live in peace, my kind and yours. Then a prophet came along and said my kind was evil, we did witchcraft and magic. We were an affront to God. HA/ As if your God was any match to us." He snorted. "But we had grown comfortable, complacent. Some of us even learned to live mortal lives and took mortal lovers." He sneered as if the thought disgusted him. "Weak fools, even then I didn't understand why anyone would choose to be mortal and have a short life and die. They started coming in the night, at the darkest hour when there was no moon shining. They would drag my people from their beds and into the street and slaughter them like animals. The corpses were left to be ravaged by animals."

I stared at him. I didn't even know what he was talking about. He wasn't making any sense with his talk of mortals and immortals. I was still trying to wrap my head around him not being human, I couldn't handle the rest yet.

"We caught on, too late to do anything but go into hiding and lick our wounds. We used our gifts to hide in plain sight. We made the pockets, little pieces of your world only entered by the doors, and most humans never even noticed. And we watched and learned and waited."

His hands clenched on the table. "When the time came to destroy man, some of my kind protested, they said that it wasn't worth it. That we lived just fine as we were and should let it rest. The past was the past."

He unclenched his hands and looked at me, "But some of us knew the wrongs of the past had to be righted. We made a plan. We would take female lovers, the children born of that union would be stronger than men and we would have our revenge.

"You see the cross, as we call them, can be immortal too. Not all of them are born that way, but enough that we have built an army with them." He grinned maliciously at me, but there was pride in his tone.

I made a disgusted sound, "Seriously? You want me to believe that crap? That you're some kind of ancient being? What like Fae, UH! Are you a Fairy? Do you have wings?" I was again trying to bait him, I had to buy time to think. He was giving me so much information to process. Phae, and pockets, and armies. I had known at least most of that, but not that he was one of them.

He growled at me, and leaned forward claws forming on his hands and his teeth elongating to fangs. I saw the otherworldly then, I couldn't deny that he was not human. And my stomach began to hurt. I stared at him, my mouth falling open, there was not refuting the evidence in front of me now. No human could do that.

I blinked collecting myself again, we knew the doors had been portals. But was it possible they weren't to another land just pockets in our own world? That deserved some thought when I wasn't faced with an angry male who had long before proven he liked to hurt me.

"Phae, are an ancient immortal race that lived on this earth before you humans came to be and stole it. Fairy," he spat. "You've made jokes of us for centuries, never realizing the true predator that you laughed at."

"I called you Fae," I said. I hadn't known what they were called, we simply said creatures.

"It is pronounced Phe. P hea," he growled at me, he had taken my bait, I grinned at him.

"Pay?" I giggled, a look of innocence on my face I topped it off with batting my lashes at him.

He growled and lurched from his seat, "You are my chosen mate, but that doesn't mean you won't suffer for what you have done."

Faster than should've been possible he was around the desk and his hand closed around my throat pulling me to my feet. "Starting now..."

I jerked awake, and cried out putting my hands to my head. It felt like my head was tearing open, that it would truly explode. "Jack!" I said in distress, "Jack my head!" I fisted my hands in hair and pressed my knuckles hard to my temples.

The dream was fresh and raw and it felt like it was breaking something inside me. Everything began to wobble as my head continued to feel like it was splitting in half. I felt tears streaming from my eyes and landing on my thighs, but I was powerless to stop them.

"It won't stop, Jack!" I cried, "the pain won't stop, it's like it's tearing me in half." I started to pull on my hair, as if I would help the split in my head and relieve some of the pain and pressure.

I felt the truck pull off the road, and then my door was opening and Jack held my head. "Kel," he said in panic, his words sharper. "Kel, don't. You're not ready yet. Stop thinking about it!" Jack sounded completely panicked now.

His words didn't fully register, but a part of me acknowledged what he said. Like it made sense to me, though it didn't.

He yanked my hands down and before I knew what was going he had begun to kiss me. His lips crashed into mine, and his hands held my head. They should've held my hands, in shock and fury and fear I slapped him. The memories of the last man to kiss me were raw wounds. If you could call what Alex did to me a kiss.

"How dare you!" I almost screeched. He had kissed me! I had sworn off kissing, and had had plenty in my very recent past that was unwanted, and still here Jack was kissing me! I had been sleeping, and though I knew I shouldn't keep passing out on him, he didn't have to kiss me awake!

He stepped back from me, not an ounce of apology on his face. "Why did you do that?" I demanded hot anger, setting fire in my blood. I used all my anger at what Alex had put me through and the violations he had visited on me to make the kiss from Jack an unforgivable crime.

"How is your head?" He asked me calmly. Either not understanding why I was upset or not caring that I was. I don't even know why he was asking about my head.

"Don't change the subject!" I demanded. "Why did you kiss me? I didn't want that!" To my shame I started to cry. "I didn't want that," I said again quietly. I wasn't sure why I was crying; it wasn't that the kiss was unpleasant.

He didn't approach me, probably worried I would slap him again. "How is your head?" He asked again softly. There was concern, and sorrow in his voice but no guilt. It didn't appear Jack was worried about kissing me.

"What do you mean?" I asked, the tears making my voice rough. "Why do you keep asking about my head? You assaulted my lips. Don't tell me you bashed my head into the door first." I righted myself in the seat and as I slammed the door it sounded like he sighed in relief and in sorrow.

Jack got back in the truck and we continued driving in silence, he still hadn't turned any music on. "Someone will report me as kidnapped," I finally said to break the silence. My tears had stopped and I had been brooding about the kiss in silence.

If I thought about it carefully I really liked the kiss. I had enjoyed the feel of Jack's lips against mine, I had just been so startled. No one had ever woken me up with a kiss, and then he had just gone on about my head. I still didn't know what that was about.

"No they won't," he said calmly, again he used a tone of superiority like he knew something I did not and could not understand.

"What do you mean, no they won't? I'm not so unimportant, my absence will not go unnoticed!" I huffed in indignation. "Where are we?" How did Jack seem to know there would be no one to report me missing? Why was I such an open book to him?

"Close," was all he said. "Try to get some more sleep." His tone was gentle but commanding.

"Why? So it's easier to slit my throat?" I demanded angrily, "Or maybe just so it's easier to address unwanted attention on my person!"

"Kel. Stop with the dramatics, and when did you get so doom and gloom? I'm not going to kill you." He huffed in exasperation, and his lips pressed into a thin line. Fine, maybe he wouldn't kill me then. He certainly was offended by the idea.

"Nothing to say about unwanted attention?" I snapped. "And stop talking like you know anything about me!" I looked out the window and closed my eyes. Had there been a dream? I couldn't remember if there was or not. Why had he asked about my head? For that matter, why was I even in his truck?

I sighed, when had my life gotten so tangled. I just wanted a quiet simple existence. No one to worry about but myself. I used my calming techniques and quieted my thoughts, drifting back to sleep.

"We're here," Jack said, startling me awake. I jumped and immediately wiped my face checking for drool. Sometimes when I was as tired as I felt that happened, and I didn't want to give Jack anymore ammunition to use against me.

I looked out the front window of the truck. "Right, so no woods or swamp, just a giant mansion. Is there a little torture chamber in the basement? Gonna try to make me spill all the worldly secrets? I don't know anything, you know? My life was quiet and boring until you showed up." I was rambling to hide the fact I was terrified.

I wasn't scared in the same way Alex scared me. No this place and Jack scared me in a different way. I couldn't figure out how, or what or even why. But I did not want to enter the house.

Jack snorted. "Your life has never been quiet or boring," he stated matter-of-factly, like he actually knew anything about me. He looked at me in that superior way again that set my teeth on edge.

I snarled. "Stop that! You. Don't. Know. Me!" I emphasized every word, and got out of the truck slamming the door. I stomped around to his side, and slammed his door since he had just gotten out.

I crossed my arms, forgetting the bruise, but not for longer. With a hiss of pain I dropped my arms. Concern crossed Jack's face.

I growled at him, "Well," I said "Take me to your leader then. Oh mighty serial killer."

Jack sighed and looked at the sky as if asking for patience, "Always with the titles," he said quietly. Grabbing my hand Jack started to walk towards the house.

I yanked my hand back. "I'm not a child to be led around!" The truth was I had liked my hand in his, but it felt too close to Alex leading me to my own door and I had reacted in anger and panic.

He rolled his eyes and started walking without me. I followed five steps and stopped. The air felt wrong here. Thick and sticky, but cold and light. It was familiar in a way that added more fear to growing apprehension.

"Scared?" Jack asked. His tone was teasing and mocking, but for once I didn't get angry at him for it.

In a moment of weakness, I nodded. "Terrified. I... I... I can't do this." I turned to run, but Jack had caught my wrist.

"Kel," he said calmly. "I won't let anything happen to you," he said the last firmly, a promise with bounds I didn't comprehend.

"That's just it, Jack. It already happened to me." I felt again that I was speaking in riddles I didn't understand, but the devastation that passed over Jack's face said he knew what I meant.

"Well, I'm here now. And I'm not leaving your side again." He stepped forward and pulled me with him. I didn't have time to react and pull away before we were going through the door.

The air was Jell-o made of clouds. It felt wrong the way it slid over my body, and I wanted to stop and go back. Then it was over, and we were through it. I turned and looked behind me at the door, where I had been able to see this and the house from there, I could see only empty air. No glimpse of the pocket we just left. I turned back and stopped dead in my tracks gaping.

The house was more impressive on this side of the air. House was so understated though. Mansion wasn't even correct; it was a palace. Soaring towers, and long halls. It looked like something from the days of kings and knights, but made of wood and not stone.

I faced Jack, "For the love of everything, tell me you really are NOT a knight with a white fucking horse." I felt the panic start to take over again. I am such a wreck, it seemed I was either crying, passing out or panicking.

Jack pulled me into him, facing me away from the palace. "Breathe Kel. I am not a knight, and my horse is black actually. That's twice you've sworn at me, decided to leave the goody-two-shoes behind?" His tone was the light teasing tone he used to rile me up.

I knew he was baiting me, and I still went for it. " I am NOT a goody-two-shoes, I choose to speak politely!" I turned and stomped towards the palace. It wasn't that I wanted to go there, it's just that was the direction away from Jack.

I heard his chuckle and the sound of his footsteps as he caught up, I slowed down and let him catch up and even get a step ahead. I didn't actually know where we were going anyway. So there was no harm in following.

Jack walked right up the steps and through the front door. I made it just inside and stopped. There were people everywhere. Running back and forth across the entry, up and down stairs. People carrying papers, or computers. Some with food, some empty handed.

I must've made a sound, because suddenly everyone stopped and all eyes focused on me. I felt like I had truly walked into the lion's den. I wanted to hide, or run. I'd have been happy if the floor just swallowed me up.

I stopped breathing as I stared back at everyone, I was going to faint. I felt it coming, my vision was tunneling again and the buzzing was back.

A sharp whistle pierced the air, and as if that were some magic cue, everyone went back to rushing around. I fell back against the wall and slid to the floor, gasping for air. I heard multiple footsteps approaching me quickly, but I couldn't dredge up the energy to look up.

Mary spoke. "Kel! Oh god, is it really her? Jack! Where's Jack?!" I hear the sound of feet moving, like she was spinning in circles. And people always think I'm the crazy one, I thought sourly.

"Stop your yelling woman! I am right here, I had to get the doc." I picked my head up enough to see three pairs of feet in front of me.

"Carly!" There was a tone of warning in Jack's voice. "She needs to be seen by doc before you overwhelm her." I heard what sounded like a hand connecting with something, and guessed Jack had grabbed her to stop whatever she had been about to do.

The woman huffed and I saw a foot stomp to my left, that must be her. The movement made me flinch and I instinctually curled protectively over my ribs. I was overwhelmed and on the verge of a complete panic attack. So I focused on the name Jack had said, funny he had gotten it wrong.

"That's Mary," I muttered, not sure if it was even loud enough to be heard over the noise. I tried to clear my throat and discovered my mouth so dry it didn't work. I gave up, either they heard me or they didn't.

Three forms squatted in front of me, and I was not at all surprised to see she was exactly like the woman in my dreams. Directly in front of me was Jack, my nightmare and savior. To my right was a man I didn't know, but he had soft, kind eyes and a wrinkled face. I liked him instantly.

"I'm sorry, what did you say?" she asked, a weird, twisted look on her face like calling her name had insulted her.

"I said you are Mary, not Carly." My voice choked out in a hoarse tone. I was really feeling strung out and exhausted, and having to tell the woman what her own name was made my jaw clench.

Jack laughed. "No, love, you are confused. Mary um..." He trailed off and looked uncomfortable, like he didn't really know how to say his thoughts.

Not Mary snorted, "Mary is a traitor and abandoned us. She said you were better off and we should leave you." She frowned as if talking about Mary was an offense to her sensibilities.

I shook my head, "So you're not Mary?" I asked her, before turning to Jack. I thought about when I had named the women from my dreams, how the names hadn't quite fit them. Maybe I had gotten it wrong. "And don't call me that!" I snapped at him, coming back to what Jack had said.

She chuckled, "No, I am Carly. Mary hasn't been around in a while. Even before you disappeared." She grinned at Jack. "Been fun huh?" She gave him a knowing look, and I felt the strong desire to kick my foot out and knock her over.

He gave her a sour face. "Yea, let me tell you all about it. After you get me whiskey. Doc?" He looked away from Carly.

Jack drew our attention to the wizened man by his side. "Kel, I am Dr. Jonathan Wallis. Most people call me Doc. You may call me whatever you are comfortable with, can I take you to the exam room?" He had a grandfather's voice.

The kind that makes you think of being a small child on the porch listening to stories, sitting on a lap in a rocking chair. It was comfort and love. I stared into his sky-blue eyes, the wrinkles at the corners showed years of love and laughter.

I nodded and let Jack help me to my feet. I followed Doc down the hall, watching his back but I still saw everyone stop and stare at me. I felt like I was under a microscope. The walls of the hall were painted a cream that reflected everything and seemed to shift colors based on where you were at the time.

We passed door after door; some closed some open and still more people bustled about. It was like a hive in here, busy little bees going back and forth. But everyone noticed me, it was disconcerting.

Doc stopped in front of a set of stairs set off the hall that led down.

"There really is a torture basement," I whimpered. I didn't know if that would be worse than if I had stayed with Alex but I couldn't think straight yet either.

Doc, clasped my shoulder. "Kel, nothing will happen to you that you are not okay with. I promise." His tone and words were said in a practiced soft way that would set all patients at ease.

I believed him, so I followed. The stairs wound around twice before ending in what looked to be a waiting room. Big sofas and overstuffed chairs, tables with magazines. "Not a torture dungeon," I said quietly, unreasonably relieved at the normalcy of the waiting room.

"That's on the other side of the hallway upstairs, sweetheart," Jack whispered in my ear. "We'll visit it sometime, you and I." His voice held a promise that some part of me wanted to explore while the rest of me again was angry he kept being so familiar.

I shuddered and stepped away from him. "Stop that!" I said through gritted teeth. "Don't call me pet names, stop insinuating we know each other. We don't!" I hissed at him angrily keeping my voice low so the Doctor wouldn't overhear.

I pushed Jack for good measure and hurried to catch up to Doc across the room. He paused at a closed door, and produced a key. Unlocking it he opened it with a flourish and stepped aside for me to enter first.

"Please, please don't let it be a prison cell," I whispered quietly as I stepped in. I didn't realize I had squeezed my eyes shut until the lights came on, and all I caught was a shift in darkness. I peeked one eye open, and peered through my lashes.

My initial impression was not of a prison chamber, so I took a breath and fully opened my eyes. It was a nice room, with that sterile exam feel. The walls were white, appliances white or chrome and the lighting overhead fluorescent.

There was an exam table in the middle, with mobile gadgets and machines all around it. But different from other doctors' office rooms were the plump double chairs around the outside. Actually as I looked closer this room was the size of three regular hospital rooms.

Jack moved off to one of the plump chairs, and I looked for Doc. He was walking to me from across the room with a hospital dressing gown in hand.

"There's a private change room, over there." He pointed to my right, "When you are ready, we'll begin. I need to do preliminary exams, and I want to do a full physical. Then we'll need blood work, CAT scans, MRIs... etc. It will be a long process, and some of it will require me to anesthetize you. Are you okay with that?" He was so kind and talked so gently that I nodded again.

"Yes, thank you Doc," I said quietly. I took the garment from him and went to the changing room. The changing room was what would be considered a regular sized hospital room, it also sported a toilet shower and sink. Whoever these people were that Jack belonged to, they did not lack money.

I changed slowly, the bruise on my ribs pulling and pinching with every movement, and I was still weary and at this point over-stimulated. I finally managed to pull the gown on, but I couldn't tie it. I almost started crying again. By sheer willpower I stopped the tears and headed out. I had left my socks on, because I hated when my toes got cold.

I shuffled back to Doc, not even expending the energy to pick up my feet properly. Mary, no Carly, had returned while I changed and it appeared she brought the whiskey Jack wanted. At least I assumed that is what he was drinking. She smiled at me, and I tried to return the look. By the way her face fell I'm guessing I gave her more of a grimace than a smile.

"All yours Doc," I said, punctuated by a yawn. I felt overwhelmed and exhausted, despite the nap in the truck. The one Jack had decided to interrupt with a kiss. I was still processing my feelings. I was angry still, but there was something else there too.

"Do you want the curtain pulled? It'll be just us behind the curtain then, I am sorry they need to be in the room." He smiled kindly, and nodded his head to Jack and Carly. Doc seemed to understand that I was uncomfortable with them and feeling completely out of my league.

I did a quick glance at Jack and Carly. They had their heads tucked together and didn't appear to be paying attention. "Please, Doc, that would be amazing. I didn't want to offend anyone. I mean I think Jack saved my life. I'm not dead yet."

Doc laughed and patted my arm, leading me to the exam table and pulling the curtains. "On ya get," he said, all cheery business. I could see myself becoming fast friends with this man.

I quietly obeyed, climbing onto the table and arranging the gown while I sat. "Oh, lie back dear," Doc said, while he moved machines and set up tables. I stared at the ceiling and tried to empty my head.

"I'm going to connect these electrodes to you, they will help me monitor you and do some of the testing for me. I'll need two under your collar bone, one for each side of your ribs, and one for the inside of your wrists."

I flinched when he said ribs, and my hand jerked to press the gown to the bed. Doc missed neither motion. And his eyes flicked to my side.

"Let me see?" He asked so kindly and with so much concern that I didn't ever contemplate not shifting the gown aside. I didn't feel any shyness with Doc, and something inside me wanted to let him see.

I opened the gown exposing my side. I had removed both bra and underwear, but it didn't feel awkward with Doc here. He was businesslike. A low whistle escaped through his teeth. I think it was unintentional.

"I bet he forgot how much more fragile you are than him," Doc murmured.

I didn't respond because I don't think he meant me to hear and like many other things lately it didn't make sense. I furrowed my brow but chose not to acknowledge I heard. His tone seemed to imply more than the fragility of females against males.

I felt the cool touch of fingers on the lump and it was like a red-hot fire poker touched my skin, I screeched a wounded animal noise and jerked away so fast I almost fell off the table. Instantly Jack and Carly were there. The motion of pulling away had completely dislodged the gown and when I sat up Jack and Carly saw all of me.

Jack's face went maroon, Carly looked embarrassed, Doc was apologizing and I was trying to cover up.

"OUT!" I screeched at Jack, horror, shame, and shyness warring for my attention. Jack was seeing all of me, and worse I knew there were probably bruises other than the large one on my ribs.

Jack had the decency to look chastised and Carly shoved him out of the curtain, but not without an angry glance at my side. Doc rushed over and pulled the curtains tighter. I was overwhelmed with shame that Jack had seen so much.

He looked embarrassed and upset as he said to me, "I'm so sorry Kel. It looks a week old at least, I did not realize it would hurt so much. At least one rib is broken, when did this happen?" His voice was quiet and apologetic.

"No, I'm sorry Doc. I knew you would touch it; I just didn't expect that pain. I didn't mean to react so violently." I paused, ashamed I had caused this kindly man so much distress. "It happened Monday evening," I finished quietly.

Again, I realized I was crying; I should save these tears I could sell them in the desert and make bank. I sniffled, "He was angry, Jack had tried to stop me leaving work. And Alex, he was going to hit Jack so I interfered and I told him that I just wanted to leave." I sniffled again as the words poured out of me. "I was mad at Jack, I thought he had been hired by Alex to find me. And I said something in the car about paying Jack before threatening him." Another sniffle. "I have bruises from that comment too," I showed him the fingertip marks above my left knee. "He said I wasn't worth the money it would've cost to find me, and I thought that was it. He would just insult me."

I was crying harder now, and Doc helped to sit back on the edge of the bed. "But we got to my house, and he shoved me down. And he was mad that I had interfered with Jack, and he kicked me."

Doc produced a Kleenex, and I thought I heard Jack swear and Carly shush him. I flinched, embarrassed to think they had heard my sobbing and the story. One was bad enough without the other.

"I'll be right back Kel." Doc hurried through the curtain, and I heard muffled voices. Then two sets of feet leaving. "Kel," Doc said and I looked up as he re-entered.

"I'm going to insert an IV and give you a sedative, I need to examine your ribs more closely. And I don't want you to be in pain. I'll place the electrodes after you are asleep and remove them before you wake so as not to add discomfort."

I nodded and lay back on the table. Doc placed a soft pillow under my head and prepped my right inner elbow to set the needle. A sharp jab was all I knew before Doc started to tape the needle still.

"Now, you may feel a tingle or slight sting when the medication enters. But after that you won't feel anything for a long while. And with luck, there won't be dreams either." He said the last as if he knew about my dreams. Maybe Jack had said something.

I felt a little tingle and my head got light.

"I feel something… Doc…" I managed before the world went dark.

CHAPTER 9

I roused to whispered angry voices. I did not know how long it had been or if Doc was still doing tests. I felt out of sorts from the anesthesia and couldn't quite get the world back to functioning reality, so instead I just tried to listen.

"What do you mean, Doc?" Jack's voice growled.

"I mean I can't fix her memory, Jack," Doc replied, not sounding angry.

"Why?!" Carly demanded. "What did they do to her Doc?"

"I don't know," he said quietly. "It's nothing I've encountered before. We know little to nothing of their magic, and I suspect that magic is at play here."

"I don't understand why though." Jack's voice growled. "And why her? That thing talked like he had history with her." I heard the bitter angry tone that sounded like jealousy. Jack was jealous of Alex and mine's history?

"You never told me that," Carly snarled. I could almost see the posture she would be in with that tone. Half up on her toes, fists curled and her lips twisted to match the snarling tone.

"It's not important," Jack snapped back. "He's Phae, it was probably a lie!"

"Enough." I heard Doc say and there was some bite in his voice. "Jack is right, no don't look at me like that Carly. Say the Phae isn't lying and they have a history, we don't know that history and I doubt she does either! And say your history with her gave an ID, it wouldn't make a difference. Their human personas are untraceable."

"Listen, her ribs are thankfully only fractured. Just in multiple places. It will take a long time to heal, her body will heal Jack. Her mind is another story. Tell again about this dream in the truck." Doc's tone had lost its bite, he now sounded like a scientist digging into the secrets of the world.

"She had just asked me what was wrong with her, but she didn't hear my answer because she had passed out again. I don't think she slept around *it*, not that I blame her. Yea yea, I'm getting on." Jack said with annoyance in his voice. "Anyway, she mentioned Alex and Phae in her sleep. And I thought she was dreaming about before. You know she disappeared. Something she had said made me think that was something that happened."

There was a long pause and I wondered if he would continue. I heard a deep breath and then the story resumed. "Then she screamed, and I never wish to hear that sound from her again. It was pain, fear, terror. And I thought I would wreck the truck. It scared me so badly. I had already started to slow down and pull over, when she grabbed her head and yelled my name. She said 'Jack! Jack, my head!' And she had her hands clenched at her temples. She was moaning and mumbling things, I was terrified for her. So I managed to pull over and got stopped."

There was another pause and deep breath, "I thought maybe she was remembering things and her mind was rejecting it so I told her to stop thinking that she wasn't ready. And she kept crying, and said the pressure would explode. So I, ehhm, I distracted her."

"You distracted her?" Carly said, with a hint of snideness.

"Yes dammit!" I heard him snap back.

"How did you distract her Jack?" Doc asked.

Jack cleared his throat, "I kissed her," he said quietly.

"Jack!" Carly said with a tone like a schoolmarm.

"Shove off Carly, I've been around her for a month unable to touch her or kiss her. Every time she sees me she sees a stranger, and she hates me. You have no idea what it has been like!" I heard the desperation and despair in his tone. "She was in pain! I didn't know what to do!"

"Okay, Jack, okay" Carly said soothingly. "I'm sorry. You're right I don't know. I don't think I could've done what you did. I can't imagine it, to be around her and not know me. And for you..."

"Yea," he said bitterness lacing his tone. "Anyway, I kissed her and she slapped me. And she started yelling about me assaulting her, and didn't seem to remember her head pain. It was weird, the kiss seemed to have distracted her from the pain and she couldn't remember it."

"Intriguing," Doc said, and his voice sounded like his thoughts were miles away. "There may be something in whatever was to her that would cause a lapse in memory like that. Though I have no idea what or why. The whole thing makes minimal sense to me. I don't even understand why *they* would erase her memory to begin with. I feel like we are missing something, something big picture. I'll run more tests, Jack, but we need to face the possibility she will never remember."

"But all of this, everything here that's because of her! She did it all, she is the reason we know anything!" Jack sounded distraught.

"We will show her Jack." I heard Carly's soft tones. "We'll remind her who she is, and," she said sharply. "What she means to us."

The conversation continued, but I was falling back into the dreamless sleep again. I floated in a dark void for an eternity, and eon. There was no pain, or feeling. Just blissful blackness. They must have lowered the dosage of the sedative at some point, because blackness became nightmares. Followed by blackness again, in circles it went.

Alex featured prominently; he was always there in my dreams. Whispering and laughing, telling me he would find me and I could never escape. I would thrash about and could hear my screams, and then the blackness would return.

The dreams continued on and on a never-ending cycle of terror and nothing. I finally woke up what felt a lifetime later, and felt raw and tired and my whole body ached. I tried to open my eyes fully and take in my surroundings.

There was a chair to my right and a person occupied that chair.

"Water?" I croaked. "Please?"

The body stirred, and Carly came into focus. She looked haggard and care worn. It seemed at first she didn't process what I had spoken, because she stared at me with a heart broken sadness.

Her eyes opened wide as she realized I was staring at her. "Oh my god! You're awake!"

She leapt to her feet. "Doc!" Carly shouted, spinning towards the door then back to me and back to the door again like she couldn't decide if she should leave to go get Doc or yell again.

"Oh, my head..." I murmured. "Please don't be so loud, Carly, I need water." I wanted to bury my head under the pillows to get away from the sound and light and pain.

"Just a minute, Kel. We can't do anything until Doc is here."

The sound of running footsteps followed by a hurried shuffle, and Jack with Doc on his heels burst through the door. Jack had a look of panic and sheer terror on his face. Doc appeared calmer, but worried.

Jack slid to a stop in front of Carly, eyes wide and unseeing. "Carly!" He said, and seemed to be able to say anymore. He just stared at her, there was panic and fear I couldn't understand. I didn't understand why he didn't look at me either.

Doc however, approached the bed. "Kel," he said softly. "Welcome back to the land of the living, we didn't think you would be back." His tone was brisk, but not unfriendly and he set about checking the machines and monitors.

Jack whirled and the motion unbalanced Carly tipping her over and back into her chair. Jack hit his knees beside my bed and as if he couldn't control it he clasped my hand. His grip was light, as if he didn't want to hurt me. His eyes held a tortured horror and sadness.

"Good, good," He murmured. "Yes, very good. Ah! Excellent!" He turned to the bed with a triumphant smile on his face. "She'll be fine Jack."

A noise like a strangled cat came from Jack and he disappeared from my view entirely. "Water?" I asked again, trying to see where Jack had gone. Did he faint?

Carly was there then, and she bent over where Jack had vanished to. The distinct sound of a slap reverberated around, "Wake up you jackass. You fainted like a girl!" I heard a grunt from the floor, but a motion to my other side caught my attention and I saw the water Doc was holding.

He pressed a button on the bed and the upper half raised me to a sitting position, the movement was slow but even that caused me pain. A low whimper slipped past my pressed lips and Doc's face tightened.

"Why does everything hurt?" I asked the gravel in my voice, making it crack and whisper. My throat felt raw. I must have really screamed, a lot.

I took the water from Doc, and sipped carefully. It was a soothing balm on my raw throat. "Ah, yes that. Well, that would be from the poison," Doc said, and no should be allowed to deliver news like that with a cheery tone. It's an abomination.

"Poison?" I choked. Horror stealing through me, "what poison?" I had been poisoned? Alex had really decided to kill me?

"That's just it, we don't truly know," Carly answered.

"We just did everything to counteract anything, we don't even know what was the final key," Doc said, his tone was heavy and tired.

"But how was I poisoned?" I asked. I couldn't make sense of the world yet, and the poison idea seemed to be causing a short circuit in my thoughts.

Doc sighed and Carly gave an angry kick towards Jack, they seemed to be blaming him for something.

"We think it was something you consumed," Doc said. "Something given to you." Doc gave me a funny look, like I should've known how I had been poisoned.

Did they blame Jack for me being poisoned? Surely that wasn't possible, unless Jack had said something about his confrontation with Alex and that was what they thought had made him poison me. But I didn't think Alex had done it because of Jack.

"He really was trying to kill me," I whispered. I had said it once to Jack, but I hadn't let myself believe it. I didn't think he would really go that far. But here I was in a hospital bed and I had been poisoned.

"No I don't think so," Doc hurried on. "It was slow acting, like it was given in the morning and an antidote slipped in at night. We assume it was Alex. That it was his fall back if you ever ran away."

"Again," I said hoarsely. My head hurt like someone had tried to use it for a drum. But my thoughts were starting to clear up.

"Pardon?" Doc asked politely.

"He wouldn't have wanted me to run away again," I replied. I flexed my fingers on my free hand. Even that was uncomfortable.

"What do you mean again Kel? Have you tried to escape before? It didn't sound like, I mean from what Jack said, you weren't with him very long." Doc's tone was cautious.

"I left him five years ago. He was at work, and I left. He had only just recently found me," I said. I caught the uncomfortable glance they shared, Jack now on his feet. "What?" I asked. "What is it?" No one said anything. "Tell me!" My voice cracked again and my throat felt like a cactus had been shoved down it.

"Kel," Jack began carefully but Carly cut him off.

"You couldn't have run away five years ago. That's impossible," she said and her tone said that there could be no argument. That made me angry, I was getting very tired of these people telling me I didn't know my own life.

"Oh and I suppose you, like everyone else, knows everything about me then? It's like it's my life and I was living it or anything!" I snapped. I was angry that everyone kept talking like I was the crazy one.

Jack threw her an angry look. "Kel you couldn't have run away five years ago, because five years ago you were with us. Here, in this house. Well, not this house. We were somewhere else; this place is rather new actually."

"This isn't a house!" I snapped automatically. "And stop that! That's not true!" Fear began to crowd in my senses. He was again speaking like he knew me and that I had just been confused and dreamed up the whole world.

"Kel," Doc said quietly. "You went missing six months ago. We've been searching and only just found you when Jack infiltrated a month ago. Five years is a lie. A lie planted by *them*," he said "them" with an inflection of fear, disgust and hatred. I couldn't begin to comprehend the meaning behind it all.

I looked slowly at everyone in turn, they had mirrored looks of worry and concern. *Holy gods, they are serious! They actually believed I had false memories and they knew more about my life than I did!* I thought.

I cracked, like a lunatic I laughed. I laughed so hard I bent forward and pulled at my ribs. I couldn't stop myself though every laugh was a pain somewhere. What kind of ego did these people have to have to believe in some fantasy other world crap?

"Well, that's it then. She's fucking cracked!" I heard Carly snap, and then footsteps left. I was laughing so much I didn't see who the footsteps belonged to. I heard her say other things as she left, but non clear enough to make out and her tone suggested they were unpleasant.

I continued to laugh, I laughed until I cried and couldn't see or hear anything. I think they put some sedative in my IV, because my head went fuzzy and the world was again dark. I was not plagued by dreams or visions or anything of the sort. This was just a calm black empty dark, I internally rejoiced while in this place.

Nothing could harm me here. No Alex to hit me. No Jack or Carly or Doc to say I was some brainwashed victim of a fairy tale existence. Nothing could harm me, because this was nothing. I felt the pull of consciousness, but I fought it. I didn't want to go back; the dark was soothing and addictive. Like a lover's touch could be, or well I'd heard could be. I lacked the experience. I heard voices murmuring, and like an unwanted duty they pulled me to the surface.

I could tell by their tones, no one knew I was awake yet. So I lay there with my eyes closed and listened. Maybe I would hear something that confirmed they were lying to me.

"How do we fix this Doc?" Jack asked, again desperation sparked through his tone. He sounded so lost and sad. What did he need fixed, a part of me wanted to do whatever it was just so that sadness would go away.

"Jack, there is nothing I can fix. She's healthy and alive. There are no broken or sick pieces." Doc sounded tired, like they had been arguing this some time. They were talking about me, then. Jack thought I needed to be fixed.

"Her head is broken!" Jack almost yelled. I watched his face twist in anger and even a touch of fear. "She doesn't even know who she is! She doesn't know who we are!"

"Hush!" Carly snapped. "What if she woke to hear that? Think, Jack." Carly seemed to be the voice of reason for Jack. I imagine he often needed a voice of reason.

I heard a growl of danger and warning, and I assumed Jack was making the sound. I cracked an eye and with a leap of excitement realized my head was turned towards the speakers. As I had already figured Doc, Jack and Carly were there.

I was also correct that Jack was making the growl, he faced Carly his back mostly to me. I observed him for the first time unnoticed. He had a truly magnificent form. I could happily admire that all day, especially if he kept his mouth and didn't notice my staring.

His defensive stance had his feet spread slightly, and the muscles in his legs from ankle to butt tightened and flexed. He looked like he might jump at any moment. That butt, though, a girl could get used to walking behind it. His hips were narrow, but the kind of narrow that said he was an active man.

My gaze continued up his back, watching as it moved and the muscles jumped under his shirt with every breath. His shoulders were broad and defined, but not over done like a man who lived at the gym. No, I could tell looking at Jack that he worked. Probably a physical job, that would be a sight to see.

I let my gaze trail his arms, and saw his fists were clenched. Was he going to hit Carly? He didn't strike me as that kind of man. I knew that kind of man, and Jack just didn't fit that bill. I kept my eyes on him, curious if I had actually been wrong.

"Jack," Carly said, using the same tone that would be used to soothe a wild panicking animal. "Jack, trust me, I get it okay? I've known her my whole life. Now more than ever I regret the falling out we had all those years ago. I can't get that time back, and she may never remember any of it. You are not alone here, okay? But we have to think about Kel."

He jerked when she said my name as if she had landed a physical blow to him, though she hadn't even twitched a hand. My heart ached at that, seeing him flinch away from my name being spoken. I couldn't figure out all these feelings, it's like the anesthesia was doing weird things in my head. I had always fought the feelings Jack brought out in me, except the anger. I let the anger boil through me constantly. Part of that in the hopes it would burn away everything else.

But now, still half conscious, I couldn't fight them, and I truly felt sad that Jack was hurting and angry, and I wanted to fix it. I just didn't know how since everything seemed to be because of me.

I started to fight for full consciousness, at least then I could be angry and I could wipe away the guilt that I had hurt Jack. I was the one who had been hurt, why should I have to feel guilty for anyone else?

"Doc," she said turning to him, obviously she didn't believe he would hit her either. "What can we do?" She also had sadness coloring her voice but it had a different quality than Jack's did. The dreams had shown Carly like a best friend, and her sadness seemed to be similar to what I imagined someone felt when a friend died.

Doc sighed heavily, and as I looked he appeared to be a man defeated. "Honestly, I don't know. Maybe try showing her around, slowly introduce her to things. Show her we aren't lying. Give her pictures and talk about the past."

Jack must have given some que or made a noise I missed, because Doc suddenly focused full on him. "Not at all once Jack. We have to do this slowly. You have to go slowly." Doc emphasized "you".

"I can't just not love her, Doc. I want her back," He said the last word with a fierceness that made my heart quicken and I was afraid the machines would give away my eaves-dropping.

"Then maybe you need to be somewhere else Jack. If you overwhelm her, I don't know for sure, but I think it could shatter her mind. Whatever they did is tied to her human lover. I'm sure he didn't know you anymore than you knew him. And we have a small grace to thank for that. Lord knows what would've happened if he had recognized you...." Doc trailed off. I didn't understand any of that except that Doc had told Jack to leave.

Would Jack listen though? And did I want him to leave? I didn't know, there was so much going on. I needed space, but there was that small part of me that was always wanting Jack around.

Silence so heavy and thick I felt choked settled in the room. Carly wasn't looking at Jack, she seemed to be studiously avoiding him. Doc was busying himself with a clipboard I hadn't noticed he held.

"You agree, don't you Carly?" There was deep anguish in his voice. "You think I need to leave." His shoulders hunched, and he appeared a man who had been whipped and broken. I felt my heart squeeze for him. Angry or not, I was saddened by his reactions.

Carly's face crumpled, "No Jack. I think we both do. We expect too much from her, and I don't think it will help her for us to be here." Carly took a breath so deep she gained an inch in height, then she grabbed Jack's hand and they left the room neither looked back at me.

Doc sighed, and appeared as if a world of weight had settled onto his shoulders. He looked so much older and frailer then that I wished I was who they thought me to be. I so desperately wanted to be her, that a tear slid from the corner of my eye.

Doc checked the clipboard again, set it on a table and he too left with a look in my direction. If they had looked, everyone would've seen I was awake, they would've known I had heard. Heard, and still didn't believe.

They saw me as some heroine who made a big discovery. I was a friend, lover and apparently some kind of leader. They spoke of a world that couldn't exist, magic and fae... I rolled that word in my head. Jack had said it differently.

Pfay? Phay? Pay? I shook my head, it was more soft p and the fae. I kept playing with the word, distracted from my original train of thought for a time. This was like trying to name Carly and Mary, only to figure out they were real and I had gotten the names backward.

Right, Carly and Mary were real. They existed, so did Jack. I hadn't just made them up in my dreams. But that didn't mean they were right. I mean alien invasion was more believable that magic beings. At least Aliens made sense, there was no possible way in the entirety of space that our planet held the only sentient life. It was sheer arrogance to think so.

But if I could believe Aliens, why not them? I pondered that thought. Why couldn't I believe what everyone was saying? Why did I fight them and scorn their words? *Because it was impossible that's why!* A sharp angry voice in my head sounded.

But was it really? The idea wasn't, I used to believe there was magic and power in the world. But believing them meant I was who they said. I couldn't be this girl they expected me to be. I didn't even know what they expected, except that it wasn't me. That was the impossible part. I wasn't the woman they expected, I couldn't be. So maybe they were only part right. Maybe the idea of magic and Phae wasn't far-fetched and maybe it was even true. But they had just gotten the wrong girl.

I considered that a moment longer. Maybe it wouldn't hurt to let them show me how they were right. Then I could show them that they had gotten the wrong girl, and when they realized it and got the real Kel they wanted, I would just go on my way then. They could help me really hide from Alex.

Alex, just thinking the name caught my breath and panic tried to overrule my senses. If I believed them about the Phae, that meant he was one of them. Did that mean he might always be able to find me?

The thought terrified me, I would spend the rest of my life looking over my shoulder fearing he would be back. The shadow of his memory haunted me here in this place. There were so many people that even if he were magic he wouldn't get to me.

A hazy image started to defog in my head, a fear in between bouts of blank emptiness. A part of me shied away from that memory and didn't want to bring it up. But I had to see, I had to know. I focused on the vague images, and sounds came back.

His laughter, that cruel cold laughter he would use when I acknowledged pain he had inflicted. Sometimes if I cried or whimpered he hit harder, but always he had that laughter. My body began to tremble, but still I focused. I started to see his face coming back, the words that were whispered in my nightmares getting louder.

I will find you, Kel. You won't escape me. I am not done with you yet. Those words over and over and over, and he would chant my name. Kel, Kel, Kel... It was a death chant. He was calling for me so he could kill me.

"Kell!" Doc's voice broke through my focus, I heard my harsh panting breaths and could feel I still trembled. The machines attached to me for monitoring were screaming warnings, and nurses were flooding into my room.

"Doc?" I gasped, "Doc... I... I... I... can't... breathe..." I scrambled at the bed sides with my hands, fisting the sheets and dropping them. I felt wires and cords under my fingers, and still my breath wouldn't come to me.

A rescue breathing mask was set over my nose and mouth, and nurses grabbed my hands holding my arms still. Doc's face filled my tunneling vision, "Listen to me Kel. Hear my voice, focus on the words. There's a girl. Now breathe, in and out. In and out."

The shaking and trembling slowly stopped, my hands loosed the sheets and cords and my breathing began to level. I kept my eyes locked on Doc, but in my periphery I saw nurses scurry all around the room. Monitors and machines stopped screaming their warnings.

Finally Doc removed the breathing mask, and in some silent language known to medical professionals he got the nurses to leave the room and the chaos stopped. The room emptied and stilled as if by the magic Doc had spoken of earlier. That was a pretty cool trick.

My bed was raised to sitting and I was on eye level with Doc. "Kel," he said. "What happened?" His voice was soothing and calm, and he pulled a chair to the bedside. A chair I had not noticed before. It's like a cafeteria chair.

I frowned at the chair, "Why not use the comfy ones Doc?" I asked him, still looking at the chair as though it was offensive.

He chuckled as he sat down, "These old bones love the cushions, but I don't get up so easily from them anymore. This chair allows me to stand and move easily." He crossed one knee over the other and looked at me with patient expectancy.

I looked at the ceiling, I didn't want to see his face when I explained. "You remember when you all said I had been poisoned?"

"Yes." He answered. A look of concern on his face at my question.

"How long was I under?" I asked, I was afraid of the answer that was why I hadn't asked before. I didn't want to think of how long Alex had had to look for me while I'd been unconscious and helpless.

"Two weeks," he said quietly. "We thought we would lose you several times, your heart would just stop. And then like a miracle it would go again, and we would add more antidotes or antibiotics or whatever the anti of the moment was." His voice was heavy and tired.

"I thought Jack and Carly would kill each other, and they are best friends," He added with a wry tone. "But they worried for you, and when they worry tempers run hot." He chuckled softly, I imagined Doc breaking up a fight between Jack and Carly and almost chuckled as well.

I swallowed hard feeling a lump in my throat. "Two weeks..." Tears started. "He's trying to find me Doc," I whispered. I was afraid and the realization wiped any trace of amusement from my thoughts. I was afraid that despite everything Doc and Carly and Jack did and said, he would still find me.

I heard the chair move suddenly, and then Doc was standing at the bed. "Kel, you don't know that. We have assumed it was probably so, but you can't know that." He had his soothing tone, like he was comforting a child woken up by a nightmare. Except the tone didn't work on me this time, because I did know it.

I cried harder, "But I can Doc. There's something here." I touched my head. "A... A... connection or something. I didn't want to believe you with the magic and everything else, but I can't deny he's here. In my head." I covered my face with my hands.

"I can't see him, or hear him. I mean at least not right now. It's weird though, like I should be able to but I can't. But I can... it's like I feel him. Like I get impressions." I struggled to explain. "I don't think it goes both ways, and I don't think it was supposed to be like it. It's like...umm... Like a tracking beacon? Umm, like a ping to him that I still live."

I cracked my fingers apart and peered at Doc, his face had gone paper white. He had the clipboard again and his grip was white knuckled. "Kel, we've never heard of anything like that before. You are not the first rescue, and none of their captors was capable of such a thing."

"What does that mean Doc?" I asked. Curiosity and horror battling for domination in my head. I was truly afraid of the connection, and sickened by it. I didn't want any part of him, and yet his presence was there.

"I don't know. But I think it means your captor may be the oldest one alive we've ever encountered, and that is not good. Their memories are as long as their lives. They can't let go of past wrongs, because time never fades the sting. A wrong done a millennia ago, will still be as raw today as when it happened." He swallowed and put an effort into trying to smile. It didn't work.

I sighed, and closed my fingers over my face again. "In the weeks I was sick, I floated between drugged emptiness and nightmare unconsciousness. I would see *him*," I whispered him like even that would make him show up.

I cleared my throat, "He was always laughing a cruel and cold laughter, and his eyes burned with fury and vengeance. He told me," I swallowed hard "He told me he would find me, and he would chant my name over and over and over."

I dropped my hands and turned my head to Doc. "He wants to kill me, I think," I said with terror so thick I could taste its bitter sting. I didn't want to die. I wanted a long life, even the lonely life in that place Jack had found me was better than dying.

Doc placed a hand over mine, "Kel, I'm going to tell you something. And you will not like it." He gave me a look that said if I told him no he wouldn't continue, but I had to know so I nodded. He sighed as if he wanted me to tell him no. "As I said, you're not the first woman to be rescued, and what I have to say will explain why I don't think death for you is his plan."

I shuddered, the idea of not killing me felt worse than if he did. I didn't want to contemplate what it meant, and yet I needed to know what Doc thought was worse than him killing me. Needed to understand what it was that was worse than death in Doc's eyes.

He released my hand and pulled his chair closer, then sitting down he captured my hand again. "You are the first to be in such bad shape, though none of the other girls were well off, none were like you.

"See, it seems that the Phae and humans have a long bad history. And when it came down to it, the Phae went into hiding. Humans then passed stories of them like they were fairy tales. Never allowing the real truth to be known. So they passed from true memory to myth.

"But they've always been here. Always watching, intertwined with our society's." He clasped his fingers together and looked like a grandfather telling a story by the fire.

I interrupted him, "Pay?" I think he said it differently but the two words were so close, I still hadn't been able to roll the sounds right.

"P-hay, yes, the creatures, the ones like Alex. We only in the last couple of months learned what they called themselves. Think Fae, with a Ph sound. It's hard to wrap the tongue around." Doc used a coaching voice when he pronounced Phae like I was a student learning a difficult medical term.

He took a deep breath. "Anyway, six years ago, a girl disappeared from her home. There was no sign of break in, the locks were intact, she just vanished. The police were baffled. They searched the whole area and could find nothing. They talked to neighbors and family, no one had any information. So the case went cold.

"But a small group of people got curious and they started to poke around." He got an ironic and sardonic smile at that. "They found the first known door." He paused and looked at me. "Do you remember the door?"

I scrunched my brows, "that weird air pocket thing?" I asked.

Doc nodded, "Precisely. Those are what we call doors. They lead to a pocket of our world protected from humans. Each pocket is different, some are little cities with a lot of Phae in them. Some are like a simulation, where there are only a couple things that are real." He gave me a pointed look that I decided to ignore.

"So the group found the door, okay? What kind of pocket was it?" I asked him, pressing to continue.

"It was a Phae city. Now the Phae have lived so long in their protected pockets, that they didn't realize they had been discovered. And so it was easy to rescue the girl. But there was a problem." He looked so sad when he said problem that I felt my own heart break.

"She was pregnant." His eyes held a world of horror and sadness in them. He looked a hundred years older, it even appeared as if his shoulders hunched forward with a heavy burden.

I gaped at him. "What?!" I felt horror and disgust, "They kidnapped and raped her?!" I was angered but I found I wasn't surprised, after all Alex had always just taken what he wanted. If I believed he was one of them, it stood to reason they all would do the same.

He nodded sadly, "Yes. She'd only been gone two months, but by human standards was eight months along. Apparently Phae gestation is two to three months." He scrubbed his free hand over his face. "They brought the woman back, and enlisted a trusted doctor friend, not me by the way, to check over the woman. Everything seemed to be fine, so they asked her what happened.

"She told them that two men like beings had appeared in her room one night, and that they had grabbed her and then vanished. They stopped in front of a door, and had to walk through. Even Phae can't magic through the doors, they have to walk.

"They took her to the lead for that city, and he then locked her in a bedroom. A Lead is just the highest ranked Phae in the area, we don't know how ranks are chosen." He paused and reached under my bed getting a bottle of water he offered one to me, then got one for himself. I took a small sip and waited; Doc drank down half the bottle.

"The Lead was an arrogant fool, the better for us, he came to her that night and took from her..." he trailed off. Seeming lost for words, Doc appeared to struggle for a bit on how to say it.

"It's okay Doc, I get it you don't have to explain," I said to him gently. "I know what you are saying, please continue." I didn't need Doc to put the acts into words, I knew better than he understood what had happened.

Doc nodded his thanks. "When he was done, she asked him why? Just that one word. And to our advantage he told her everything," Doc sighed, and the weight of the world seemed to rest on him as he looked back at me and continued.

"He explained about Phae, though he didn't name their kind to her, and how they had been around longer than humans. Not him specifically he was only a few hundred years old not thousands. He said that humans had started war on the Phae, and the Phae had gone into hiding.

"He told her that some of the more cowardly of his people were okay with this. But there was one, he was older than anyone knew. He was not happy with the way of things. He wanted revenge for a past wrong. Remember what I said about their memories and time not faded them like it will with humans?" I nodded, and Doc continued. "He had been watching humans for centuries in secret like the rest of his kind but he had never liked hiding, it felt like exile to him.

"So he came up with a plan, and over a few decades started to act on it. The Phae would wipe out the humans. But in themselves they were too few, we outnumber them you see. He needed more numbers, but Phae did not have children often, and their children grew slowly. To try and make a Phae army would take millennia or more. And he didn't wish to wait that long, excluding the complications of taking the Phae children from their families.

Doc's face twisted. "He began to experiment with human Phae children. He learned that humans impregnated by Phae males, had the same gestation period as a pure Phae. But the children grew at human rates. At eighteen, the children stopped aging. That was the key to his plan, unlike Phae females, humans could conceive at least once a year. Some females would conceive every time.

My horror grew, "He was breeding an army?" I asked in a shocked whisper. He was not only kidnaping and raping these women, but he was using the offspring to build an army? What kind of twisted monster thought like that?

"Not was, is, Kel. This is happening now," Doc answered me. "The rescuers began to check historical records and they found cases of hundreds of disappearances like the woman. They began to suspect that the Lead had not been foolishly bragging.

"Two weeks after she was rescued the woman went into labor," Doc cringed. "Phae children need Phae magic to pass through the birth canal. Neither mother nor child survived the process." His head dropped and I saw a tear hit the floor. "I have never heard of a case where the mother and child survived with Phae interference.

"The rescue party was anguished, but none more so than the youngest of them. She had known the woman; they had been close friends. The woman was named Selaina Weir." He stopped, and there was a long pause. He looked at me and there seemed to be an expectation there.

"And?" I asked, impatient for him to tell me more. I ignored the expectant look. I didn't know what he expected when he said the name, it was unfamiliar and I was tired of defending my lack of the knowledge they expected me to have.

Doc's face fell and disappointment showed in his eyes but he continued. "Selaina became a sort of battle flag, the group started to recruit others and tell the story. They watched the news and searched for missing women. They found quite a few, but not enough. Over the last six years they have grown to what you see now, but worldwide.

"This is a fraction of the group now fighting Phae." He took another long drink. "We know he plans to use his bred army against us, but we don't know when or how. One of our members almost figured it out, but they disappeared and the knowledge is probably now lost.

"The point of this Kel, is I don't think he wants to kill you. I don't know why there was the mistreatment and torture for you but I think they still want you for the purpose of bearing children." He sat back slightly and looked at me.

His story had been incredible, and I wanted to believe him because it would add sense to a lot of my messed-up world. But, I was skeptical. I had been lied to a lot in my life, and I wasn't about to start believing without some kind of proof to Doc's claims.

"Doc," I said, and something in my tone must have alerted him to my next words. I had been into Doc's story but I couldn't quite believe it. "This is a nice bedtime story, it might even qualify as horror, but you'll forgive me for not blindly believing it. Even if he did want me as some kind of baby making factory, it doesn't fit into anything else."

He sighed, "When you are ready to leave that bed I will show you. In the meantime, you should rest more." He patted my hand and stood up placing the water on a table near my bed.

Doc lowered my bed and before I could protest I felt the pull of sedative, I would find that bag and throw it away so it couldn't be used against me anymore. That emptiness waited, but somehow my mind held back and instead circled over everything Doc had said.

Why had I dismissed him so readily? Two figures appeared in the blackness. They were me, I watched in shock as they drew closer to my mind's eye. Carbon copies of myself stood there looking at me.

"Close your mouth," the one on the right said, as if she saw me and I was actually staring open mouthed. She was dressed in dark clothes, and had a no-nonsense vibe. I knew she would be the one who believed everything Doc had said. She would believe him and would be ready to act on that knowledge.

"Don't be so awful!" The left one said, that must be where I got that word. I hated her instantly, I knew her. She was the one who never fought back, who questioned everything and wanted to believe everything was a dream.

I hated her. Hated her because I was her. I wanted to be Right. And instead I was Left, a shell of a girl who was scared of the world. A girl who let people hit her, because it was easier than fighting. A girl who ran instead of facing the problem

Right started talking. "You know it makes sense, what Doc told us. You know somewhere inside he is right." She began, folding her arms and looking at me.

"There is no us, we don't exist!" Left said with a pouty whine. "We are just figments in a drug induced sleep world." Left stomped her foot, and flopped her arms. A child having a temper tantrum.

Right threw her a glare hard enough to wither stone, and Left shrank away. "You know they have to be telling the truth, and you know Alex is the big dark Scary. He's the one behind everything. You know why too, you just forgot and you let yourself keep forgetting!" There was a sharp accusation in her tone.

I wanted to refute her words, of course I didn't know anything. But it seemed I was the observer only in this, and I couldn't speak. Hard as I tried, only the two images of myself could speak. I couldn't even make them vanish.

"Don't say that," Left whimpered, I hated her more. I saw who I was in her, and disgust at myself and what I was rose inside me. "Don't talk about things like that. Of course she doesn't know anything."

Again Right glared, and again Left shrank away. "There's something we are missing here though. Where do we fit in?" Right began to pace around. She turned to face me. "We have to remember!"

"No we don't!" Left squeaked, apparently forgetting she was supposed to argue about their being an us or a we. "It was a mistake. We aren't what they think! We don't know anything!" Left was in a panic, and in a deja vu kind of way I saw myself start to hyperventilate,

Right paced back and forth, "We fit in here somewhere, we need to remember!" She was ignoring Left now muttering to herself and trying to find the piece of the puzzle that would fit her claim.

"STOP IT!" Left shrieked in hysterics. "Why won't you ever leave well enough alone, we can just get better and leave! You don't have to be nosy for us!" Left began to sob, and internally I recoiled from her.

Right watched her in disgust, "That's you, you know," she said matter-of-factly, facing me. "You hide from me, and instead you become her." She pointed an accusing finger.

I knew what she meant, and I hated that she was right.

The two images of me faded, and Alex's face appeared. But he was different, there was a kindness in his eyes. If you didn't look too closely. This was an Alex I didn't know, but seemed so familiar to me.

He seemed to be smiling at someone and laughing. Real laughter though, not the cold and cruel laughter that had been part of my every day with him. It was strange to see him this way. I had forgotten that once he had been a kind and thoughtful person. That once he had truly cared and taken care of me.

I studied the face I knew so well, but that was different. He still had the haunted eyes, but instead of embers burning with hatred, there was a softness there. I didn't understand, he had no softness. The vision shifted and I saw what Alex was looking at.

It was me. A younger me, the me from my memories of when I left Alex in that other place. But this was when we first met. When he was gallant and great. Before the hitting and cruelty happened.

My mind shuddered, and I mentally fled for the empty black. I didn't want more visions and memories. I wanted everything to just go away, I fell into the emptiness offered by the medications.

CHAPTER 11

I spent a week in my hospital room recovering, but by day five I was literally chomping at the bit. And day seven nothing was keeping me there anymore. I had not talked about what Doc told me, nor had I told anyone what I had seen right after our talk either. I spent my days surrounded by nurses and doing physical therapy. At night I thought about everything I had heard and learned here. I couldn't puzzle out my own feelings on the whole matter yet, so I didn't say anything.

The morning of my seventh day I got out of my bed before the nurses could appear and locked myself in the bathroom. I would NOT come out until they agreed I could be let out of this room. I needed air, I needed space, I needed to move. I didn't think about my actions and what they would mean when my bed was found empty.

I listened as the nurses started to enter, I heard a screech and the sounds of panic. Running footsteps sounded, and more panicked voices. I sighed, maybe disappearing wasn't the best idea. I was desperate though, and desperate measures made bad choices.

I opened the door, and stepped out. The room went still, and all eyes turned to me. Some in relief, some in anger. I closed the door and stood there awkwardly.

"I just uhhh, I uhhh..." I shuffled my feet and looked at the floor. "I didn't mean to worry anyone," I said lamely. I continued to stare at the floor, I didn't know what else to say.

A nurse with a round face, and kind demeanor came forward. "We just didn't know where you were, deary," she said, taking my hand.

I pulled out, "I need out," I whispered. "I need to leave this room. I need fresh faces." I flinched. "That didn't sound right."

She smiled, "Let's go talk to the Doc." She gently took my hand and started to lead me away.

I followed her not looking at anyone, I realized when they had begun to panic that it probably felt like the women who disappeared. I felt ashamed. I needed to learn to think through things before acting. She led us out of the room that had been my only safe place in a long time, and stepping out of the doorway took all my courage.

I wanted to leave. I was desperate to leave. But the room had provided safety and shelter. I hesitated and the nurse paused, turning to smile at me. I wish I remembered her name; I would've said it.

She seemed to understand though and came back taking my hand. "I'll help," was all she said, and with a soft tug on my hand she got me through the door.

The nurse took me through the waiting way to a little hidden away door. When she knocked I heard Doc's voice call to enter. She opened the door, ushered me in and shut it. She didn't follow me.

"Kel!" Doc said, surprised and rising to his feet. "Is everything alright?"

I nodded and looked at the room, I assumed this was his office. It looked like an overcrowded miniature library. The ceilings were at least nine feet and every wall had floor to ceiling shelves. Some were crowded with books, some holding odd gadgets. Some with pictures.

I approached a shelf with pictures, drawn there by some inexplicable urge. I heard Doc draw a sharp breath when he realized where I was heading. "Kel, wait."

But I didn't stop. No until I was in front of the shelf. The pictures showed people, some I had seen, like the nurses, others I didn't know. I looked at every picture slowly studying the faces, trying to find some semblance of sense or recognition.

The last picture on the shelf was people I recognized, and I stopped breathing. Carly and Jack were center frame, it looked like a southern plantation style house in the background with large trees everywhere else.

Mary stood to the left in the picture on Carly's right side, she smiled but there was something off about it. She didn't look as bold and happy as Carly, and certainly not the vibrant woman I had had dreams of. My eyes followed along the picture and my heart stopped too.

It was me. Standing next to Jack. No, I was holding hands with Jack! I couldn't deny that it was me. But it was wrong, that was the me I saw in my head. The strong version, the tough girl. Not the shell I was now.

I turned to Doc, shaking and my voice trembled. "When?" I asked him, it was the only word I could get out. I didn't understand how this picture existed. I had never met Jack and Carly before Jack barged into my life and brought me here. But here was a picture that said that was not the truth.

Doc slowly approached. He looked like I was a cornered rabid dog, and would bite him if he got too close. He looked at the picture still watching me from the corner of his eye. "Ah." He said solemnly. "Yes. That is..." He lifted the picture and turned it over. "June, three years ago." His tone was cautious.

I felt numbness start in my feet, and sweep up my legs. My ears rang, my body was cold. "That's not possible... that's... that's not right..." I said, before my knees buckled and the world went dark.

Alex pushed me back with his hand around my throat. I expected to hit the wall again but we passed through, it was either by magic or there was a door. I couldn't tell.

I was barely able to move my feet fast enough to avoid being dragged by my throat. We passed quickly through a narrow dark hallway and then we were in another room. There were more of the Phae in here, all males at least a dozen of them.

Alex shoved me to the middle of the room, and they circled me. Alex stood slightly in front. The looks on their faces told me what would happen before a word was spoken. These were males like Alex, the kind that would enjoy hurting someone.

"You're despicable," I spat venomously at him. I half crouched ready to fight to my best ability. I would not let this be easy for him. I knew logically I didn't stand a chance. The odds were beyond stacked against me. But I didn't care.

"Oh, come now Kel. Fighting will only make it worse for you." He smiled a dangerous smile full of promises of suffering. "See before we start, before I begin my revenge for what you did to me my friends want to get to know you a little... better." He grinned maliciously and there were chuckles all around me.

"Go to Hell." I snarled. A slap stung my face, and Alex was right in front of me again. He could move so fast that I hadn't been able to track the motion. One second he was feet away, and the next he was inches from me.

"Rule one, darling, respect. You will control that tongue, or you will suffer." He grasped my chin and forced me to look up at him. "Understand?" He used a tone like a parent talking to a disobedient child.

I snarled, and being a rational thinking person spit in his face. I would not give into him again. I was better than that. Better than him, and this time I would fight with everything I had. I would fight until there was nothing left in me to fight with.

His lip curled as he wiped his face, "It seems a lesson in manners first then." His tone was mild, but I picked out the hidden depths of anger and maybe even a little glee at what I had done. Like he wanted me to fight him.

The first blow came from my right and knocked the wind from me, another from my left. A hit to my head, pulled me from Alex's grasp and I landed on the floor. I tried to crawl away but someone caught my ankles and yanked me back.

Feet started flying at me, and I started not to know where I was hit anymore. The blows were hard and came from everywhere. I couldn't pick out a single impact point because it seemed I was hit in many places all at the same time. The pain started to take over my thoughts and I blacked out.

I came to when something cold and wet splashed over my body. My head pounded and everything hurt. The floor was cold, and as I focused on that sensation the horror of what happened slammed through me. Not only had I been kicked to unconsciousness but I now awake with my clothes missing.

I sat up and pulled my knees to my chest, still trying to get my eyes to focus. I could hear them laughing through the buzz in my ears. Everything hurt, from head to feet. I felt sticky dryness across my face and arms, and guessed some of the kicks had broken skin.

"Kel!" Alex's voice snapped right in front of me. He sounded impatient, and I tried to dredge up enough emotion to care or snap back. My mind moved sluggishly and I put a hand to my temple.

I blinked and he slowly came into focus, a grin of wicked delight playing with the corners of his mouth. He looked like he had just had one of the best days of his life. I believed that look and shuddered, if that had caused that look... I tried not to think about what that would mean for me.

"Why?" I croaked. I didn't understand why. Why me? Why the torment? Why did any of this happen? Why the vendetta, and the decade long search? What was I to him?

He smirked, "Well, when you left me. I tried to find you. And the more I looked the more vague your past became. I kept digging though." He chuckled like he knew some great secret. "I should've known, really. With how I was drawn to you, a mere human female. I should've guessed."

"Sp... it... it... out... Alex." My mouth felt heavy and dry as I tried to speak. My mind was clearing only a little, the pain was still everywhere. Still taking up most of my concentration.

"Why, Kel. It's like you were literally born for me." He grinned. "Your mother was one of our breeders, she escaped. How she managed to birth you with Phae help is a mystery.

"You know what we are doing here. You were meant to be one of my army." He put a hand on my cheek. "But you are special. You are different from them. I was drawn to the Phae side of you."

I shook my head, "You're lying Alex." But why would he lie about that? It made less sense than if he was telling the truth. I didn't want to believe he told the truth, that would change everything.

"Am I?" He laughed. "Well there's a simple test, Phae instinctively knows their blood kin even the half human mutts. So let's get your father in here."

My blood chilled further as the door opened. A male crossed the room and stopped, looking down at me he sneered. "Yes Lord, she's mine." He looked disgusted, and turned on his heel walking out.

I knew he hadn't lied, deep in my soul I knew that I had in part come from that creature. I shuddered and felt tears sting my eyes. Alex had been telling the truth I was a cross. I was one of the enemies. And Lord?

I faced Alex horror growing, "Lord?" I asked. I didn't want him to confirm what I knew already. If the Phae called him Lord, that meant he was the leader of their plans to wipe out humans. He was the one who started the creation of the cross.

"Yes, darling. Lord. Lord of Phae, bringer of justice against humans. Leader of the army." He smirked. "It's sad really, I did like you so much before you left me." He rose to his feet, towering over me. "It would've been so different if you had just stayed."

I snarled and curled my lips. "Eventually everyone leaves and abusive Prick, Alex." I smirked at him, I knew I should probably stop goading him for a while and maybe get the chance to heal. But I didn't, I kept fighting him.

He grinned at me, "Oh, Kel. Manners lessons will be hard for you." He turned his back to me and walked towards the exit. "No permanent damage," he said over his shoulder and the door shut.

I screamed and fought. I got some hits in but I was overpowered. I was one human girl to a dozen Phae males, and I never stood a chance. I woke in a room like the first one I had entered in this place.

The room offered no light, and I had no way to tell time. I was never left alone long, and hardly given time to rest. The only sleep I got was when exhaustion finally overtook everything and I passed out.

Hours, days or maybe even weeks later I was strapped into a chair, the straps were so many and so tight I couldn't move anything but my fingers and toes. Even my jaw had been clamped shut and a strap ran over my mouth.

I had been kicked and beaten and passed around until I didn't know who was who anymore. I hadn't seen Alex since his last comment of 'no permanent damage'. My world had been a haze of sleep deprivation and abuse. I have no idea if I had been sleeping when they brought me to the chair or if it was just another waking black out.

"Good! You're awake!" I hear Alex croon excitedly, "We've been waiting!" He strode into my view and I remembered why I had fallen for him. He truly was an extraordinary looking male.

I glared and tried to speak, only mumbling was heard. I pulled against the bonds, and tried to scream. That failed too. I couldn't move or speak no matter how I tried.

"Oh no, darling," he said. "This is a delicate procedure and you must be very still. See this is where the fun begins, I will start by breaking your spirit. That won't be difficult, we will just erase you and implant a new self, with ques to bring you circling in self-doubt." He grinned in triumph.

"When your spirit breaks the machine will send a signal, then," he paused and wagged his eyebrows. "Then I break your mind. And when you are mine, like you always should've been, I will find out who that human lover of yours was and send you to kill him."

I screamed into my bonds in fury, and he laughed cold and cruelly. The laugh that had started everything ten years ago when I left. The laugh that was the first sign, before he hit me.

"This will be fun darling, when the machine shows a broken spirit, I will enter into the program with you. It will all seem real, that's the joy of magic and technology." He walked to me, until he was right in front of me. "When you've killed that human lover, you and I will lead the army to wipe out humans for good. And you will be by my side for eternity."

He walked away from me, and I heard him talking to another male. Then there was silence. I strained my ears, and tried to twist my head.

I was startled when Alex's voice sounded in my ear, "This will hurt, Kel. And I will enjoy that." The strap over my mouth dropped and the head harness holding my mouth clamped shut removed. But before I could say a word, pain exploded across my mind. I was being ripped away, shredded into nothing. I screamed. And kept screaming, I couldn't stop it any more than I could stop the pain.

I felt ripped in half, and each half was run through a tree shredder. Part of me fled, I felt it. Part of me hid inside of me, in the box I had used to protect myself from Alex all those years ago. I felt that was the real me hiding, and through the screams I feared what of me would survive.

The pain stopped when a door opened and male walked in. He dragged a woman behind him, Jane. I had left Jane in charge of taking vital information to everyone and protecting them. Now she was here, I hoped she had gotten to my family first but I doubted it.

"Apologies lord, we caught this one," He flung her forward. "Sneaking around a door." He shot her a look of disdain and disgust.

I locked eyes on Jane begging her silently to tell me she had done it, that she had gotten the information out. I could handle this and would find a way to survive if only she had gotten to them.

Jane looked at me and shook her head, Alex didn't miss the move or my gasp of pain and fear. Everything had failed, my coming here did not save my family. "Oh, Kel? Do you know her? Was she going to rescue you?" His words were falsely honey sweet. "Too bad. He turned to the male, "kill her."

I watched as he drew a knife and I don't know whether I began screaming for my friend or for the pain in my head that started again when her body hit the floor. The only thing louder than my screams was Alex's cold laughter.

The screaming everywhere. In my head, my ears, even in my throat. Screams and pain. The world was pain, and the screams were proof. There were raised voices barely heard over the screaming. A detached part realized I was the one screaming, and wondered why I didn't just stop. But I couldn't stop, the pain needed to release the screams being that release.

The same detached part of me watched as Doc and the nurses held me down, and someone gave me a shot. It watched as the medication sank in and the screams stopped. It was like the world emptied of noise when they did. There was nothing without the sounds of my screams.

The silence was more deafening than my screams. The Doc and nurses rushed around and spoke quickly but I didn't hear any of it. I was numb, numb to pain and sound and everything outside my body.

"You know what it means, don't you?" Right's voice sounded in my head she sounded self-righteous, "It means I am the real us. It means, you are broken. It means, everything has changed. I am what was guarded when he ripped us apart!"

Right's voice faded, and I thought I heard Left crying. I wanted to cry, and I hated her. I hated Alex, I hated what he had done to me. And I hated myself, I had become what he wanted from me. I had been broken, and shattered.

The sedative wore off, and still l lay on the floor of Doc's office. My body was heavy, I could feel tears track down my cheeks. I could hear the murmur of voices, but I didn't think. I forced my mind to stay blank, Right and Left now seemed permanent presences. The two sides of me I realized. The before, and what he had me.

I shoved that away, before real thoughts formed. I tried to will the world away, tried to wish it gone. I wanted that empty anesthesia existence, but all the time and without the medication. More tears tracked the side of my cheeks.

That's enough! Right yelled. Get up! Stop being her! She flung her hand at Left, still curled up and crying. GET UP! She screamed in my head. Be strong! Be what we are supposed to be, Damn you!

Woodenly, I obeyed. I rolled over and pushed myself to my hands and knees, the movements were jerky and short like I didn't know how to work my body. The buzz of voices in the room stopped. I slowly lifted my head, there in front of me an empty chair. I crawled for it. It seemed to take a lifetime, but I reached the chair and with great effort pulled myself into it.

I heaved in a breath and lifted my head again. Doc was seated at his desk, a dozen nurses crowded around. How did this room hold so many people? It was like a Dr Who box come to life, internally I laughed at myself. Externally no noises escaped my clamped teeth.

Doc did a motion with his hand and like wisps of smoke the nurses left. He came around his desk slowly and approached me like I would run away or have another episode of screaming. He didn't know I was too numb for that. I was too numb for anything but to watch him approach.

He sat in a chair across from me and looked hard at my face. I don't know what he was looking for, but I don't think he found it. I felt shattered, and empty. Everything I had thought I knew was a lie, I was a lie.

"Kel?" He asked softly. When I didn't reply his face fell. He looked like a tired, beaten old man. "Kel I'm so sorry, if I'd known you would come in I would've moved the picture. I didn't know, I didn't even think it would cause such a reaction." He seemed to be struggling for words and finally just closed his mouth hanging his head.

If he had removed the picture it wouldn't have triggered the memory. Whatever magic had been done wouldn't have crumbled. I would still be clueless and arguing the truth with everyone. I don't know which existence I preferred.

I wanted to reach out and touch his arm, I wanted to say it wasn't his fault. None of this was his fault, he couldn't help what happened. I couldn't say that though, that required too much feeling. I said instead, "You took the picture." It was a statement, I remembered him being there.

"Yes," He whispered, tears on his cheeks. "Yes at the first place we looked for to be headquarters. That was when Mary first started to break away. None of us saw it, but looking at the picture now I've always wondered how we were so blind to it."

I flinched, Mary. Mary had been my best friend since we were in middle school, Mary had been my rock for so long. Then she crumbled, two months before I left she went willingly with a city Lead. She had agreed to bear their children to create an army to destroy her own people!

After *everything*, Mary had decided that the Phae were right and she would help their cause even if that meant she was used in creating an army. We had fought, I had told her she was stupid. She said I didn't understand, we hadn't spoken since.

A comment from Carly floated in then, '*Mary is a traitor and abandoned us. She said you were better off and we should leave you.*' Mary had known I was gone, and Carly had spoken to her. But no one knew the real truth, that I was half Phae that I was an abomination and that Mary had been right and they should have left me.

"Kel?" Doc asked cautiously, and I realized I had been silent a long time. I looked up at him, at his sad eyes. I knew he blamed himself now, for all of it. Somehow Doc was even managing to blame himself for my leaving.

The memory took hold of me before I could stop it and I was watching a scene from the past. I was there again that night that I had made the choice to hurt everyone I loved.

It was a cool evening and Jack, Carly, and I were scouting. We were sure there was a door somewhere here if we could find it and gather intel our night would be a success.

I squeezed Jack's hand tightly, and reached to clasp Carly squeezing her. I pointed with my chin when they looked. There it was, if you knew to look you could see a door. It looked like an out of place patch of air really. Not easy to distinguish.

I pulled them back behind a dumpster. "I go in," I whispered. It was my turn. Jack had gone the last time and Carly the time before. We never all went in at once.

They nodded, "Ten minutes." Again part of our deal, the person who went in got ten minutes before the other left. We couldn't risk us all dying or being captured.

We approached the door, and Jack and Carly squeezed my hands before finding a place to observe on either side.

Taking a deep breath, I pushed the heavy cold feeling. I entered a field. I was always thrown off by the differences each door had. Some were buildings, some cities, some like this. The problem with the field is that I was exposed and with my first step I knew I hadn't come in unnoticed.

I whirled trying to make it through the door but when I turned it was yards away instead of a step. Hands caught me from behind.

"Well," said a cold voice. "This will be my lucky day." He laughed in my ear.

I felt a blow to my temple and the world fell into silent darkness.

I came to on the other side of the door, no longer in the field. My head ached and my vision swam. I moved my arm to place my hand on my head and heard a crinkle of paper. Blinking my eyes I found the paper and held it up. Every line dropped a lead stone in my stomach.

'We know where you came from, and that you aren't alone. Our Leader wants you to come to him, in trade we will leave your facility in peace. Write your reply here, if you are in agreement meet at the woods on the edge of town tomorrow. Fail to show and you and yours won't see another sunset.'

I had been handed an ultimatum, go back and leave everything I knew and loved or watch it be destroyed. I had seen these creatures in action and knew nothing would survive an attack. It was why we were on the mission tonight, to find a way to beat them before they destroyed our world.

I felt heavy, there was only one choice. I got to my feet preparing my story of sentries and having to wait before I could come back. It had happened before and would be believed. I had information I hadn't shared with Jack and Carly yet. I needed to get it to them, but if I told them would they be suspicious?

I wobbled on my feet as I headed back in the direction of HQ, I would have to walk the five miles back but that was okay it gave me time to plan and think and get steady on my feet. I figured the information about their armies' size and locations would be safe to give to another member, and I would just say I had another mission and no time to deliver it myself. Also believable.

Jane was my best candidate. New to our ranks she was one of the rescued and had decided to fight back. I would give her the information and slip away. The woods mentioned were within walking distance of HQ so I wouldn't even need to try and sneak a car.

My plan made I headed back to HQ and bed. If I was lucky I would see no one before evening when I sought out Jane.

"Doc," I said quietly. "I left. I chose to walk out the door. I thought I could protect you all, so I left a note to Jane about the army. I wanted to find her but I ran out of time. It told of the when and how. And the numbers."

Doc cut in, "Jane vanished, right after you did. We think they got her." I could tell he was upset by the thought and dreaded the next words I was going to say.

I nodded, "I know, they did. I'm sorry Doc," I sighed heavily. "They killed her. I think she guessed what happened and came to find me. Jane was always too smart, and she didn't deserve that." I hung my head; I couldn't look at Doc anymore.

"Kel," he said sharply. "Do you... Do you remember?" He sounded hopeful and excited.

I nodded, "All of it Doc. All of it."

The door opened and a nurse entered with a tray of food and water. She set it down, cast a worried glance in my direction and bustled out closing the door behind her. I had watched her enter and leave, quickly, quietly, efficiently. A well-oiled routine.

"But that's good Kel!" Doc said, some life and excitement back in his voice. "Tell me everything!"

I turned my head to him, "Where did Jack and Carly go? How soon can they be back? I only want to say it once, you understand right?" I couldn't bear the thought of telling my story multiple times, excluding the fact I figured I would be exiled when they learned the truth anyway.

He frowned slightly, stood and walked to his desk. He opened a drawer, rummaged around and came out with a cellphone. I watched him punch the screen a few times then hold it to his ear. His face had no emotion, and when spoke it was a flat dead tone.

"Come back." He said and hung up. He put the phone away and returned to the seat across from me. "We don't know if they can listen in to calls..." he started.

I smiled a little and waved my hand. "I know Doc, they couldn't fully erase me, though as you saw they tried. I had a cellphone and always left it in the truck, I never could bring myself to carry it. I had a mom in that reality, and she always yelled at me about carrying the phone on me." I chuckled.

He grinned at me. "I don't know how long it will take them to get back, or to even get the message. Also that does sound like something your mother would do." Doc gave a gentle smile.

I hadn't spoken to my mother since we discovered the truth about Selaina, I had told her enough to keep her on guard but not enough that she would be in danger. I had thought that was the right thing, now though I was questioning that. The revelation of Alex changed the playing field entirely.

I nodded, "I just want to tell it one time Doc." I closed my eyes. "I need to be busy, please let me help. I know a lot, especially about the army." I took a deep breath, and slouched in the chair. I felt centuries old and bone weary.

Doc led me to a control room on the third floor of the 'house', I could get no one to actually call it a palace. This place had been finalized on the day I left, so I had never been here before. I was lost before we left the second floor, and dizzy before the stairs stopped on the third floor.

We had had a different HQ before this one, the picture in Doc's office had been a prospect but we decided on its smaller neighbor. We utilized that, building and adding on as we grew, until Mary had left. The scramble for a new HQ was mass chaos. I was supposed to be here when the doors opened the first time to our family.

That's how we thought of ourselves, those of us who knew the nightmares were real and fought worldwide to stop them. I had been thought of as the founder; some of my closer friends even jokingly called me the Queen.

When we got to the control room, a map was spread on a table at least fifteen feet square. Heads snapped to the door when we entered, and everyone rushed to their feet. I knew every face, and some were missing. I turned to Doc.

"They never came back from trying to find you." He said quietly. "Everyone in this room searched, Jack is the one who found you, that's part of why he went there. But every person here wanted to go." He nodded to people in the room. There were twenty of them, there used to be thirty.

"Kel?" A short man round as he was tall came forward. "Kel, it's me. It's..."

I rushed forward and cut him off with a hug. "John." I breathed.

He sighed and the relief in the room was palpable, everyone rushed in and I was crushed in a press of bodies. My resolve broke and had it not been for all the people and hands I would've fallen to the floor crying.

Emotions overwhelmed me. Joy at seeing my family, my friends. Sorrow at the faces I would never see again. Anger at everything that had happened to me. And fear, fear they would hate me when they all learned the truth of who I was.

CHAPTER 12

Eventually I pulled my emotions back in, but the numbness never came back and I was more raw than ever before. Every emotion coursed through me with sharp edged fullness. The joy would push tears of happiness to the surface, anger would make vision tint red. It was a roller coaster and I struggled to stay afloat.

"I have some news, it will help. But it's not good news." I said finally, pulling back from John and feeling the others retreat. John was beaming at me even though my words were solemn and heavy. It was like he couldn't help himself.

John nodded, "Let's hear it my girl." I told them about the half-breed army. The problem was the numbers, at thirteen, they were putting these children in ranks and training them. And had been doing so for centuries. There was one Phae cross bred child to every three humans.

"Okay," I walked to the map in the center of the room. "Exact numbers are iffy, but I gathered there probably one of them for every two humans, at least. There could be a lot more." A gasp echoed through the room. I sighed, I understood. We were too few.

"Exactly, we don't even have a quarter of the human population on board with us." I grabbed some green army men from the edge of the board, they must have been John's doing. Placing one army man in every location I learned of, I showed where the doors would be.

Always near a big city, but never in the city itself. There are seven continents and the Phae planned to unleash an army on nearly everyone. They thought to overwhelm the cities first and then work out to less populated areas. Thinking that it would be easier to destroy the human race that way.

"That's not very many doors," Doc said behind me. He peered over my shoulder studying the map. "Asia general, Alaska, Europe, Africa, South America; Brazil area, nothing directly in the U.S though..." He trailed off. I didn't understand that either, but that was what I had learned. They planned a South American Gate and an Alaskan gate and for both forces to meet on U.S. soil.

I shook my head. "You misunderstand Doc, that's where they intend to put the doors. They have ways to travel between pockets without entering our realm and they can make and close doors at will." I pointed to the army men again, "That's the strategy for attack, take out the big cities where all the largest human populations are."

Groans sounded through the room. "So far, Kel, you're telling us we're screwed and should go home to kiss our wives and babies." John said from my right. His tone was unreadable and his face carefully blank.

I smiled slightly, "Not yet John. I have a secret they don't know I know. The Phae cross army stops aging at eighteen but they have human weaknesses." I looked around the room, "AND!" I said the word with emphasis. "Naturally produced Fire Opal is instant death to the Phae crosses." I let that sink in as I surveyed the room. If we were lucky that weakness could tip the scales in our favor.

Murmurs started around me as my news sank in. I looked to John who was studying the map and frowning in thought. I could see him coming up with a plan, already he was thinking of a way to use this information.

John turned to me. "So if we can powderize the opal and set up ambushes at the doors we can, at the very least start to even the playing field? Does this opal work against the pure Phae as well?" There was a hopeful note in his tone.

I shook my head, "Sadly no, it will not work against them. But they are far fewer than the army. I didn't have time to learn their weaknesses." I made a face, I wished I'd gotten that information too. It was luck that I had learned about the opal.

It seemed that one of the Leads had taken a liking to a cross girl, and had tried to gift her with a bracelet made of opals. The primary stone had been a fire opal from an extinct Volcano in Mexico.

He had placed the bracelet around her wrist and she had gone into seizures, and within seconds died. The Lead had not known the cause except that the bracelet had triggered it. So he experimented with the different opal on other crosses until he concluded it was the fire opal that had killed her.

He started to spread that information to ensure no one else made the same mistake, I happened to overhear about the opals on the reconnaissance mission prior to us being found out. That was part of the information I had left for Jane. I hadn't found the time to tell anyone and then everything had gone wrong.

The thought of Jane brought guilt and sorrow; she had been a fierce friend. After her rescue she had dove into the work of bringing the Phae's plans to an end. I was sorry she was dead; I was even more sorry that it was my fault.

"What is our timeline like Kel?" Again John was pressing ahead, not discouraged by my answer. He was a positive person, and liked to find the bright side of things instead of focusing on the doom and gloom and death. I had always loved that about him, and now more than ever needed that in my life.

I did some mental calculations. "I've been gone for six months..." I trailed off again. "Four months, June 20th." I looked around again. "It's not a lot of time, my friends. We have to make due and get as much prepared as possible."

John gave a sharp nod, "Kel." He said, "this is a great start, and I can see you want to be here to plan their demise. But I also see that you are exhausted, and something is weighing on you. Have Doc show you to your room, and get some good rest. We are so glad to have you home with us." He hugged me tightly, and his words drew tears to my eyes again.

I conceded without much fight, normally I would argue with someone ordering me to rest but John was right. I was exhausted, and my world had again changed completely. There was only so much a girl could take and expect to still be sane. I was almost at my limit.

"Doc?" I asked, facing him. I yawned hugely as I turned, I was feeling the need to be alone again. For just a moment a tiny part of me missed the lonely existence I had in the pocket. Miserable as it was, it had been simple and I hadn't been aware how close the world was to destruction.

Doc looked relieved, as he nodded at me and I followed him from the control room. Personal rooms started on the fourth floor and Doc led me again up a winding stair and down a corridor. I stopped myself from chuckling at the look he had, Doc was probably thanking every God everywhere I had complied.

Halfway down he stopped and nodded to a door on the left. "That one is yours. Jack is here," He pointed to the door on my right. "And Carly is here." The door on the left. "They wanted it to be like it always was even when you weren't here to set things up."

I smiled sadly, yes Jack and Carly would want that. I slowly opened the door, holding my breath and closing my eyes as I stepped through the doorway. Doc must have turned on the light, because beyond my eyelids was bright where it had been dark. I carefully opened my eyes and started to look around.

There was a queen bed, at the back in the center of the wall underneath a window. The blinds were closed and curtains drawn. A bedside table held a lamp and a couple books. The dresser had an attached mirror and there were pictures all over of the three of us.

I took a step farther in and saw doors on opposite walls. I glanced at Doc in question and he laughed. "Those are an addition. Jack and Carly built them, they said when you came back the doors would always be open."

I wanted to cry again; my two best friends had never believed I wouldn't come back. Jack had never given up on me, and Carly probably hit anyone who suggested I was lost forever. I hoped they would still want me around when I told them everything. I didn't realize how much I needed them until recently. But the thought of their rejection almost broke me.

Another step in and I found a creaky floorboard. I looked down and frowned at the floor marking the spot in my memory for future avoidance. Barking exploded behind the door to Jack's room. I whirled and stared at the door.

"Doc?" I asked in trepidation. "Is that... Is that who I think it is?" I pointed at the door. I couldn't bring myself to say the names of the dogs, what if Jack had gotten new ones? Or what if there was only one dog? It felt like my heart stopped, and I held my breath waiting for Doc's answer.

"Yes Kel, Jack wouldn't go anywhere without them. I'm sorry to say the older girl passed while you were gone. But the two boys are still around. When Jack leaves we take turns caring for them." Doc's tone was quiet and solemn.

I approached the door, when I had been captive I had missed having dogs. Dogs that then I didn't know I had had. The magic was supposed to erase the old me, but it hadn't erased Jack and Mary and Carly. And it hadn't erased the dogs, not completely anyway.

Ten years ago, when I actually had left Alex. I was angry and frustrated with men, and I got a door. A young chihuahua puppy as round as he was tall. I had named him Gordito, the Spanish word for fat. He had become my constant companion going everywhere with me. Often riding on my shoulders so he could properly survey his kingdom.

When Jack and I met and started to date five years after that, Gordito immediately accepted him and claimed him as ours. He would ride on Jack's shoulder's and even grace him with nose bites, a sign of true affection from this little dog. We called them mouth hugs.

A year later while at work we found King Charles Spaniel and Dachshund cross. Despite Jack's protests we brought the dog home and named him Kujack. Kujack quickly became Jack's dog in the way Gordito was mine. As far as Kujack's world went his guy was most important, and then me (the one who actually rescued him).

When the world went crazy and Selaina disappeared we had talked about giving the dogs to family to protect them but we couldn't part with them. So they went with us, and when we had missions through the pockets we would leave the dogs at the safe house. I was relieved that even with my disappearance Jack had kept the dogs.

I opened the door between mine and Jack's room and crouched just as two small blurs of color raced through. One black and one red/orange. They charged past me initially heading for Doc, but Gordito halfway to Doc realized he had passed me.

He spun on his heels and charged back to me barking and crying. Kujack caught on and came back right after. Both dogs jumped into my lap and pushed each other to be the one to lick my face first and most often.

I laughed and cried, and felt a small part of myself become whole again. While I had my worries that my human family would reject me when the secret was out, I knew in my heart that these little dogs would love me forever.

Eventually the dogs settled enough I could get off the floor, and I realized at some point Doc had left. I yawned and climbed on the bed. The dogs followed me and when I lay down they curled up with me, Gordito against my belly and Kujack at my back. I felt the exhaustion weigh me down and pull me to sleep.

Alex, snarled at the Lead in front of him. "It has been three weeks! Where is she?" He shouted. His face was turning red with fury, and that look meant death to someone.

"We don't know Lord," The Lead said cautiously, taking a tiny step back. He was right to show fear, Alex didn't tolerate mistakes. Mistakes meant someone would pay, and the Lead seemed to understand that about his Master.

"How did a human even get into my pocket!?!" Alex roared, and everyone took steps back. "I knew something was off about that man but I thought it was a computer glitch on her memory." He seethed much quieter. "We've never done this on a cross, I didn't realize it was a human interfering!" His quiet tone was gone again.

Alex turned to a male dressed like a scientist. "Explain to me what happened! When I went in it's because you said she was broken, and it was time for phase two." His nostrils flared, and eyes turned even colder. His face spelled death.

The male swallowed audibly and paled. "Lord, I believe because of what she is, a cross I mean, that the magic to erase her didn't work fully. Somehow she retained bits of her old self, but the computer read the new self. And when the other human joined the pocket, the computer got confused."

Alex clenched his fist and slammed it on the table, "How did the human get in?" His voice had become calm, and I knew the scientist would die even if he answered Alex. He seemed to know it too.

"There was a connection between them," He whispered hoarsely. "When the erase went awry that connection became part of the pocket program and it recognized him and so he was able to enter the door."

Alex never moved, but the scientist began to gasp and claw at his throat. It was slow, as if Alex were drawing it out as long as he could. Finally the male collapsed and Alex turned to a different Lead.

The Lead had paled and was looking at the scientist in horror, but when he realized Alex's attention was back on him he straightened and wiped all emotion from his face.

"Make sure everything is for the attack, get the Army moved. I don't want there to be any problems. Four months gives plenty of time for something to interfere, and I will not have that. Understood?" The male snapped a salute, and seemed relieved to run out of the room.

Alex faced the first Lead. "Find her Maximus, and get her back. I don't care who you have to kill, and if you come across that man, bring him too." The malicious glint in Alex's eye said what would happen if he got ahold of Jack.

The male nodded. "Yes, Lord."

I came awake at the sound of a knock on my door, and the dogs barking. Blinking, I tried to make sense of my surroundings, "Hello?" I called towards the door.

The door opened, and an unknown face entered. "Miss Kel, I am Mike, I got her after you disappeared. Doc asked me to bring you some food." He set a tray of food on the bedside table and was out the door before I got to say thank you.

The food was simple fare, a meat and cheese sandwich and a glass of water. I had slowly been working my appetite back in the last week. I chewed each bite slowly mulling over what I had dreamed.

It hadn't been a memory like the other dreams, where they felt familiar this was new and Alex had spoken of finding me and the attack. He also spoke of Jack. I wondered if this new dream or vision or whatever it was had to do with my admission of the connection. If somehow I was able to actually things when Alex was most angry.

I got halfway through the sandwich and my stomach turned. The pocket where Jack had found me had been made specifically for me, it was meant to be my prison until Alex had fully broken me. I felt sick at the thought, Alex had meant to break my mind and spirit. The shell that I was in the pocket was what he wanted permanently.

But something went wrong. I thought about that, and I remembered with mental and physical clarity the pain of the erasing. I had split apart, and part of me locked away in an internal box. Right, as I had named her when confronted with my two selves.

The erase had failed and the pocket had never functioned properly, I had always dreamed of Jack. In the pocket world I had believed I was there for years, and had felt lonely for Mary and Carly. But the dreams were only months old.

My head started to hurt as I tried to mesh the two realities. The years in the pocket had been a lie twisted by Phae magic from my own memories. They had literally used my life as a weapon against me. So it should have worked, I should've been broken when Alex came in. But I wasn't.

Jack had found a way in and had started confronting me with the truth that the world was wrong, and it had made the computer believe I was broken. Or something like that. I shook my head.

I didn't understand what had happened any more than that scientist. Maybe he was right and being a cross made their magic work differently. Whatever had happened it had saved my life and if we succeeded, the world.

CHAPTER 13

Over the next two months I was either in the control room with John going over ways to weaponize the Fire Opal and how to get it, in the hospital for physical therapy and strength training or in my room sleeping. Days blurred into each other, and sometimes I didn't know if it was actually day or night. I hadn't had any more dreams or visions since that last and I hoped that meant good news and that Alex had not changed his plans.

We decided on crushing the opal to powder and air releasing it. The logistics were harder to plan out. We talked about everything from cannons to air planes. The problem with cannons being how well dispersal could go, or rather that it wouldn't disperse well at all.

I brought up the idea of old Bi-planes that they used to use to for crop dusting. "We can use the same theory, we'll put the powder on the planes and fly over the army once they've reached a designated zone. That will allow for max dispersal and if we choose the right spot there is the best chance of maximizing the damage done."

Everyone went silent and looked at me, and I began to feel uncomfortable. I don't like to be the center of attention, and twenty pairs of eyes locked on me had me wanting to squirm like a toddler doing the potty dance.

"Kel," John said slowly. "That may just work." He began to talk of locations from the doors for release and everyone looked back to the map. I had felt like the weight of the world would crush me with all those eyes on me. I had questioned my idea and wanted to take it back immediately.

I heaved a sigh of relief, and shrank away from the map. This was more John's area than mine and with my idea in place he didn't need me there. I could go and leave the planning and discussions to John.

The door opened and Mike came in, he saw me and made a beeline in my direction. Ever since he had brought me that sandwich Mike had acted like a personal secretary, bringing me messages making sure I ate. Even caring for the dogs if I was away from my room too long. I smiled at him and met him halfway.

His look was solemn and serious and my smile started to fade. "Mike? Is everything okay?" I was worried that something bad happened. Had the Phae acted? Was there another disappearance? Or was it a death this time, to spite me for my escape.

"They are back Kel; Doc is setting up a conference room and wants me to take you there." He turned then and walked out the door, leaving me to follow. He didn't look over his shoulder to see if I did and I would forever be grateful to him for that.

I felt the blood drain from my face, and where I had felt happy accomplishment moments before I now felt a cold dread. I felt the cracks inside me start to grow like they had in the pocket. Like they would overwhelm me and I would fall apart again. It was time then. Time to tell them my story, and let them pass judgement.

A cold sweat started at the base of my skull and slowly trailed down my spine, I knew this had to happen. They had a right to know, but I was afraid. And selfishly didn't want them to know. I didn't want to risk losing the only thing that had kept my sanity for six months. I don't think the pocket was supposed to take that long to break me.

I had come to the conclusion that the reason it took six months was because of my dreams of Jack and Carly and Mary. Because I kept a hold on them Alex never got his hold fully on me. Now I was faced with possibly losing that lifeline.

I followed Mike to the second floor where the bigger rooms had been made into conference chambers. Some small and cozy for only six of fewer people, and some converted to hold at least fifty people.

We were set up in a small conference room. It was dominated by the round table in the center that left just enough room to get in and move around if the chairs were tucked in. Mike opened the door, and when I entered I saw Doc was the only one there yet.

I felt the knot in my stomach grow hard, and thought I might be sick. I grabbed a chair farthest from the door and sat, laying my head on my arms on the table. I didn't want to do this anymore, but it was too late now.

I heard Jack and Carly laughing before they entered the room. I listened to their voices, memorizing the happy sounds, I would hold those forever in my heart. When they rejected me and cast me out, I would cherish the happy joy in their voices.

"Doc!" Jack said loudly upon entering the room. "Why do we need a conference room?"

I hadn't lifted my head when he entered but I heard his footsteps stop and Carly's oof as she walked into him. I could feel his eyes on me, boring holes into the top of my head. I wanted to slide under the table and get out of his line of sight.

"Dammit Jack, get out of the way!" She said, I heard her huff of annoyance.

I lifted my head then in time to see Carly shove Jack hard from behind and him stumble sideways as, in truly Carly fashion, she barged through the door. Carly hadn't noticed why Jack had stopped and before glancing around she flopped into a chair.

Jack was unmoving after he regained his balance, and his eyes were locked on me. I met his stare, and smiled at him. "Hello, Love." I said softly. Jack's eyes widened and he looked at once relieved and terrified it was a trick.

Carly hearing my voice whipped her head so fast she should have gotten whiplash, and looked at me. "KEL!" She screeched, trying to get out of the chair and around the table, but in the same instance Jack had moved and they tangled together with limbs and chairs. I don't know how disaster was averted, but no one managed to crack their skulls open on the table.

When they had righted themselves I held my hands up. "Please, my dearest companions. Before you get excited about me, let me tell my story." I gave them each a serious look, and Carly shoved Jack again.

"Sit Jack," she said. "We can hug her when she has delivered the doom and gloom that has her so worked up." She sat heavily with an eye roll. Carly was trying to lighten the mood.

I made a face at Carly. She knew me well. I just hope that with that knowledge of me she would be able to forgive me too. I needed her and Jack in my life.

I looked at Doc and he nodded. "Jack shut the door please," he said. "Kel, as you asked, this room is one of the sound proofed spaces." Doc had suggested it a few days ago, saying it would give us privacy for my story.

I nodded gratefully, though I was sure eventually everyone would know I wanted to tell these three people alone first without being overheard. Then I could leave and they could spread the story. But this way I had only three faces to judge me instead of hundreds.

Jack shut the door, then all three looked at me. Taking a breath I began. "Everyone here knows that years ago Carly and I had a falling out and we didn't speak for a long time." There were nods around the table. "Okay, so this starts during that period. I didn't have many friends left after Carly and I quit talking. Mary had moved away already and even before that she was Mary, very wrapped in herself.

"I met and started dating Alex." There were hisses of anger from Doc and Carly, and Jack growled deep in his throat. I took another deep breath. "We dated for I think four years all together. It's a little fuzzy to me and I think I've blocked a good bit of it out. The first two years were perfect. He was attentive and caring, always there when I needed something. I was truly happy and at the time didn't think I could be happier.

"Alex left for a business trip right around the two-year mark, he was gone for close to a month and we didn't talk the whole time. I don't remember what he said the reason was that we couldn't talk, but I remember missing him terribly.

"When he came back he was different, but it was really noticeable at first. But subtle things started to change. He was quick to anger, and at some point the physical started. It was minimal at first, slapping my hand away when I would reach for him. Pushing me. It got worse over a six-month period, and finally he broke my arm. Earlier that day I had been riding and fallen off. I don't remember what triggered him, but it didn't go well for me."

I looked down at the table, I couldn't handle the intensity in Jack's stare. "Like all foolish women who get caught up like that I had convinced myself that it was my fault. But when he broke my arm I decided to leave." I felt the burn of tears and cleared my throat. "I planned for a year to get away, I saved money and stashed things away. Then out of the blue Alex had another business trip, and my opportunity was presented.

"I ran. I moved out of state. And never told anyone I was leaving, not even my mom. I couldn't because then I would have to admit to the abuse. And I was a coward. So instead I ran, and I wound up more than fifteen hundred miles from home in Mississippi.

"About six months later I got an email from Carly." I looked up and smiled at her. "It was the start of our friendship repairing. And a few months after that Jack, I met you." I couldn't look at him yet and went back to studying the table.

"I never questioned my choice to run, for the first year my mom would tell me that he had asked about me but then even that stopped. And I thought I was free from him.

And life was perfect, with Carly back. And having Jack that the abusive ex-boyfriend went the way of old trash. Out of sight out of mind.

"That wasn't the case for him, he never stopped thinking of me and never let go of the fact I had left him. I didn't know this of course and you guys remember how involved things became after Selaina.

"Alex was obsessed though, and he started digging into my past trying to find clues to find me. He eventually figured out how to find my father. I thought my father had died before I was born, that's what my mom always told me. Anyway, Alex located him.

"When we did that last recon mission and I went in I was found out." Carly's eyes widened; she'd been getting paler the longer I talked. "I was knocked unconscious, and after you guys had left, I left outside where the door was with this note." I had found the note in the jacket I had worn that night, and carried it every day for the last two months.

They passed the notes between themselves and when everyone had read it they looked back to me. My voice choked, and my throat felt thick. "Go on Kel," Doc said gently.

"They knew who I was," I whispered, unable to make my voice any louder. "Alex had provided a full description and while they were searching for women for the cross breeding they were also to keep an eye out for me." I felt a tear run down my cheek.

"I don't know why they didn't just take me immediately to him, maybe it was another of his games. Making me choose to give up myself or place everyone in danger. Either way, I'm sure he knew what I would choose."

"You chose to leave!" Jack's voice exploded through the room and I flinched. "You chose to walk away from us!" I nodded my head. His accusation rang through the room every word a dagger to my soul.

"Yes," I said quietly. "I knew I had to protect you. I tried to get as much intel as possible you guys, I left Jane a letter explaining everything and telling her to tell you. But Jane tried to follow me. She figured out what happened." Another tear hit the table.

"I heard you that night looking for me, and I hesitated. I almost went back, but they threatened you again and I kept going." I finally lifted my head to look at Jack. The look of anguish and despair and anger crushed my heart.

"I was taken through a door, and then they closed it immediately, it's why you couldn't find me." I saw Carly nod at that, and Doc's face puckered with displeasure. I couldn't tell if it was directed at me or the door being closed immediately.

"I was taken immediately to Alex, and that's when I learned he was one of them. And not only that but the leader of the rebellion against humans. He said he would make me suffer for leaving him, and after I had suffered and was broken he would make me come back and kill you guys, then lead the army to destroy humanity.

"He also told me about my father. My father..." My voice choked and cracked. "My father is Phae. I am a cross, the only cross born without the magic of the Phae to help. My mother escaped when she was days from birth, and somehow we both survived."

I let the words hang in the air between us all, I watched the shock of my revelation register on every face. Jack looked angry and before I could say another word he had stormed out, slamming the door. Carly gave me a strange look and followed him.

I hung my head expecting Doc to also leave, but when I didn't hear him move I looked up. He was smiling sadly at me. "I already knew Kel," he said by way of explanation. "When I did your exam and tested your blood, I figured it out."

I stared at him dumbstruck. "And you didn't tell anyone?" I asked incredulously. Doc had known, and yet he had said nothing, not even to me. He had let me help and plan the counter attack.

He smiled at me. "Dear Kel, what difference does it make? You are still you. Your heritage doesn't change what you have done. You started this resistance and have played a key role in our success."

I truly cried then, Doc had known what I was and not thought ill of me. He had remained my friend, and steadfast and loyal. He hadn't even mentioned it once, I wasn't sure I had deserved that loyalty but I treasured it.

"Do you think he'll forgive me Doc? Will he tell me to go? I can plan to be out front when we launch the opal. To be at one of the doors I mean." I looked at Doc. My own proposal was hollow in my ears, it was not what I wanted but I would do it if it spared my loved ones more pain.

I saw the moment when I had said registered. Doc paled and a look of horror passed over him. "Why would you plan on that Kel? It would kill you too," he said. He sounded angry and hurt.

"I know," I replied simply. "I shouldn't exist Doc, there should never have been crosses. And whatever else I am, there is a connection to Alex and I'm afraid that while I live he could discover it and use it to hurt the ones I love. I don't know if he could ever use it, but I know he knows I'm alive by it. And that puts everyone in danger. It would just be easier if I was gone, permanently." I looked at my hands and a couple tears splashed my clasped fists.

I still didn't want to die; I wanted a long life. But I would die, I would again make the choice to be the sacrificial lamb if it saved everyone else.

"Then we destroy him!" Doc snarled fiercely. "I will not hear any more of you sacrificing yourself, it nearly killed us all when you disappeared. Whether you like it or not, you are the heart and soul of this organization." Doc's look of determination started to lift my spirits.

"What if they all find out the truth? Not everyone is as accepting as you Doc." I looked pointedly at the two empty chairs. The two most important people in my life had not been able to accept my truth, how could I expect everyone else to?

"Jack will come around, I'm sure he just needs to process. He hasn't been okay without you. And Carly, I think she went to straighten him out." I knew Doc was trying to make me feel better, and so I let the words comfort me.

"All the same Doc, can you have Mike fetch Gordito? I think I need to temporarily not be in my room." I gave him a sad smile, and he nodded. I closed my eyes and took a deep breath before looking at Doc again.

"If you wish." He stood and walked to the door. "Kel," He turned back to me. "Don't do anything rash, okay? We need you. This plan will not happen without you." He left the room and I sat in silence thinking.

Doc did not come back so it was just me until Mike arrived. I thought about Doc calling me important, I had trouble believing him. The plan would still work, and could still happen without me. I was just one person.

Mike came in a short while later, Gordito in his arms and I placed him on my shoulders. "Thank you Mike," I said to him softly. Standing to leave the room, I needed fresh air.

"Miss Kel," he said before I could walk away. "No one will hate you, you know? In fact I bet they think more of you for helping mankind." He turned and left before I could reply. Mike knew then I didn't know how he knew but he did and he accepted what I was.

Strangely that was a comfort. I walked down the hall to the stairs and decided Gordito needed a run outside. We crossed the massive entry and as soon as we were outside I set him down. He took off like a shot heading for a tree to pee on. I laughed and followed him. I had no need to run. I knew Gordito wouldn't go far from me.

We walked along the woods, the same woods where Alex had had a doorway made to take me. I found a quiet secluded spot just inside the tree line. You had to practically crawl through a bush to get to it, but I managed. I leaned against a tree and Gordito crawled into my lap and promptly went to sleep.

I stroked him from head to tail down his back and leaned my head back against the tree staring up into the foliage. That's the thing about the south, even though it was barely spring the trees and bushes were thick with green growth.

Gordito picked his head up and wagged his tail staring off in the direction of the house. I heard them then, male and female voices coming our way. When they got closer I picked out Jack and Carly, and it sounded like they were arguing.

"You don't get it Carly! Everything is different now!" Jack was saying. I could hear the anger and hurt in his voice, his stomping footsteps like a marching rhythm.

"How Jack?" Carly asked back. "How is it different?" She sounded annoyed like she had been trying to make him explain this since they left the conference room.

"You heard what she said!" He snarled, and I knew they were talking about me now. They were talking about what I was, and Jack was saying he couldn't accept that. My heart started to crumble and shatter. I had still held out hope they would forgive me, but it seemed like at least Jack could not.

"Yes Jack, I did. And I watched you storm out. You didn't see what that did to her! So tell me how things are different?!" I heard the anger in Carly's voice, she seemed to be defending me. That caused me too, I was putting a wedge between them with my revelation.

I didn't hear Jack's reply because they had been moving quickly and were now past my range of hearing. My heart clenched. I knew Jack wouldn't forgive me for what I was. Tears silently rolled down my cheeks, and Gordito in distress licked my face. He never liked it when I was upset.

With sheer force of will I stopped the tears. I wished for my memory to be broken again, it was easier to take the disdain from Jack when he didn't mean so much to me. We were supposed to have been married. I even had the ring in the room between him and Carly. I had stared at it every night hoping and praying he wouldn't hate me when I told them the truth.

I sat up suddenly as that thought ran through me. June 20th the day of the army attack, that was the day we were to get married. I didn't think it was a coincidence that Alex had chosen that date. But if not coincidence then it meant he knew.

It hit me then, that Alex had specifically said *"Then I break your mind. And when you are mine, like you always should've been, I will find out who that human lover of yours was and send you to kill him."* He had known about Jack.

But Alex hadn't been a part of my life in a decade, so his knowledge of Jack should have been the first warning bell. Stupid Kel! I cursed myself silently, I had been so wrapped up in my own misery I had potentially put us more at risk by missing the key signs.

Not specifically, but enough that he chose the date I was to get married for his attack and he planned to send me to kill Jack when he succeeded in breaking me. But that meant that someone had been keeping him informed. The date of that attack I had known before I had been discovered on our mission.

I drew in an angry breath; the only way Alex would know that was if someone told him. And that meant someone in the family had betrayed us all.

CHAPTER 14

"Doc!" I ran into his office out of breath Gordito right behind me.
I had practically plowed through the bushes and I felt the sticks in
my hair. I bent over and placed my hands on my knees heaving my
breaths in and out.

"Good lord, Kel. What is it?" Doc asked in alarm jumping to his feet. He was surprisingly spry for an older man.

"We have to talk," I said urgently. "Not here. Nowhere inside." I shook my head and
continued trying to catch my breath.

I turned and hurried from his office not waiting to see if he followed me. Once outside again I halted my pace and waited. Thankfully Doc was fast for an older gentleman
and caught up quickly.

"Kel, what..." He started but I shook my head sharply and headed towards the woods
again. I wouldn't say a word until I felt we were far enough away that no one could be
witness. He followed a couple paces behind, and I led him deep in the woods.

When I felt sure we had gone far enough, I stopped and turned to face Doc watching
him approach. I forced a calm into my mind that belied the fear of my epiphany. I
watched Doc carefully.

When Doc caught up to me he looked annoyed and out of breath. "Kel! I am an old
man!" He said admonishingly. "We don't do long hikes at fast paces!" He placed his
hands on his knees and I felt a small tinge of guilt when I noticed he was shaking.

"I know Doc. I know," I said, also out of breath. "I couldn't risk us being overheard." I folded my arms across my chest and looked around again.

Doc's face paled, "what do you mean Kel?" He said cautiously. He stood a little straighter and watched me closely. I couldn't tell if it was suspicion of me that made him look so careful, so I decided not to take it that way.

"I mean Doc, I think we have a mole." I looked at him carefully judging his reaction. I didn't believe it was Doc. But his reaction would confirm or deny my belief.

Doc's eyes went wide, and his face managed to get more pale. "Why do you say that Kel?" He asked me in a choked whisper. He no longer had the strange intent look on his face as he stared at me. I had shocked him.

I studied him closely as I delivered my next words. "The attack is scheduled for the day I was to marry Jack. He knew about me. About this operation, and he knew I was with Jack. I haven't seen him in a decade, so someone had to tell him that." I watched for a flicker of guilt or recognition, anything that would say Doc was at fault. To my relief no indication came.

Doc gave me a look of horror as my words sank in. As the truth I had just come to realize slapped us in the face. "That means everything is about you Kel. All of it now is about you." He looked more horrified as he said those words.

I nodded. "Yes, the attack would have happened regardless. Alex hates humankind. But the date was a message to me. One I missed. Oh! I could kick myself!" I turned and kicked at the ground not wanting to kick sticks and dirt at Doc.

"The problem Doc is everyone here knows me, and everyone knows when the wedding should have been! It could be anyone! What if they have told him about the Fire Opal? If he knows, we're doomed. We don't stand a chance." I covered my face with my hands. "I've been so busy feeling sorry for myself that I missed our biggest clue and now the enemy might know our plans."

A soothing hand landed on my shoulder and I turned to see the kindness in Doc's face. "Kel, any of us should have caught the significance. Especially when you disappeared. We've all been short sighted." He was trying to comfort me.

"But I'm supposed to be the leader!" I said in despair. "You all tell me so, you even said so earlier. The plan wouldn't happen without me. If I'm so much a great leader, how did I miss that? That one detail should've been a huge red flag!" I threw my arms in the air and dropped them down to my side.

"Doc patted my arm. "Well thank God you have some faults. I was starting to think the worst I could get you for was that wicked temper." He grinned at me. "Kel, if you figured out there was a mole, why did you come to me? What made you think it wasn't me?" He was giving me an odd sort of look as he posed this question.

I huffed a laugh. "Honestly Doc. I wasn't completely sure. That's part of why we are so far out here. But I trust you, and you're the only one left that is speaking to me. I took a calculated chance it wasn't you." I gave him a wry smile.

He laughed then, loudly and both of us who had forgotten Gordito were startled when he barked his protest at Doc for making so much noise. I picked up my dog and placed him on my shoulder.

"So if I had been the mole, I would've just disappeared then?" He asked a little too casually. A shrug was my only response and he answered with a small shake of his head.

Doc nodded suddenly and his face tightened. "Kel, you won't like this. But I may have an idea who it was." He paused and looked at me, like he expected I would reach the same conclusion. But I had already, I was just afraid to voice it.

I sighed heavily. "Yea, Doc. I thought that too. It would make sense, she left not long before me and told Carly to leave me. I think it was Mary too." I felt a piece of me break away. Mary had been my best friend for years before she left, and it broke my heart to think she was the one who had sold me out. But it made the most sense.

"For now," Doc said. "I think we need to treat this revelation with caution and though it was most likely Mary, we need to be more careful who knows what plans. Maybe even have John shift things around just to be sure."

I nodded thoughtfully. "That is going to be a headache. John won't be happy." I looked imploringly at Doc. "Can you tell Carly and Jack? I'm not ready to face them, and I don't think they want to see me either." I felt like a coward again, that inner me that was what Alex made was showing through.

He patted my arm in a fatherly fashion. "Of course Kel, of course," he said. We stood there a moment longer in companionable silence each going over what I had said.

"Shall we go back to the house?" Doc asked, offering his arm to me. I wrapped mine through it, and looked down. Gordito showed no interest in wanting to ride on my shoulders, he was too busy sniffing around.

I shook my head, "you're all crazy. That in no way can be thought of as a house." I laughed and leaned over to kiss his cheek.

He started walking back and gave me a cheeky grin. "It's a large house for a large family Kel," he said, and a softer, more fond smile curved his lips. "A large happy family, and all made possible because of you."

I shook my head and sighed; I hadn't set out to start anything. Jack, and Carly had merely gone with me to find Selaina. I had never been satisfied with the police not finding anything about her disappearance. So I started poking around, I had just wanted to find my friend and we'd found a world of trouble instead.

Doc and I walked back to the house in companionable silence, comfortable and settled with each other. Gordito got in front of us and sat looking at me expectantly so I bent down and placed him in his spot. Like the princeling he believed himself to be, watched the world pass him by while he rested on my shoulder.

I again looked at the palace as it came into view, in the full sunlight and with my knowledge of the people who lived here I could see why everyone said it was a house. It felt closer and more comfortable than the Palace. Though as the unofficial Queen, I enjoyed the thought of living in a palace.

Doc and I entered the front entry and Mike appeared at my side. "Please get John, and bring him to the meeting room we were just in." I asked him and with a nod he disappeared into the mass of moving people. Doc and I made our way up the stairs and back into the small soundproof conference room. John joined us minutes later.

"Kel! Doc!" He greeted us in exuberant cheer. John was always a cheerful person; it took a lot to bring him down. "What's the good news? Why do we need the special meeting room?" He asked as he took a seat and Mike shut the door behind him.

I nodded at Doc, silently asking him to tell John what we had come up with and the idea that plans needed to shift in secret. John listened in silence the whole time, face never changing.

"Lord..." He finally said as Doc finished. "That's a lot to take in." John sat back in his chair and looked up at the ceiling. Doc and I stayed silent while he thought.

The silence drew on for long moments while John thought about what had been said.

"We'll make adjustments," he said decisively. "I'll be damned, if I let them beat me out. I've still got some years and use left in this body and I plan on having them." He looked at Doc and I and smiled. "You both look like I was going to disbelieve you." He laughed then, and Doc and I let out a relieved sigh.

"It does sound far-fetched John," Doc commented mildly. He was watching John carefully though as each second passed he seemed to relax a little more.

"True, but there's a couple too many coincidences for it to be completely unbelievable." John rose to his feet, and I made a split-second decision.

"Doc?" I asked. "Can you spare John and I a few moments?" I tried to convey with my eyes what I intended.

Doc searched my face intently, and seeming satisfied with what he found there he nodded. He worked his way around the table and out the door shutting it quietly. I knew he would probably wait on the other side.

John sat down again, looking quizzically from the door to my face. I had felt the blood drain when Doc shut the door, and my courage almost failed me.

"I need to tell you something, John," I said quietly. "And then when you're caught up, Doc will come back and I'll finish my story." I looked at him, and prayed silently that he wouldn't turn away from me when the truth was laid out.

"That sounds ominous, my girl." Was his only reply. He clasped his hands together and gave me his more attentive and serious face.

I quickly relayed what I had told Jack and Carly and Doc just earlier today. Today? It felt like a lifetime ago. A different version of me, perhaps. Maybe by telling the people I loved I was finally defeating Left and fitting back into who I should be.

John listened quietly, and when I finished he let out a low whistle. "All the heavy news today, my girl, all the heavy news," he said quietly.

I watched him anxiously waiting for his judgement, waiting for him to leave like Jack and Carly did. I felt sure he would leave, and every moment he stayed I felt like a death row victim granted another day of life.

John sighed when he caught sight of my face, I must be a truly open book today. "Kel!" He said in reprimand. "Don't tell me, you divulged that great dark secret in the thought that I would then cast you off?" He sounded offended, and a touch hurt. His face fell as he read my expression.

I dropped my gaze, the guilt written plain as day. That was exactly what I had thought, it was how Jack had reacted and I just couldn't see how I wouldn't be seen as one of them, the enemy. My heart broke and healed in the same instant, John was going to cast me out.

"Lord have mercy, Girl!" He sounded angry and exasperated then. "What made you think that the happenstance of your birth would mean one damned lick to me?!"

I looked up and saw the hurt in his eyes, and felt worse. I moved around the table and sat in a chair closer to him and took his hands in mine. They were large hands that could engulf mine, but they had always shown me kindness. I had done my friend an injustice and I was grieved by that.

"I don't know who I am anymore, John. I barely know what I am. When I told Doc, Jack and Carly this morning... Well only one of them stayed in the room with me. I'm afraid. I'm afraid my family will wish me gone when the truth is out..." I trailed off and stifled a sob, the tears I had spilled today were bad enough. I refused to start sobbing.

"I'm one of the enemy, how can they not want me gone?" I finished on a hoarse whisper.

I had closed my eyes and so I was surprised when John laid a hand on my cheek. "My girl, Jack... well he hasn't been right since you left. I imagine he was overwhelmed and reacted poorly. That don't excuse him now, and I have half a mind to whoop him for causing you such distress. As for Carly, for months her world has been keeping Jack sane and alive. I don't think she meant you any ill will, it was just a habit to go care for Jack." He patted my cheek and wiped away a tear that had slid out. "Now, now. There's no need for tears."

I heard the door handle turn, and Doc's footsteps re-enter. It seemed some kind of silent conversation passed around me as I was again crying. I'd get a hold on these tears eventually.

The door opened again a few moments later, and the smell of food had me opening my eyes. There was a plate of spaghetti and meatballs for me, a large steak with potatoes for John and a plate of grilled chicken for Doc. A glass of water was placed before us, then to my surprise some wine glasses and bottles.

I laughed at the array, and turned to thank the food delivery people. I wasn't surprised to see Mike there and I gave him a grateful smile, he only nodded back and shut the door. The three of us dug into our food, and for a time there were only happy sounds of contented eating. I slipped meatballs off my plate to Gordito on the floor.

I finished my plate of spaghetti and already felt a hundred times better. Setting the plate down for Gordito to lick, he really does live up to his name. I grabbed a bottle of wine and opened it, pouring some in each glass.

I waited quietly, sipping my wine while the other two finished eating and in true family style also gave their plates to the dog. I smirked. "I thought Gordito seemed a little fatter than when I left." They gave me guilty smiles.

"That little dog was a vile tempered, rotten, pouty, and bitey little monster. If you wanted to keep fingers when he was around you paid the food toll." Doc laughed. Then his face sobered. "None of us did well without you Kel. You are the backbone here."

I sighed; I hated being told I was important. "There's more to my story Doc, John," I said, instead of replying about my place among them. "Jack walked out before I could finish, and then I slunk away to lick my wounds. The epiphany..." I nodded my head and sighed again.

"I would like to tell you what happened, after I discovered who my father was." I gave them both an honest look, a look I hoped conveyed that if they wished not to hear that was okay too.

They nodded, grim faced and already braced for my unpleasant tale. Each sat back in their chair a little and watched me as I began to tell them the rest of the story.

"After Alex so delightfully showed me I had a father and was half Phae, he left me to his men." John drew a sharp breath and Doc gasped, I nodded. "It's as bad as it sounds and for my sake as much as yours I won't give details. I have blocked most of it out anyway.

"I don't know how long that arrangement went, I lost track of days and almost never was allowed to sleep. My rest consisted of passing out and getting whatever I could before someone managed to wake me again.

"It could have been hours, days or weeks I don't know. I think maybe it was just a week or less. Alex was impatient to 'get me back', so to say. I gained full conscious thought and awareness one day and realized I had been so securely tied to a chair I could barely move my fingers and toes. They had even clamped my jaw shut and secured a strap over my mouth.

"That was when Alex went on about breaking my spirit and mind and sending me back to kill Jack before leading the army to wipe out humankind. The chair was attached to some kind of machine, and by Alex's magic and the machine it was supposed to wipe my memory of me and implant the false me."

I took a long sip of wine, emptying my glass and pouring another. Neither man had yet touched theirs and as if I had given some cue each downed it in one gulp and also refilled their glasses. I stared at the wine in my glass a moment, swirling it slowly inside the rim and gathered my thoughts.

"I don't know how the machine was supposed to do this, I never got to ask and no one explained. But it felt," I shuddered at the memory, the pain blazing through me. "It felt like I was ripped in half and that each half was run through a tree shredder over and over. And when I thought I couldn't take anymore the pain stopped."

I swallowed back tears. "A male had entered the room, and he had Jane with him." I looked at Doc. "That's how I knew she was dead. Alex made the connection and he killed her in front of me before the machine turned back on.

"I used to have this trick, when I was dating Alex, he would start to hit me and I could lock a piece of me away. And that part remained untouched and the world and pain would never hurt or break me as long as that part was safe.

"Alex had wanted to hear me scream when the machine was working and he had removed the straps. Somewhere inside while I was screaming I felt one of those halves of me go into that protected place.

"The part of me that was left, was the cold lonely and angry person that Jack rescued and brought back. The coward who denied everything because it was too scary to believe the truth." I finished my second glass of wine, and poured a third.

"Whatever it was that pulled me apart, I think that saved my life. I had no memories of this life when I was in that pocket, but I had dreams of Jack, Carly and Mary. I had little habits like putting plates down for the dogs. I had a feeling that my life used to be full of love and people, where it was then empty and cold. It was a constant battle in myself that never made any sense, and I spent a lot of time feeling out of place.

"They had managed to change some core part of me, and I feel that change still. But they never managed to erase all of me." I sighed. "Jack doesn't know it, but he was literally my lifeline. As tortured as I was by the dreams, and then when he entered the pocket by him, I also cherished them. They showed me that something in life could be happy and complete, even if I didn't believe that was a life meant for me.

"I craved for that dream's existence to be real, and as much as I was terrified to admit my feelings for Jack there, it began to feel like he was the only real thing. But when Alex came back," I shuddered. "There was no doubt he was real and I questioned everything again and I started to push Jack away. I don't think either Jack or Alex realized the other was a real being.

"I think Alex thought Jack to be made from some distant memory of mine, since the pocket was taking its cues from my memory and twisting them to suit Alex. But that's why Alex hated Jack so much. Jack I think was just disgusted that I was made to have a 'lover' there when I didn't even know who he was. Or who I was. That bothered a lot Jack, he always made little comments, and talked to me in a familiar way that bothered me.

"Truthfully that was the best thing that could've happened there. If they had known about each other..." I shuddered. "Anyway, I think something else besides the split in me happened."

Both men had been watching me in horror as I spoke. But at those words they sat up straight and gave me such intense looks I thought I might crumble to dust. I almost lost my courage, and had to swallow hard taking a few deep breaths.

I looked down at the table, picked up Gordito who had started to scratch at my knee and took a deep breath. "It's like a part of... him..." I couldn't bring myself to say

Alex's name just now. "Like a part is in me. Somehow with the magic and the way I split something of him is in me.

"I never told anyone this part. A couple months ago I had another 'dream', but instead of the dreams I had in the pocket this was like a vision of current events." I explained about seeing Alex demanding they find me, and the other events of my dream.

"I don't know what it means, that I saw it. I haven't seen or dreamed anything else since. I always feel just a little of him though. His anger at me and hatred towards humans. But only since I 'woke up'," I finished my tale and hugged Gordito close, pressing my face to his smaller one. One of the best things about Gordito is he never smells like a dog; he has always had a fresh clean smell about him. And I took in deep breaths of that smell, comforting myself with his love.

"Kel?" Doc's voice was tentative, and I looked up. "Kel, I can't begin to imagine what this means." He smiled wryly, though I am glad to know he doesn't know where to find you." He reached across the table and offered his hand.

I took it and clung on like it was a lifeline. John clasped my other hand. "I think, Kel," John said. "That for now we do nothing about the vision. If it was just the one, then we should be okay. But we need to know as soon as another one happens. If you are getting glimpses of him all the better for us, especially if he doesn't know."

Doc's face turned thoughtful. "Perhaps it's your Phae heritage that made the machine react the way it did, and that heritage also caused part of Alex to splinter and subsequently latch to you. His obsession." He fell quiet and I watched him as he thought.

Could he be right? If they had never used the machine on a cross before they wouldn't have known. I got the idea that Alex and other true Phae had no regards for the crosses. We were cannon fodder in a war they couldn't wage themselves.

If we had the time to spare I would enjoy turning the cross against the Phae. I must've grinned at that thought, because both men went still, and stared at me.

"What?" I was a little defensive. Their looks made me feel like I had done something suspicious or wrong, and after baring my past and my soul I didn't like it.

"What are you thinking there, Kel?" John asked me, with as much caution in his voice as I had defensiveness. He was giving me the 'don't you dare do something crazy' look, like I would leap up and jump out the window or something.

I started the laugh then, "I was thinking it's too bad we don't have the time to turn the cross against the Phae. The cross are not well treated, they are thought of only as cannon fodder for Alex's war."

Doc chuckled. "You would be the person to do that too. If there was time. I regret that so many will perish with our weapons. They've been raised only to kill us for one male's hatred." A sad smile crossed his lips then.

I sighed, "Yes." Was all I could say. Doc was right, it would take more time than we could imagine to turn that hatred some of it taught for centuries, against the Phae instead of humans. We would just have to stick with the original plan, I was saddened by that. It was not the cross's fault; they had been used by the Phae and would now pay the price.

John clapped his hands together. "Well, shall we adjust our plans then?" And just like that, it was back to business.

I convinced John to allow me to go between our sites and oversee the set-up of defenses, it kept me away from HQ and away from Jack. The voice in my head said I was running away again. But she wasn't entirely correct, I was only avoiding a short time. I had to go back two weeks before the invasion was to happen.

It was amazing, travelling literally around the world. I had always wished to travel and with the mess the world was the last few years it just never happened. But now here I was going from country to country, seeing and experiencing everything.

My travels started in Alaska, there was to be a gate in Anchorage. Alaska in April is gorgeous, just coming out of the winter and starting to be a warm real place. Someday I wanted to come back in the summer and really see it. Our team there was well set up and only needed me for the details we didn't trust to anything but personal transfer. Technology was too easily hacked; the pockets were technology and magic. And if they could manipulate those, we weren't taking chances on the internet.

I spent two to three days in each location making sure the plans were in place, the personnel understood the situation and everyone was comfortable with their role. In a couple of my stops I had to alter personnel so that they were better fitted for the jobs. Some of the people didn't want to deploy the opal and watch the mass death that would entail, they were moved to a communications spot instead etc.

China and Japan were flashes of color and strange foods and things I could never explain. I didn't have enough there to satisfy my curiosity. I kept in constant contact with Doc and John, informing them of progress and we kept the changes to our plans to a need-to-know basis only. It felt good to be out and doing something, to see the plans we made put in motion. I was never good at idle supervising.

I made the rounds of every location twice, and so I was ending my trip in Anchorage where I started but I would only be there a final night before going back. All too soon my deadline hit and I was on the way back to HQ. I really didn't want to go. I was more comfortable out in the world than I was at home now. But, I resigned myself to my fate and so got on the plane that would take me back.

I couldn't believe how normal it was to get on a plane and be crowded by people, none of them realizing the danger the world was in. If we didn't succeed how many of these people wouldn't survive? Would anyone survive? I think if Alex got his way all human life would cease, and then he would probably kill the cross for the crime of being half human.

I sighed inwardly. Heavy thoughts seemed to take over my life lately. I walked onto the plane from the terminal and found my seat. I had an aisle seat and hoped my row-mates weren't the kind of people that needed half of my seat and all of theirs.

One thing the pocket had right, I didn't like to be crowded by strangers. Of course the pocket had made it all people, because I had no friends there. I stretched my legs and observed the chaos that was always the boarding process of a plane. A man approached, vaguely familiar though I couldn't place him, and said he had the seat next to mine.

I stood and stepped into the aisle, allowing him to get in. I was still trying to place where I knew him from, I was literally half way across the world from everyone I knew well, when a woman came up and said she had the window seat.

The man and I both exited the row and allowed her in. She got settled, and stored her purse under the seat in front of her and the man settled back into his seat. I followed, and now that everyone in my row was seated I got a lap blanket from my bag. I get cold on airplanes and so always have a jacket and blanket easily available.

I settled the blanket, latched the seatbelt and tilted my head back closing my eyes. It didn't either of the people sharing my row wanted to spill into my seat and I was relieved by this small stroke of luck. With a little more luck they wouldn't want to speak either and I could take a nap. I needed to rest and relax before I got back. The idea of seeing Jack and Carly was making me feel sick. By my own request neither Doc nor John had mentioned them the last month and a half I was away.

I adjusted in my seat, stretching my legs ahead of me and under the seat in front of me. John should be at the airport when I arrived, I couldn't wait to see him and Doc. Even if the other two made my anxiety ratchet up to a hundred.

The pilot came over the radio and made his announcement, then the flight attendants did their announcements and safety presentation. And finally the plane was on the runway for takeoff. I love roller coasters, and the feeling of going fast enough to leave your inside behind, so I had always enjoyed the feel of an airplane taking off and landing.

Once up in the air, I settled my mind and tried to get some sleep. The woman against the window wouldn't close the shade so it took longer than I liked to fall asleep, but eventually I managed it.

"Lord, we found her." Maximus's voice rang through the conference-like room where Alex sat a brooding angry stare plastered across his features. His head snapped up.

"This is pushing it awful close to the deadline, Maximus," Alex growled, a feral angry tone slipping through the space between them.

Maximus bowed his head. "Yes, Lord. I understand. We will get her though." The submissive head bow seemed to appease Alex and his face lightened slightly.

"What of that man? Jack?" He asked a bit too casually. His curled fingers gave away his irritation.

Maximus' face paled slightly. "We cannot find the man, Lord. We only managed to find her, because she seems to be on a world tour spree." Maximus had reached the far end of the table where Alex sat and only the length of the table separated them, it was about six feet.

Alex uncurled his hands and drummed his fingers. "Bring her to me Maximus, perhaps she will tell us where to find him with a little persuasion." He grinned maliciously, and I wanted to run from that smile. It told of pain and punishments yet unimagined.

Maximus raised his head, and I could feel the hair on my arms raise even in the dream. Maximus had a thin frame, and narrow face. His eyes were dark, and seemed empty of all feelings. He had black hair kept at about two inches long.

It was a handsome enough face, but empty and cold. It was also the face of the man who sat beside my body.

My inner voice started to yell at me to wake up…

I jolted awake just as the announcement about landing was coming over the speakers. I didn't look at the man next to me, worried that if he saw my face he would know I knew him. As steadily as I could I took my blanket and folded it to store in my bag. I would need to lose Maximus in the airport and make it John as fast as possible.

I put extra focus into remaining calm and as if nothing had changed. I didn't want to give Maximus reason to be suspicious of me. The flight attendants did the final rounds and the plane started its descent. My mind continued to run in circles of how best to lose Maximus.

I had bags in baggage claim and that is where John would be waiting. I needed to get there and to him unnoticed by Maximus, we had to be able to get away before he caught up and could follow. It seemed that despite the note that had started this roller coaster, they didn't know much about us or where we were. I could kick myself at that revelation.

If they had truly known, they would have found me and Jack and everyone else long ago. I had left assuming they really did know and that everyone was in danger, but if that were the case then I wouldn't now be on a plane. I would've been taken back already. It took concentrated effort not to growl aloud as all this came clear.

I had been so afraid that night, so sure they did know and I had acted before thinking through it all. That was what they had wanted of course, to scare me into acting before thinking, and they had been successful.

When the plane landed, a tiny sigh of relief escaped me. "Yea I don't like flying either," Maximus said as if we had been friendly chatting and I had said I didn't like to fly.

I decided to go with his assumption and nodded at him a tight-lipped smile. "It thankfully didn't make me sick this time. I'm usually asking the flight attendants for a bag as soon as we are in the air." For effect I placed a hand on my stomach. "Well it didn't make me too sick anyway..." I trailed off and made my face blanche by conjuring an image that made me really want to be sick.

Maximus leaned slightly away from me and I stopped a smirk from showing. Good he was now worried I might throw up on him. That would certainly help. If he was worried I would throw up on him I had a better chance of getting out of reach when the plane stopped at the gate.

The plane taxied to the gate and all the passengers stood up, I grabbed my bag and quickly rushed forward before the aisle filled. Lady Luck was blessing me today, it seemed as soon as I passed a row they would stand and get the aisle. Adding people between me and Maximus.

I concentrated on continuing forward and not looking behind me to see if he had managed to follow or get past the other people. I didn't want it to be obvious I was escaping from him. I hoped he would think the rush was that I didn't feel good and merely wanted to find a bathroom.

As soon as the people started moving, I made small quiet comments to those ahead of me about being sick and could I please pass. I almost cracked a smile at everyone who leapt out the way like I had threatened them. Apparently they all thought I would be sick on them.

I managed to get up right to the door as it opened and was quickly through it and up the jet bridge, my row had been almost the last row of the plane and the plane had been full there was now a lot of people between me and Maximus, and I was betting he didn't want to draw attention to himself.

Thankfully no one worried about someone running through an airport, as it happened often with people trying to catch flights and just generally being in a hurry. I think I made record time as I raced through the airport and down a level to baggage claim. I never looked over my shoulder, I just prayed I was still not being followed.

If I was extra lucky, Maximus would assume I was in a bathroom and would wait outside the nearest one from our terminal. I crossed my fingers that my luck held out as I rushed over to find the claim where my bag would come out.

I saw John standing by the baggage claim and my focus narrowed to him. I should have paid more attention than I would have noticed John was not alone. I would have seen that Jack was with him. I would've been able to prepare for what he did, but I didn't pay attention and so I didn't see Jack until I had run into him as he stepped forward right into my headlong path.

I collided with Jack, and we fell to the ground, me landing on top of him and our foreheads colliding. I saw stars, and Jack swore. People around stopped and some asked if we were okay. John rushed over and managed to shoo the people away as I tried to disentangle myself from Jack.

"Dammit woman!" Jack said, glaring up at me. "I know we didn't last see each other on good terms, but you seriously did not have to charge me down and head butt me!" He had a hand pressed to his forehead. And though I wanted to tell him off, I started laughing instead.

I laughed and my head hurt so bad from the collision I started to cry too. I finally managed to get separate from Jack and used John's proffered hand to stand up, leaving Jack still prone on the floor. "Face it, Jack, it's karma for being awful to me." I sniffed in a superior way, and turned away from him at his groan.

John was trying to hold in his own laugh, but his face sobered when I looked at him. "They found me John; we have to go now. Someone else can come get the bag or the airport can burn it whatever but we have to go. Now." I felt the seriousness of the situation press in around us again, and Jack got to his feet.

John nodded and hurried to the door, exiting the building. I followed fast behind, and Jack behind me. I hadn't seen Maximus since the plane and hoped he was still stuck somewhere. I couldn't bring myself to look around.

I figured that looking around would make it appear we were running from someone or something and that would draw attention. If we just moved quickly it should only appear we were late for a meeting or generally rushing.

John had parked in short term parking and even managed a place close to the door.

I ran faster putting myself ahead of Jack and jumped right into the front seat, closing and locking the door for good measure. He growled as he climbed in the back, and John laughing got in the driver's seat.

I looked over my shoulder and stuck my tongue out at Jack as John pulled out of the parking spot. For a moment, everything was what it used to be and Jack and I were comfortable and easy around each other. Things were normal and fun.

Then I saw Maximus on the sidewalk, watching us drive away. Fury and fear written across his face. He wouldn't be able to follow us, I had been able to give him the slip and the salt in the wound was him watching me leave.

I understood the fear he would have to report to Alex he lost me, again. A report that quite likely would cost the male his life. Alex didn't give second chances to those who failed him. I almost started to feel bad for Maximus, before remembering he was literally hunting me down. His death would end things quickly for him, nothing was intended to end quickly for me.

I turned forward, and we rode in silence for a time. "John?" I asked him, turning slightly in my seat.

"Hmm?" He replied in a distracted tone some drivers get when they would rather drive than talk.

"May I play music?" I was dying for some noise to distract my brain. I could literally feel the holes starting in my head from Jack's intense stare.

"Mm," he replied, it was neither yes or no so I chose my own interpretation and turned the radio on. Another thing the pocket got right, my music tastes. I found the hard rock station and concentrated on every song. I was intent on ignoring Jack.

I looked out the window and started to sing every song in my head, pretending Jack wasn't still staring silently at me.

CHAPTER 15

My intention to ignore Jack got us through most of the drive, before even I could handle it anymore despite my best efforts of distraction. I couldn't ignore it any longer, it was like a sore tooth that you just had to poke with your tongue.

"What, Jack?!" I asked, turning around in my seat to look at him. "Why are you trying to bore holes into my head!? Spit it out!" My heart pounded, and I started to breathe a little heavier as I stared at him.

Jack continued to stare at me, keeping whatever he thoughts he had silent. I felt my nostrils flare and my temper rise. I prided myself on turning around instead of hitting him. I guess no matter what reality this man could flare my moods like a matchstick.

I suppose as I look back it had always been like that, though usually I wasn't angry. The pocket seemed to have changed some fundamental part of my person. I was faster to act on anger than to settle in and let it ride. I need to work on that.

I turned the music louder, trying to drown the stare from Jack. It didn't work, I could still feel him. But, since I had broken last time and he kept his silence I determined I would not give in this time. I kept my eyes straight ahead and couldn't even watch the scenery as we passed.

The ride to HQ was only an hour long, it felt like a lifetime and I'm sure by the time we pulled up the tension could've been severed with a knife. I leapt out of the car and tried to make a break for the house. I wanted to see Gordito, I had missed him but traveling by plane was not practical for a dog.

I had not learned my lesson earlier about paying attention, as I tried to run around the front of the car Jack was in the way again. He caught my arm as I passed, thankfully he had been watching and we didn't collide again, though I almost fell over when my forward momentum stopped so suddenly.

Jack was prepared for that outcome too and had pulled me to him to steady me. I growled and pulled out of his grip turning to face him. I tried not to focus on the butterflies that started in my stomach when he had grabbed my arms, and that had gotten worse when our bodies met. I had been in a rush and almost panicked in the airport.

But here, without the distraction I was responding to my attraction to him. I yearned for things to be so simple like they were before. When just a smile from him could have us secluding ourselves from the world.

I willed the butterflies to stop, I couldn't deal with that right. It didn't work, so I instead focused on being mad at Jack. He had run away from me; he had told Carly everything was different because of what I was. He had hurt me deeply.

I grasped that thought with every ounce of will I could muster, and glared at Jack. "What, Jack?!" I said again. "This strong silent thing doesn't suit you. You're far too assertive and have too much mouth not to just say it aloud." I crossed my arms, and in a deja vu flash his eyes dipped. I wasn't in a real showy shirt, but I had plenty to show regardless.

I had the urge to uncross my arms again, like I had once before, but I wasn't that girl anymore so instead I stepped closer to Jack and snarled, "eyes up! You have a question to answer." I heard a snort behind him and knew John was watching the confrontation.

I refused to give into the temptation to drop my arms and react like I had in the pocket when Jack had given me that same glance. I would stand here arms crossed and demand an answer instead of shrinking away.

I saw Jack's temper rise, and his jaw clench but before he could say anything I cut him off. "No, Jack. You don't get to be mad at me." I narrowed my eyes further at him in challenge. I was prepared for him to yell or fight. I might even have been prepared for him to hit me. I was not prepared for him to kiss me.

But that's what he did. In a move so swift and sudden I couldn't respond at first, Jack had wrapped his arms around me and his mouth crashed into mine. I was caught against his chest, my arms trapped in their crossed position.

I felt the anger and fear start to melt away, as the kiss continued. Jack's lips were warm and full and soft. His taste was familiar, and the man knew how to kiss. I started to soften against him tilting my head to deepen the kiss. I had truly missed this man, and was just beginning to realize how much I had felt empty without him in my life.

Centuries passed, worlds began and ended, the war started and was finished... Or that's how it felt while Jack held me to him. And then in Jack fashion he then ruined the moment for me, "I'm glad I still know how to shut you up. At least I am assured that hasn't changed." He chuckled against my lips.

The words were slow to sink in, they had to filter through the heady rush of bliss his kiss had stirred. But they sank in. I yanked an arm free, and raised it to slap him. He caught my wrist and grinned at me.

"Yea, I remember that little trick of yours," He smirked. "That's a new one, but I'm a fast learner Kel." He grinned then and released me, stepping out of range of my strikes quickly.

"Well, now that that is over." John said from behind us. "Can we go inside? I'm sure you two can finish whatever that was at a later time. At least now I don't fear there will be blood on the carpet of our conference room."

I glared at John's back as we turned to follow him inside. I fought an internal battle the whole way to the conference room, equal parts wanted to kick Jack and kiss Jack. I wanted to stop him and have it out right there in the middle of the hall, and I also wanted to drag him into a dark corner and kiss him until we both forgot the last ten months.

John led us to the same small conference room that had housed both my confessions. I was unsurprised to see Doc and Carly already there with Mike stationed sentry outside the door. He gave me a small smile and I returned it with a big grin, I had missed Mike's company. Jack gave him a possessive glare and growl as he walked into the room behind John, and I rolled eyes and made a face at his back. Mike chuckled and pulled the door shut once I had entered.

Everyone shifted around the table to claim seats, leaving me closest to the door. I gave a half wry smile. "Letting me have a quick escape?" I asked no in particular. Doc and John grinned at me. Carly was too busy trying to decipher the scowl on Jack's face.

I sighed, stuck my tongue out at Jack and took a seat. As if that was the cue everyone else also sat. Then all faces turned to me, and I felt the blush creep up my neck.

"What?" I asked, slouching in my chair. "Why does everyone do that?" I covered my face with my hands, I felt like Jack's kiss was written all over my face and that everyone was now seeing what a mess it had left me in.

Doc broke the tension by laughing. "We're waiting on your final report dear," he said kindly, and thumped the table causing everyone else to look away from me.

I sat up a little straighter in my chair and uncovered my face. "Everything is as ready and planned for as it can be. The final round showed that the practices have been going well and everyone is ready for this to come to a head one way or the other." I rested my arms on the table and looked at John. "Your people are good, John. They can handle this." He nodded his appreciation.

"So, with that settled," John began. "Tell us about the incident at the airport." He folded his casually on the table and looked for all the world as if he had asked about the weather, not that he had just dropped that mass bomb on us. Trust John not to let me weasel out of that one.

Carly's head whipped to me. "What incident?" She demanded.

Her full focus on me, I could see the hurt, frustration and worry in her. I knew some was for me, but I wondered how much more was Jack. I had never been bothered by their closeness; in fact, I relished it. I made a mental note to thank her for being here when I wasn't.

Jack turned towards me, "Yes, I too want to know what incident. Since it was my face you tried to break." He gave a look half scowl half exasperation. It was a look I was familiar with and very fond of. He used to give me that look when I had been extra silly, or he thought I was overreacting to something.

Doc also looked inquisitive, I sighed heavily. "I fell asleep on the plane and had another vision. It seems tied to when he is most... errmm emotional?... Over me," I said, trying to find the right words. It was hard to do when I saw Jack's face redden with every word I spoke after 'vision', he sure could make things intense.

"What vision?" Jack demanded. His brows furrowed and he tightened his jaws to a painful looking clench. I wondered how he had any teeth left with that jaw set; it seems they should all crumble away under the pressure.

"What do you mean again?" Carly asked, their voices overriding the others as they spoke simultaneously. Their voices crowded the room, and bombarded me like they had shouted, though they had only barely raised them in agitation.

"We don't have time for me to explain the 'again', Carly," I said a touch of annoyance in my voice. "I've already been over that, it's not my fault you and you," I pointed at them both, "decided to run away because you didn't like part of my story."

She looked a little hurt but I ignored her and pressed on, explaining about Maximus and how he had found me because I was travelling and that he was sitting next to me on the plane. I explained how I had come to realize they knew nothing of us or this place.

"I wish I'd realized that last part months ago," I finished quietly and more to myself. I sat back in my chair and leaned my head back looking at the ceiling rather than the people in the room. What would they think about that last revelation?

"Kel?" It was Carly who spoke first, and she seemed cautious. I could picture the look that went with that voice. A slightly clenched jaw, and she would be partially leaned towards me as if she would rest a hand on my arm.

"Hmm?" I replied, not looking at her. I was picking out shapes in the popcorn on the ceiling. Popcorn is a truly terrible finish but if you're creative you can find shapes and patterns in it. It was a pastime of mine and a good evasion technique when I didn't want to look at anyone.

"Kel, no one blames you for leaving. Well, not really. We're upset and we thought we'd lost you, but any of us would have done the same." Her words hit me like a waterfall of cool water, I hadn't realized how much I wanted to know she didn't hate me for leaving.

"Agreed," Doc said. "We all would give everything to protect this family." His kind words reverberated in me, setting another small piece of me at ease. I felt like I was slowly starting to heal, and it gave me hope that I could be whole again. That I could be me, again.

John murmured his agreement, but Jack was silent again. I dropped my gaze eyeing him carefully. "You blame me, don't you?" I asked, and I felt tired. I knew he blamed me; the accusation was all over his face.

I had hurt Jack deeply, and he was still angry with me for it. I dropped my gaze to the table. I didn't know how to begin repairing the damage. I wanted to erase the hurt from his face, and make everything better. I just didn't know how.

Our friends averted their gazes and pretended they weren't here, but Jack didn't answer my question. He stood up, and I heard the door open, then felt him grab my hand and pull me to my feet dragging me from the room.

"Okay, meeting's over!" I called over my shoulder to the conference room. Mike gave me a look that asked if I needed help and I shook my head. It looked like it was time to have it out with Jack. I hoped we would survive this confrontation.

Jack opened the door to his room and gave me a pointed stare until I walked in. Kujack and Gordito came charging from the bed to meet us, and I dropped to the floor to hug my boys. I laughed as Kujack licked everything he could reach, my nose, my mouth or even Gordito if he got in the way.

The door shut and I heard the lock click, my body tensed and for a moment I was in the pocket with another shut and locked door. Some of the panic I felt must have shown because Jack was suddenly behind me and as he had once before, he covered my nose and mouth and started to coach me on breathing.

I hadn't realized I stopped breathing, my head was fuzzy and my ears rang. But his voice sounded through it all and like before he calmed me. I felt the panic ebb, and reminded myself this was Jack not Alex. Jack had never hit me, for all he could be he was never abusive.

My breathing returned to normal and I focused on the world to find Kujack threatening to chew off Jack's arm and Gordito actually tugging on the sleeve of his shirt. I started laughing and both dogs halted their attack to check on the crazy woman they thought they needed to defend.

"I'm okay boys," I said soothingly, when Jack dropped his hand. I scooped the two dogs into my arms and pressed both to my cheeks. Poor things did not handle my distress well, I hoped they didn't actually bite Jack.

He was still behind me, and I realized he had maneuvered us around so his back was to a wall and we were leaning against it. I sighed and pressed back into him. "I missed this, you know? Even in the pocket, being with you was always so right. It scared me then. I had the pocket impressing on me that relationships were bad and you were no good." I took a deep breath and closed my eyes as I rested my head on his shoulder.

"I missed you too, you infuriating woman," Jack replied, his answer rumbling through his chest. "Don't you leave me again." His voice cracked. "I didn't do well, Kel. If it weren't for Carly..." I felt him shudder. "You just can't do that to me again."

I turned my head and rested my forehead against the soft spot between his neck and shoulder. "Jack, I had to. I couldn't have survived if you or anyone else had been hurt or killed because of me. Alex knew of my loyalty to love and family. Knew and used it against me. They could've just carried me off when I was discovered, but the twisted bastard made me choose to hurt you." I felt tears start and forced them away.

"You are one of the most important people in my life. Carly is close second. You're my sanity and my firm hold on the world. I couldn't bear the thought something would happen to you." I said into his neck.

"Dammit woman, you realize that's not a one-way street. That you are that for me?" He sounded broken down and exhausted. "I was so angry at you. Even when I found you in the pocket I was still angry." He sighed and I felt his head rest against the top of mine.

A little chuckle escaped him. "Remember the day you saw me in that restaurant?" I nodded. "I was ready to drag you over my knee and whoop you for having left me, but you looked so confused. Like you didn't know me, but you still wouldn't stop staring at me. And I realized that somehow you didn't know who I was." A heavy deep breath pushed his chest out and momentarily lifted my head from his shoulder.

"I figured out where you worked, and how to get a job. It was really easier than it should have been. If I'd realized everything was pretty much created because of you it would've been easier. But I thought that they might be real people, or even Phae.

"The day you showed up at the job site in that atrocious pink... hey!" I had pinched him for insulting my sweater again, and he just laughed. "I knew that whether you knew me or not, at least something of my Kel remained. Only you could ever love a color that truly obnoxious.

"When you pulled your hand away and wouldn't meet my gaze I broke inside, my girl was fiery and assertive. And you showed me this shell that was nothing like the real you. That's why I walked away and didn't look back that day, it killed me to see you but not you.

"When I came to the office that night, I had been there long enough to see Bob leave and you just sat in the truck with your head down. I was worried something was wrong, and had come over to check on you. When I scared you and you went off like a bottle rocket, I saw the real you again. That fiery little half redhead I loved so much. But the only way I saw that side was to goad you." He chuckled again.

I sat up and turned to face him, "You really were just being awful!:" I accused him. "You picked fights on purpose!" I huffed and crossed my arms, scowling at him. That was unfair, he really had known everything about me and how to get to me and used that knowledge without mercy.

He leaned forward and kissed me. "Oh yes Love, I picked them on purpose. I wasn't lying when I said I liked your fire. And when I called you a soft creature and your head about exploded it was all I could do not to kiss you then. But I promised myself I wouldn't kiss you until you knew who I was."

His face pinked a little, "I broke that promise when I kissed you in the truck, but I didn't know what else to do. I thought a distraction might be the thing." He shrugged, but still looked a little sheepish. "I was truly shocked you slapped me." He raised an eyebrow at me and I stuck my tongue out at him.

"Anyway," he said, smiling at me. "Continuing my story. You mentioned reincarnation that day we had lunch and I thought something was coming back, but then you just told me to go to a desk and I felt disappointed.

"At lunch when you proceeded to tell me off, I was honestly loving every bit of it. And the dig at your job, I almost cracked again." He broke off laughing. "You told me you didn't want your breasts getting my attention, while your eyes told a very different story."

I snorted at him, "I was so sure the universe had sent you to ruin my life. I kept having dreams of you and Carly and then you haunted my days too. I was constantly torn between physical violence and dragging you to an empty office. That's probably what cued the computer I was broken. Was that struggle inside." I shrugged and made a face at him.

He lifted a hand and placed it on my cheek, "I wanted to drag you off so bad, and bring you home. I was afraid it would have negative effects on you though. So I stayed and pushed your buttons instead. I was really glad to see you ate the same way you always did, and watching you get defensive was a cherry topping." He smirked again, I swear his smirk should be outlawed.

"You popped off with 'feed me and tell me I'm pretty', after I had insulted you," He pointed behind me, and sure enough our old wall hanging with that quote on it hung in his room. "I thought for a minute it was coming back, there were always little flashes of you. It started to drive me insane." He made a scowly face at me.

"I loved the fact you wouldn't swear very often, it was a strange quirk and it just made me smile. I loved confronting you, and watching the sexual energy ratchet through you, getting you riled like that, it brought the real you to the surface." He tilted his head and smiled at me. "I'm glad they failed to erase all of you, I don't know what I would've done if you hadn't come back." The look of deep sorrow on his face had me laying against his chest again.

"The day I got to the office and saw you with Alex..." He shuddered. "I could tell there was something wrong, but I hadn't met another real person so I thought maybe this was another part of the pocket. A bad memory made real to cause you pain. I didn't really understand the pocket, my time with Bob had given me a hint that there weren't many 'real' people there.

"But something was off, when you got sick after the meeting with him. It just seemed off. I almost left with you right then. It took every ounce of will not to. I was still afraid of the effects that might have on you." He sighed, and I saw the guilt written on his face. If he hadn't been afraid that leaving would have negative effects on me, Alex would never have had the chance to kick me.

"You wouldn't let me help or even care, you were so convinced that the only thing people could ever feel for you was pity that you pushed me away. So I tried to get Bob in, I thought even if he was fake you had some kind of relationship there." There was a deep sadness in his voice, I couldn't imagine how it must've felt to him to see the relationship I had with Boss and not with him.

His arms came around me and he held me so tight I felt my ribs groan. "You lied to Bob though, and you went with that thing over the weekend." His voice grew hoarse and angry. "And you came back on Monday and were so worn down and sick you passed out in my arms after saying he would kill you.

"I was starting to think maybe he wasn't one of Pocket's creations. So I tried to tell you it wasn't real to get you to look around and understand. That you would see the pocket, and the danger he was obviously posing to you. I hoped that might spark something, but stubborn infuriating woman that you are you fought back against that.

"But even as you fought against what I was trying to say your real self would try to break through, your random movie references gave me hope. You looked so broken though, beaten and defeated. I did the only thing that made sense that day, I picked another fight. Poked another button, and when you got angry I thought you might be okay.

"And then you start spouting off some crap about leaving him six years ago, that's when we met and I almost went off to kill him for that. So I tried to shock you by bringing up Mary and Carly. I thought if you knew me in some way you might know them.

"I felt triumphant and discouraged when you knew the names then said they were just made up." He squeezed me hard briefly. "I'll have to remember to tell Carly you thought she was a figment of your dreams."

"Jack." I growled in warning; he just held me tighter. I sighed and gave in. I was too comfortable in his arms to try to be mad. I considered pinching him anyway, but that required movement and he would catch on before I could do it.

"You called yourself broken, and I slipped up and lost my self-control and said that I wouldn't leave you again. And we went right back to square one. And then you ran away from me that night after and again I thought something was wrong with Alex. He seemed too aggressive, too real for the pocket. But I was too afraid to risk you to take action."

I heard a thump and guessed he had smacked his head on the wall. "Then Bob had to spend the week visiting jobs, and wanted me to go. I think that was a manipulation in the system honestly, but I had a cover to keep. So I went.

"I was angry every day I couldn't make it to the office to check on you, but we worked until after you had left. When we came back that Friday, you looked like death. And again you lied to Bob, but I could tell something was wrong.

"I followed you to the kitchen, I planned to confront you. Drag that fiery spark out until you spat the issue at me in anger. But when I saw the mark peak under the hem of your shirt, I started to see red. You tried to hide it from me, and I knew it was bad.

"When you wouldn't just do what I said and lift your shirt to show me the mark, I decided to distract you with a little seduction." There was a short chuckle. "You might've forgotten me, but I still knew every one of your weaknesses."

I turned my head and bit him. I was held tight enough that pinching was out so I was left with only the option to bite him. I clamped my teeth down hard, intent on leaving a large purple bruise. That little stunt in the bathroom had been a torture, and he knew it.

"OW!" He said and one hand released me, grabbing my hair and pulling my head back. "I still don't like biting." Cautiously he let me head back down to rest on his chest.

"I asked why you couldn't just do what you were told, and you surprised me when you said you like the challenge and then you looked confused like you were unsure why you said that. I almost kissed you then, but I held back remembering what I was trying to accomplish.

"Kel, when I saw the mark on your ribs..." his voice cracked again and I felt a tearing sob come from his chest. "I was angry at myself mostly. If I had acted sooner on the situation that I knew wasn't right..." He sighed and I felt tears hit the top of my head. "I decided damn the effects we were leaving, immediately."

I turned slightly in his arms, and wrapped mine around his back. "Jack, if you had tried to go earlier I might not have gone willingly." I said in a reasonable tone, trying to purge the guilt he was feeling.

"I would've just kidnapped you," he said and I could hear the smile in his voice. An image flashed in my mind of Jack doing just that.

Wearing a dark ski mask the kidnapper snuck up on the unsuspecting girl and grabbed her. He tossed her over his shoulder and ran before she could even yell her protests. I bit my lip and held back the laugh that threatened to bubble up.

"Yea, I'm sure that would've gone well. I hope you had some knockout drugs for that plan." I snorted and laughed, losing the battle to hold it in any longer. Unlike the silly little imagination I had just had, I might have actually fought against Jack.

He was the only person in the pocket who could make me go against everything that had been implanted. So I might have actually fought back tooth and nail and made him regret the attempt. That was an amusing mental image as well.

He chuckled and pulled me higher and closer against his body. "When we got here, it killed me to hear you might never recover your memories. And then poison almost killed you, multiple times. Finally Doc and Carly told me to just leave and let you rest and heal. Carly, world bless that woman, went with me and kept me sane.

"She is a good friend, Kel. She yelled at me when I needed it, let me cry when I despaired about your recovery. And she kept me busy so my brooding was minimal. I was terrified when I got Doc's message about coming back. Terrified something was wrong or that you had died.

"Instead you were alive and you told your story about the history with Alex and your heritage. And I was so overwhelmed I overreacted. And then you left and I never got to apologize. I just needed some time to think through everything, and for Carly to beat me over the head." He gave me a wry smile when I sat up a little to look at his face.

"It broke me when you walked away, Jack. I was sure you would never want me again and so I asked to leave to give us both time to heal." I sat up fully and placed my knees on either side of his thighs looking him in the eye. "How can you want me, knowing what I am?" I asked in a tense whisper.

He gripped my face with his hands and pulled me in for a hard kiss. "I never stopped wanting you, woman," he said, pulling back slightly. "I just got a little lost in anger."

The tears I had been fighting since he closed the door spilled over and I leaned in to kiss him. Wrapping my arms around his neck and my legs around his waist. I needed to hold him as close as possible. I still felt in a very small corner of my mind that this wasn't real and Jack wasn't here forgiving me.

Somehow Jack stood without untangling my limbs from his person and he made it to the bed, laying us both down and sliding up the bed so we weren't hanging off. We lay on our sides facing each other.

"I had a king sized bed in the pocket, and a house with bare walls. There was always too much room and not enough life in that world. You give me life Jack. You have always filled just the right amount of space, and brought color and light into my world. I didn't know how much I had craved that from you when I was there.

I chuckled. "I once had the thought I needed a body pillow doused in your cologne to sleep with so my bed didn't feel empty. Even with Alex it was an empty feeling." I shuddered, and pressed closer to him. I tried not to think of sharing a bed with Alex.

Jack tilted my face up and kissed me softly. "I will never let you be empty and alone again," he promised me.

CHAPTER 16

The pounding at the door startled me from the peaceful dreamless sleep that had fallen over us. "GET UP!" Carly's voice demanded through the door. "I'm tired of waiting on you too! I'm coming in!"

The door burst open, and I scrambled to pull a blanket over myself. Carly laughed as she turned the light on and witnessed this. "Please, I've seen you in your birthday suit woman." She closed the door and launched across the room jumping onto the bed and landing right between us. Thankfully she missed squishing the dogs.

"Carly," Jack grumbled, turning to face her. "You're worse than the damn dogs." He groaned and mumbled some very nasty things about Carly, none of which seemed to bother her in the slightest.

I laughed; he wasn't wrong. Carly and the dogs always wanted to be in the middle. But she was bigger so she more often got her way. She wiggled and squirmed between us, and in an unplanned move that still felt natural Jack and I each flung an arm over her.

"Stop moving," I groused. "Why did you turn the light on anyway?" I squinted an eye at her. If her intent was to just flop in the bed, turning the light on had been unnecessary.

She shrugged and snuggled closer, turning to face me. "I'm glad you're really, really back, Kel," she said and her eyes shone with torrents of emotion. "It's been bad without you." She peered over her shoulder, "Jack, turn the light off would ya?" she said, as if he were the one to have turned it on.

He growled and glared, but still got out of bed to turn off the light. I smirked. "Truly a nice butt," I said. I had missed that butt, and chuckled quietly over memories of me covertly watching him when we were in the pocket.

He tossed an extra sway into his steps and turned off the light coming back to the bed. He flopped back into spot and flung and arm over us both. "You two hush, it's sleeping time," he murmured.

Carly and I both made faces, but we stayed quiet and all fell into a deep comfortable sleep. Wrapped together and finally feeling the world was right again. I had a fleeting wonder at how I could ever have believed the pocket was reality, when this is what I had left behind.

The next morning came far too early in my opinion, I would've stayed in bed all day if given the option. But the day of the attack loomed closer. We had less than two weeks, and still much to be finalized. With plenty of grumbling, and a lot of swearing on Carly's part, we all got out of bed and Carly and I headed to our rooms to get fresh clothes.

She hugged me tight before going into her room. "You don't get to leave us like that again. We stick together, always," she said fiercely, and I hugged her back just as tight. My embrace a silent promise not to leave.

"Thank you," I said to her. "For all of it, and everything. There aren't enough words to encompass the full meaning and depth of my gratitude to you." I gave her another squeeze and pushed her towards her door. "Now let me dress, woman!" I said, in mock severity.

She laughed and disappeared into her room. I was pulling garments out of my dresser when hands landed on my bare hips from behind me, and I was pulled upright against a bare chest but could feel he had pants on.

"When this is over," Jack growled low in my ear. "You and I..." He nipped my earlobe and then whispered the things we would do when the world was safe. I was panting and feeling weak kneed when he pulled away and walked back to his room.

I threw a pair of pants at his back. "Not fair Jack!" I yelled at him as he walked away. I wasn't sure I would be able to accomplish anything today now, with those images in my mind. And Jack knew that, he had done it on purpose.

I grumbled and said some unflattering things about Jack under my breath while I dressed. I didn't realize I had an audience until Carly started laughing. I jumped, got my feet tangled in my pants and fell on my face.

"That's it," I said into the carpeted floor. "I'm not leaving this room, ever. You can't make me." I kicked my feet like a pouting child trying to unwind the pants, if anything that only made it worse.

Carly now appeared to be gasping for air, I ungraciously hoped she'd choke and hit her head on the wall or something. Her laughs brought in Jack, now fully clothed, who surveyed the situation.

Jack's face went carefully blank, completely poker face, and I growled at him. "Jack so fucking help me, I will claw your eye! Don't you dare laugh!" I kicked my feet again, in futility. "Carly! HUSH!" I yelled over my shoulder at her. I placed my face back on the carpet and began muttering about my 'friends'.

I felt a tug and some twisting, and my legs were free of the pants. I knew Jack had done it, mostly because Carly was still laughing. Jack's weight pressed down on my back, and his hands closed over my wrists.

"You won't claw my eyes, love. You like to look at them too much." Then he cracked, and started to laugh. "You make such a cute hot mess," He purred against my ear, sending shivers along my spine.

This was why he had grabbed my wrists and laid over top of me, so he could have the upper hand. I fought the shivers and the urge to just lay here all day. I kicked my feet and tried to pull my hands away. I called him every name I could come up and then started to make them up. Nothing worked, he just laughed harder.

I growled again and thumped my forehead to the floor and stopped fighting. "My friends are sooo amazing... I'm wondering why I was missing this. I didn't even know that I had such wonderful people here. I was having dreams of and longing for loving friends." I growled at the carpet.

Jack stopped laughing long enough to kiss my ear and levitate back to his feet. It was such a smooth fluid movement, one minute he was there and the next gone. I rolled over onto my back and flung my arms to the side.

"I'm cursed. Truly cursed, either you're here and tormenting me. Or you don't exist and you still torment me!" I groaned dramatically and flopped my arms over my face. My pants smacked onto my arms. The jean material left a little sting when connecting with my skin. I played it up. "Ohhh the trauma! My arms have been flayed open! The nerves exposed!"

"Put your pants on drama Queen Kel. We got to go." Jack's voice sounded above me; I should've known he was the one that threw the pants. His voice sounded strained like he was putting effort into trying to be serious. Now was not the time to be serious.

"Go on without me," I sighed heavily, falling into the drama role. "I can't even dress without falling over... I'll only shame you!" I added an extra sad sigh to that, and pried my arms apart just enough to witness Jack's reaction.

I was not disappointed, his face puckered and went a little red. He looked like he had swallowed a sour grape doused in hot sauce. I lost all self-control, and began to laugh. I had to roll onto my side to breathe, and bumped my ribs. I was ninety-nine percent healed, but sometimes it still hurt. This was one of those times, I stopped laughing and groaned.

Immediately Carly and Jack were kneeling before me. Fussing like mother hens. "Are you okay"s and "didn't you hurt yourself when you fell"s flew around the room. How do two people make so much noise while only talking?

"Stop, stop, stop!" I said flapping a hand at them. "Shoo! Let me up." I pushed to a sitting position and lifted the shirt to peer at my ribs. There was only a purple bruise left, Doc had said it might be there for a long time. The bruise itself was no larger than a dime, but it could certainly feel like a pickaxe had pierced the bone.

I dropped my shirt and looked up to see both of their faces were completely serious now, all traces of amusement gone. I sighed. "It's almost completely healed; it will just take time to finish.

It doesn't hurt often. I must have rolled over just right and poked the bruise." I lifted a hand to each of them and placed them on their shoulders. "I'm okay guys, truly. The last three and a half months have given me time to heal and think." I pulled them in for a hug. "And last night finished that when we made up."

Carly sniffled against my shoulder and Jack wrapped his arms around us. We sat like that for a time, everyone pretending Carly wasn't crying. I pushed at them, "Seriously though, I can't put pants on while you're both sitting in my lap."

Somehow I managed to finish dressing and we left to track down some breakfast. The dogs in tow, Kujack has the busiest nose of any dog I've ever met. This was fortunate when tracking down bacon, we would just follow the little red dog. He caught the scent and shot like a rocket down the hall.

Gordito gave half a second pause, as if to say he was far more dignified than Kujack. But he must've realized Kujack was heading for food and he needed to hurry too, and was also off like a rocket.

"I can see we still rate lower than human food," I said with a wry smile to my companions. We smelled the bacon then, and I had to almost agree with the dogs. Bacon was better than ninety-nine percent of people.

We got to the breakfast room and saw that at least half the family was here getting food. Most people made plates and scurried off to whatever they were doing, but here and there were people sitting at tables and laughing with each other.

I spied the two boys almost immediately and nudged Jack and Carly pointing. Kujack had claimed Doc's lap and every other bite seemed to be shared with him. Gordito was on John's lap, and appeared to be receiving the same treatment. No one had noticed us watching them.

"Those dirty rotten little beggars." I said amused shock and exasperation in my voice. "And Doc and John are just letting it happen, you see this right?" I turned to Jack who was again smiling, but his eyes were laughing.

Carly had bitten her fist, her eyes also dancing with merriment, "This is what happens when I leave, you allow them to learn bad habits!" I scowled at them both trying to be serious and pretend I was mad. I couldn't believe she was blaming this on me, they had been here and still the dogs learned bad habits.

They both just laughed at me, and when I huffed and turned around to start getting a plate ready I saw Doc and John grinning at me. I rolled my eyes, made a face and turned to the breakfast buffet bar. I loaded the plate with scrambled eggs, bacon and sausage, and a healthy amount of cheese. Then I grabbed a couple tortillas and some condiment packets. I needed salsa and sour cream. I was making breakfast burritos.

I beelined for the table when Doc and John sat, the dogs still in their laps though their plates were now empty. "Did you actually eat any, or did you let the little beggars get it all?" I asked, putting my plate down and claiming a chair.

They both just winked at me as Jack and Carly sat down on either side of me. I took a moment to look around before I started on my breakfast. I observed my table companions and the others going in and out of the breakfast room.

I watched other tables filled with laughing happy people. There was a tenseness that ran under the surface, but everyone still made the best of their lives. I smiled happily; I was so lucky not only to have had this life once but to make it back here a second time. I settled in to make my burritos, the smile still on my face.

"So," Doc said. Turning serious eyes to me, and closing one fist while still feeding Kujack scraps with the other. I scowled momentarily at the dog, shaking my head and rolling my eyes.

I waved my hands at him. "Uh uh," I said a mouthful of my first bite of burrito and shook my head. I chewed quickly. I didn't want Doc to start talking before I could finish my statement.

He drew his eyebrows in and gave me an exasperated look. I finished my bite and gave him an exasperated look right back. "No shop talk at the table. Family time. Enjoy it Doc," I said and took another bite.

Jack was watching me and I turned narrowed eyes on him. "What, Jack?" I asked. I pushed my 'don't mess with tone' into my voice, using my eyes to promise him violence if he wasn't nice to me.

He grinned, "you're not shy about food," was all he said, throwing a wink in my direction. A wink, and that damned smirk. I wanted to punch him and then kiss him, in that order. That way he would know I was mad, and then I could make him forgive me for the punch.

I gritted my teeth and growled at him. "I will break that pretty face, Jack. I swear to everything I will. Then you'll have to be nice to me, because I'll be the only one who wants your ugly mug." I took a sip of coffee and glared at him.

Carly looked amused if not a little confused, she was well used to the threats. I never held to any of them, but I made plenty. Doc and John were openly confused, and Jack... Jack sat there with a perfectly smug look on his perfect face. I waved a spoon at him. "Tempt me, Jack...I dare ya," I said before turning to our companions to explain.

"In the pocket, the only Jack was good for was riling my temper." He snorted and I glared at him. "We were at lunch one day with Boss, err, Bob the pocket's creation that was my boss." I crinkled my brows and shook my head. "Anyway, Bob orders a salad. Jack gets a Reuben. And I order a cheeseburger with everything and bacon and fries.

"Jack here." I glared at him again waving my spoon threateningly. "Decides to make a dig at my love of food, and tells me that I need to have caution because 'too much eating will detract from your pretty.'" I took another bite and sat back.

I watched my companions carefully as the words sank in, waiting for them to under-stand what Jack had said. I caught Jack's eye and he winked at me again, grinning like a buffoon and looking so proud of himself he should have been sporting a gold medal.

Carly choked on her food and turned wide eyes to Jack. Doc and John gave him shocked looks, and he just smirked at them all. Perfectly confident and pleased with himself, I often accuse Jack of finding himself to be funnier than he truly is. He would always say that I had the same problem, he was really just confused. I know I am funny.

"Trust me, if you'd see the withdrawn little thing she was you would've picked fights too," Jack said self-assuredly. His eyes were crinkling in the corners, and he looked just moments away from cackling. Say what you will, men cackle and giggle. I've witnessed this often.

"But you called her FAT?!" Carly said. "Never call a woman fat, Jack. It's like rule number one!" She appeared so comically appalled that I almost started to laugh. Carly seemed more offended on my behalf than I had been when he said it.

He shrugged. "I also called her plain and boring. I called her a soft little girl. I told her that construction was no place for a cute face with big boobs. I asked if she got the job because of her great endowments." He shrugged again and leaned back in his chair.

I was about to crack and lose my seriousness, ruining the whole thing. I needed to stay focused, but the indignation on Carly's face and the looks of discomfort that Doc and John sported almost destroyed my self control.

Carly's mouth was hanging full open as she looked between us. She seemed completely at a loss for words. Not a common occurrence for that woman. It took a lot to shock the words from her, and if I weren't trying to be mad at Jack I would've congratulated him for the accomplishment.

"Oh yes, I also told her that she wore certain shirts so that said endowments could get some attention, and that it seemed they didn't get much so she should be glad they had gotten mine." He grinned like a child handed a piece of chocolate cake.

Carly made a weird choking gasping noise. I didn't know if we would soon need to do the Heimlich and cast her a worried glance. John gaped at Jack like he'd never seen him before and Doc took a small sip of water.

Clearing his throat uncomfortably Doc said, "John, I believe we should go before the blood shed starts." John chuckled a little and they left, taking our dogs with them. They seemed to almost run for the door, it was an amusing sight. The two older gentlemen running away like scandalized nuns in a pleasure house.

Jack smirked again and crossed his arms. Carly still seemed to be struggling for words. "As I said there Jack, awful. You were just being awful." I made a face at him and stuck my tongue out. It was an old fallback, and often just said things better than words. Though Jack usually made some comment about being childish before returning the gesture.

He wrinkled his nose, "Why awful? You've called me a lot of names but awful? Where did you even get that?" He had a look of consternation, though appeared not to be worried that I had called him awful just confused.

I sighed. "From Left." I looked up and both of them were now giving me a 'okay crazy lady' look. I rolled my eyes at them. "I'm not crazy." I told them about the dream, with the Left version of me and the Right version of me and how I had started to just call them Left and Right.

I explained how Left had called Right awful. That left was what Alex had tried to make me and he had mostly succeeded. I told them I suspected that when it felt like I had been torn in two, it was how Left and Right came to be and that Right had gone into the protected space where she could occasionally influence my life.

This time both were speechless, so I took another bite and focused on my food wholly. I felt exposed having told them about Left and Right, exposed and uncomfortable. Their chairs squeaked and shifted and then each had an arm around my shoulders.

"You really went through a lot," Carly said. "A lot we may never fully understand. But," She paused and Jack raised my chin, turning my face to look at him. There was true compassion and softness there, and a love so deep my chest ached.

"But," he said, as if picking up where Carly had stopped. "We love you, and we are more happy than you can imagine that you are back. We want to hear all of it, love." He smiled softly, "the good and the bad."

"And the ugly." Carly added, causing me to giggle. She was trying to lighten the mood I knew, and it was helping. I wasn't sure when, but I planned to someday tell them everything. I knew with full confidence that I had not felt in a long time, my friends would understand and still be there when the entire story was told. I just needed to be ready to open those wounds again.

Jack kissed my nose, and Carly gave me a half hug before they shifted their chairs back and continued to eat breakfast. Jack had piled his plate with eggs and bacon and sausage, Carly had similarly piled hers though she had chosen only bacon instead. I didn't know where the five-foot nothing woman beside me put all the food she managed to eat, but I was jealous that she never seemed to get fat.

"I don't know that I deserve you two," I said, my voice thick with emotion. "But I will always be grateful for you." I smiled and we finished eating in a comfortable silence. I vowed silently that we would all survive this and we wouldn't be separated again.

After breakfast it was back to business and we ran around HQ like chicken with their heads cut off. There was so much to finalize before we were to 'meet on the field of battle' as some would say. I prayed it wasn't a true battle, that everything went as planned and we got enough of their number to not need a real fight.

We made plans for a fight though. Figuring out how to arm our people and how much. We worked over plans for the appearance or not of Phae fighters. No one knew if they would be fighting with their armies, or just directing from behind. It was really too bad the opal had no effect on them.

The days flew by, blurring into one meeting after the next. Jack, Carly and I continued to all sleep in one bed alternating who's. We weren't ready to let each other out of sight, and I knew they both worried I would act like a fool and go off on my own again. Despite reassurances that I wouldn't.

On June 18th, we had a final meeting and since this was the last before we sent our

HQ people to where they needed to go we were in a large conference room. There were about thirty people crammed inside and many different conversations going at once. It matched the regular chaos. "No!" I shouted. "Absolutely not, John!" Though there had been other conversations and we were in a bigger room my words broke through the noise and echoed on the walls. Every head turned to me, but I was too angry to feel shy.

"Kel," John started, using a reasonable tone that just made me angrier. His face was calm, but his eyes were wary. He was trying to get me to see his point of view, but had the idea I would only fight back.

"No! NO!" I said, the last now almost a scream. I was shaking and had jumped out of my chair. I now leaned on my fists across the table to glare at John.

"Kel," He tried again. A look of exhaustion passing over his features. I wanted to smack John. How dare he be exhausted with me. They had been planning this without telling me, and then just decided to drop a bombshell in my lap and I was supposed to be okay with it?!

I shook my head violently. I could feel panic starting to take hold and my breathing was getting shorter and harsher. Arms closed in from behind me and beside me, Jack and Carly were there. I kept shaking my head.

"Hush, love," Jack said in my ear, a soft whisper meant just for me. "Listen to what he has to say." Jack was the one holding me from behind and Carly was on my right, her arms wrapped around us both.

"Kel, just listen for a minute," John said. "You can't be there. The opal will kill you too, remember?" John sounded reasonable and calm, but all I could process was Jack and Carly would be on the front and I was to stay behind.

All I could hear in my head was my vow to never be separated and here we were facing separation. I couldn't speak, I could barely breathe. It was like a nightmare. John was right, of course, I was a cross and the opal would be lethal to me. But that didn't stop my panic.

"Then they stay with me," I choked out in a hoarse whisper. I couldn't explain the irrational fear I felt, I just knew somewhere deep inside that things would not be okay. Something would go wrong, it always did. It's not that I was more willing to sacrifice others in the place of Jack and Carly, I just couldn't survive without them.

Carly shook her head and I felt Jack make a similar motion. "We have to be there Kel," she said. "The plan doesn't work without us."

I felt her arms tighten; it was a small comfort. I knew they didn't want to leave any more than I wanted them too. They felt they had no choice.

The plan she spoke of, placed her and Jack on the front at the gate deemed most likely to have the largest army and potential Phae. They would be there to fight if it came down to it and to report back to HQ on the situation.

They would be halfway around the world from me, because it had been determined I would stay at HQ. Apparently everyone thought if I was close to a fight I would charge in. They might be right but that didn't mean I liked the idea.

Jack and Carly were also to be there in case Alex showed he would know Jack's face. They wanted to capture him but barring that would kill him instead. The thought of Jack or Carly in close proximity to Alex made me ill.

"I have to be there," I whispered, I knew somewhere inside I was being illogical and irrational but from the moment the plan was revealed I had felt like something would go terribly wrong. "What if something happens? I'll be here, and I might not even know. And then I'll find out too late, but I could maybe do something if I'm there!"

"Kel," Jack said soothingly behind me. "Love, we will be in constant contact. The only difference will be you won't our pretty faces." He didn't promise that nothing would happen, he didn't say that they would make it back.

My knees buckled and my companions unprepared for it let me fall to the floor. I drew my knees to my chest and stared at the table legs, conversations resumed above me. It sounded a little stilted like no one really knew what to make of my hysterics.

Carly and Jack squatted down next to me. "Never separated," I said sadly. "Never apart. You said I can't leave and you've both been planning this for a while and didn't tell me." I felt my eyes burn and a tear roll down my cheek.

Neither said anything, I don't think there was anything left to say they just hugged me while I fell apart. I was sure something would go wrong, it always seemed to when we were apart.

I felt broken inside again, but different from in the pocket. This wasn't Left and Right fighting for dominion over me. This was me and the two most important parts of me being yanked apart. Call it fate or cruel coincidence, whatever. I just knew that I needed them and they were leaving.

CHAPTER 17

Calling me a nervous wreck was an insult to nervous wrecks, I was a walking disaster. Jack, Carly and I had spent the rest of the 18th together and early on the 19th they departed for the Asian continent.

It was now the morning of the 20th. All we knew was that today was the day. We didn't know when specifically, and now it was just a waiting game until the Phae and cross showed their faces.

Jack and Carly had called last night when they landed, and I hadn't slept at all. I had lain awake half the night in Jack's bed and the other half in Carly's. The dogs had been a mess too, they just knew I was upset and they couldn't comfort me. I had broken up two fights between them.

When I came to the control room this morning I had shut Kujack in Jack's room and Gordito in mine. I couldn't risk them fighting while I was gone, and I didn't think them being here would be any better.

I paced back and forth, unable to hold still. My hands ached, partly from the fists I was constantly making and partly because I had ripped all my nails off with my teeth, and some of them went to the quick and had bled. It was a nervous habit.

The eyes of the ten men in the control tracked my progress, no one said a word. I had seen someone pass a message by paper, and someone else got so close to another's ear only that person would hear them.

John came in at about eight AM, I had been there at least hours but I wasn't really sure how long it had been. John paused inside the door and took in what was going on.

He made a little wave with his hand and the ten men turned to their computers, now studiously ignoring me.

John approached, cautiously like I might attack him. He probably wasn't far off. I didn't know if I would or not either. But as I thought about it, it would take too much effort. I was angry at John. I had no doubt it was his idea to have Jack and Carly at the door, but I couldn't find the energy to do more than be angry.

"Kel," he said kindly. "Dear, sit, you are pale as a sheet and wearing holes in my floor." He pulled a chair out for me to sit, and got settled in one himself. "Look, I brought coffee and food. I figured when I didn't see you at breakfast this is where you would be. Please sit." He kept his tone calm and quiet as if he was talking to a skittish animal.

I obeyed him and sat, not because I wanted to sit but because doing what someone else said took responsibility from me. I was not just obeying orders rather than acting consciously. It is sometimes easier to just do as a person says than to think of the action itself.

A mug slid over in front of me and a plate stacked with eggs, bacon, toast, and country potatoes followed. I made a face at the plate. "How can I eat, John?" I asked. I lifted the mug and took a cautious sip of the coffee. I wanted to make sure it wouldn't also turn my stomach. "I should be there," I said, not for the first time since they had left.

John patted my hand, "you need to eat Kel, I think it will be a long day and you need strength." He didn't respond to my comment about there, he hadn't the last times I said it. No one would respond anymore in fact, they would neither agree or disagree but I couldn't stop repeating the phrase.

I picked at the plate of food, and sipped the coffee. I managed to consume enough to satisfy John without making myself sick. Reports had been coming in hourly about no change, and I had begun to worry that Alex knew we knew and had changed tactics.

Despite what Jack had said I was not in constant contact; it was spotty at best and I vowed to punch him in his face when he came back. Around noon I heard Jack's voice report that a door had appeared, and then all stations reported the same. Nothing else, just doors, but every door was where I had said it would be.

I released a heavy breath. That was progress, and it showed we were in the right areas still. That was good, we stood a chance then. I gave a tight smile to John, who squeezed my knee reassuringly. We had placed some people in areas that might have been added just in case, and they all reported no news.

Three hours, that felt like three lifetimes crept by with the same hourly reports. No change, then from the Alaskan door word came. They were coming through the door. The comms all buzzed then with reports.

I paled and John's face tightened, it was even more than we had imagined. Tens of thousands at every door and they kept coming in. I thought I would be sick, and more desperately than ever before I had the desire to be there. To see this and protect my loved ones.

"John, this is Jack. Pick up a quiet line."

Jack's voice sounded through the speakers. A quiet line is basically just a phone call, a way to have a private talk. I scrambled for one and clicked on Jack's comm code. John was calmer as he connected.

"Go ahead Jack," John said quietly. He met my eyes, worry shining bright. What could be so bad Jack had asked for a private line?

"Is Kel there?" Jack asked and the tone said he would try to hide this from me. I frantically shook my head begging John not to tell him I was listening. I had to know what was happening. I was already falling apart, and not knowing... it just wasn't an option.

He gave a tight smile and a slight nod. "No Jack, she stepped out. What is going on?" His voice didn't crack on the lie, or give any indication of lying. I was grateful to John then, and my anger melted giving way to fear for Jack and Carly and the events yet to come.

Jack heaved a sigh, and I vowed to punch him twice over now. How dare he think to keep a secret from me at this time! I silently plotted his demise, my fear making me imagine the worst. Something must have happened to Carly then, and I would stab Jack with a spoon for trying to hide it.

"John," Jack's tone was heavy. "Mary is here, and so is Alex. This is definitely where they planted the largest force. I didn't want to tell Kel that Mary and Alex are together. It would only hurt her, and I think she's suffered enough. Carly isn't dealing well." The heaviness that followed Jack's declaration was suffocating.

Mary and Alex were together? I had long thought maybe she had been the mole, but to have it confirmed was like a punch to the gut. I had been so prepared to hear bad news about Carly, that when Jack spoke of Mary and Alex I stopped breathing.

I felt like a fish out of water, gasping and heaving. No air would enter my lungs. I tried and I tried, and still it was like there was an invisible barrier. My head started to a low buzz, and in panic I tried to focus on the last part of the conversation.

"We still plan to fight him, John." Jack said, "we'll bring him and Mary in if possible." There was a long pause. "Tell Kel I love her okay, John?" His voice sounded beaten and ragged, the battle hadn't started and Jack already sounded beat.

"Jack, that sounds like a goodbye." John said with alarm in his voice. He was gripping the receiver tight enough his knuckles went white. He was staring at me, but I don't think he saw my own panic through his.

"I really hope it's not John, we need to go. I have to get Carly and we need to go." The line clicked, and Jack's voice went silent.

There is always a part in movies when bad news is delivered over the phone, that the line goes silent. There is no tone, or static or any sign the line was ever live. Just silence, it's like a premonition of death, that sound. Anytime you hear it you know something is about to go very very wrong.

I tried to say something or do something. But my mind had gone still, and my body wouldn't respond to my commands. I sat there, holding the receiver as the horror of what was happening sunk in.

I don't know what happened next, I think I started to scream and then someone gave me a sedative, I really need to work on not being sedated all the time. Then it was just emptiness in my head. I was still in the control room and the opal was being released. But I couldn't process that, every part of me listened for Jack's voice.

I heard cheers and shouts. The opal was doing the job. By the thousands cross were dying and the playing field was evening out. There was some scuffle at every door, where a couple Phae had come with the army, but we lost none of our own.

But the Asian channels, Jack's channels, gave no report. No word came from them good or bad, and it seemed the whole world was holding its breath. And then in the way things, everything imploded.

The lines filled alternately with cheers and screams. It seemed the opal was effective but the cross were still an overwhelming number and a skirmish had broken out. The field had turned to hand to hand, knife and sword and dagger. Nothing made sense, no reports gave a picture clear enough. And Jack's voice didn't come through.

There were reports that the cross had caught on to the opal release, and some had managed to get out of drop range. It seems the cross at Jack's location were the oldest and most well trained, and things were starting to go badly for us.

I sat in my chair listening to everything and unable to react or respond, except for the silent tears that fell down my cheeks. Where were Jack and Carly? Were they dead in the field and because of the chaos no one had noticed yet? Or had they made it Alex, and he had captured them? He would know Jack's face, and Mary would know Carly's.

It felt like centuries passed while the battle raged, screams and cheers and pain and fear. It all filled my head and I felt like I would burst from the overwhelming sounds and feelings. I stared blankly at the comms devices, waiting.

Then the sounds changed again. There was less fear and pain, more elation and screams of rage and warriors on the hunt. Reports came in that the cross who had avoided the opal drop had gotten turned and were walking through the powder and dropping like flies.

Someone from our side got the idea to coat a weapon and his hands in the powder and word had spread. Every punch or stab was not fatal. I felt a trickle of relief and hope start to ebb my panic, but still there was no word of Jack and Carly.

Every other door started to report victory, any cross still alive had been rounded up and taken prisoner. All Phae killed or fled and the doors closed. It was as if they had been on a timer, and now the time was coming due and they were set to auto close. That was a new one, and rather useful knowledge.

Whatever I had been given this time to stop the panic, began to wear off and I felt my heart begin to race. Everything was coming to end in our favor, so where were Jack and Carly? I had just gotten them back, and the thought of losing them was ice water to my veins and acid to my stomach.

John got a private call, and I watched him as the speaker talked. His face paled and he went very still. His eyes flicked to me, and I knew that whatever was being said was about Jack and Carly. I knew that in the same way that I knew it was not good news, good news was reported over the speakers. Only bad news came from private lines.

I lurched to my feet, and stumbled towards him. I fell halfway to him and crawled the rest of the way, my legs were not responding well yet. I grabbed John's free hand and turned my face up to his, pleading silently that I was wrong. But I knew I wasn't and when suddenly Doc was there, I knew more assuredly than I was about my name that something was very very wrong.

No one told me what was so bad, in fact after that realization had sunk in I blacked out. The word is I started to lose it, I was yelling at John and Doc and telling them it was their fault. I said I'd never forgive them for keeping me away. They tell me I even started to throw chairs and tried to break the computers and communication equipment.

That was why Doc was there, he had brought another sedative. John's news had been so bad that he had had Doc show up ready to knock me out. I had woken in a hospital bed, strapped to it like you see in movies with the crazy person who is a danger to themselves and everyone else. I was apparently that person.

As the anger at this kind of entrapment had me thrashing and yelling, a needle was again pushed into my arm. The fluid was cold, and I swear I felt it rush through my entire body this time before the world went dark. A small reasonable side of me stood back and watched, shaking her head.

Right was there looking at me when the latest dose of sedative cooled my blood. She had a disapproving frown and was tapping her foot. I didn't see Left. I couldn't look at her, I couldn't bring myself to be faced with the mess I had become.

"You're back to being her again?" She sneered. "Back to crying and screaming and hiding? I thought we got past this? You have to be logical! We have to be strong! What would Jack and Carly say if they saw you now? Do you think they would be proud?" The catty creature had gone straight to heart with that blow.

I looked away from her, "how do we survive without them?" I asked and I realized I spoke in the whiny desperate voice of Left. I was disgusted with myself for that. I was no longer the observer I was Left.

She dropped down in front of me, "because we have to. There is no other choice, no other option. No matter what happened, we have to survive. We have to make sure the world survives." She placed her hands on either side of my face, turning it so I was forced to stare into my own eyes. Her face was set in fierce determination.

Her eyes were something I was so unfamiliar with, they didn't appear weeping and broken. They had fire and light and purpose. I closed my own so I wouldn't see hers, I didn't want to think what she would see. The lack of light, the sign of someone who had given up.

"Why do we have to take the responsibility? Why can't it be someone else's turn?" I asked her. I felt so tired of always having to survive, of having to be reasonable and in charge.

She slapped me then, and I swear a part of my consciousness felt it. "Because that's who we are. Get back with the program!" I felt the mental slap again. "Get up and do something Kel! This is not who we are!"

I could hear voices around me, and as I started to wake I felt the restraints still holding me down. Right was, well right, I had to stop being weak and giving in. I could handle whatever news they had for me. I would handle it.

I cleared my throat. "Excuse me, the resident crazy lady is dying of thirst. Can someone help me out?" I asked, I couldn't see the source of the voices with my curtains drawn so I looked at the ceiling as I spoke. I had tried to make my tone light and joking.

I knew that Right had been once again right. I had to be strong and I had to keep going, I hoped the people around me would forgive my weakness and abuse. I was still re-learning who I was and had to be. It was a painful process.

The curtains parted, and a nurse came in. She appeared hesitant and I felt ashamed. I had hurt these people, and they were just trying to help me. "I'm so sorry," I said quietly. "I know that doesn't make anything better or right, but I truly am sorry. You all deserve so much better than I have given since arriving here. I promise to get better." I hung my head.

I heard her move closer and the restraints on my wrist were loosened and removed. I looked up and smiled. "Thank you," I said. She only smiled and handed me a glass of water before leaving and closing the curtains again.

I sipped my water slowly, and a few minutes later Doc and John entered. I watched them deciphering how I felt. I was still angry, and I could tell they didn't have good news. But I no longer felt violence towards them.

I kept silent as I stared at them, refusing to be the first to speak. John shifted on his feet and Doc fiddled with paperwork and checked the machines. When he had gone through all of them and could no longer put it off, Doc looked at me.

"Kel," He began, a hesitation I didn't like in his tone. "Kel, the battle ended and we won. We lost a lot of people. The count is up to 1,000 and some are still not thought to survive their injuries. The doors have all closed, and we've almost completed recovering what of the opal powder we can." He swallowed hard. He was telling me about things I didn't care about.

John cleared his throat and I turned to look at him, "Jack and Carly disappeared before the battle broke out fully. When the battle ended no one knew where they were there was no sign of Alex or Mary." John swallowed, I had felt my face tighten and assumed by his look I was wearing my murder face. "A search was launched, and they found Jack. He was wounded and unconscious, but alive." John hesitated and seemed not to want to say the next words.

"Carly is gone, Kel," Doc said quietly. "She couldn't be found one way or another, we think..." He heaved a sigh. "We think Alex and Mary took her." He wouldn't meet my eyes as he said this, I didn't blame him.

It took everything I had left not to start screaming again, but I was working on strong Kel. Reasonable Kel. I could manage reasonable, couldn't I? I started a mantra in the back of my head. Strong Kel, reasonable Kel. Over and Over I said it.

"Where is Jack?" I asked, a steadiness in my voice that surprised even me. I looked from Doc to John. They were gaping at me. Apparently a calm question was not the response they expected.

"He's here, Kel," Doc said, cautiously. He was fidgeting with his hands, not quite wringing them but he wouldn't stop moving them either. When he caught me staring at the movements he hid them behind his back, but the muscles moving in his arms said the fidgeting continued.

"Well," I said expectantly, swinging my legs off the bed. "Take me to him." I grabbed the roller stand with my IV connected to it and moved towards the curtains. Whether they followed or not I would find Jack.

"Kel," John started, I cut him off with a violent shake of my head. My reasonable side was slipping and if I didn't see Jack soon they would probably have to knock me out again.

"No. You will take me to him, or I will find someone else that will." I hissed through a clenched jaw. Whatever emotions or look I had on my face stopped further arguments and I was led to Jack's room. I was still weak and exhausted and so I can't remember the path we took, but suddenly I was looking at Jack's face.

He was pale, and his features drawn tight as if in pain. His eyelids fluttered back and forth so fast it appeared he was reading with his eyes closed. There were small bandages everywhere, but I didn't see the wound that would've felled him.

"We've had to keep him sedated as well," Doc said behind me. "He kept trying to leave his bed, he suffered a deep wound to the abdomen and every time he would try to go, he tore his stitches out." Doc sounded defeated and sad, and for a moment I wanted to forgive him. But then I thought about Carly and that she was missing and the moment passed.

"Leave," I said without turning around. Jack was in a room with a door, and when I heard the door close I crossed over to him. I walked slowly, every step a stab in my heart. I should've been there to help and protect him.

I arranged my IV roller near the bed and carefully climbed in beside him. Jack had been almost panting since I entered the room, but when I lay next to him and held one hand in mine his breathing started to slow and his eyes stopped rolling.

"I'm here my love," I whispered in his ear, and felt the tear splash on his pillow. "You rest now, we need you to get better." I kissed his cheek and carefully lay on my side draping an arm across his chest. I rested my chin against his shoulder and cried.

I had almost lost Jack, he had almost died out there and I had been home 'safe and sound'. I had lost Carly, and I would find a way to get her back. Jack and I both would. I closed my eyes and must've slept.

A hand brushed my cheek, and I startled awake. Jack's groan brought reality slamming back in. "Oh God! Jack! I'm so sorry." I settled and kissed his cheek. I had come to comfort Jack and instead, when he was actually being nice I had only hurt him.

"I was trying to avoid that woman." He groused at me, turning his head to face me. "Why are you so jumpy anyway?" I guessed Jack didn't know that the last few people to touch me had been doing so only to give me sedatives.

I glared at him, I didn't have an answer to that, but now that he was awake I was mad at him. "Jack, when you are better I will kick your ass." I growled. I felt tears start again. "You left me here, and then you shut me out and didn't want me to know what happened! And then!," I almost shouted. "You tried to get yourself killed!" I cried harder and Jack pulled my head to his shoulder.

"I'm so sorry Kel," he said soothingly, "Please don't cry love. I'm here now. I made it back." He was stroking my cheek in a distressed way. Like he knew I needed the comfort, but he had no idea how to offer it.

I could sympathize with that, before the wall in my head had collapsed I had wanted to soothe and comfort Jack. But it had been my fault he was distressed and I didn't have the first idea how to undo that.

"But Carly didn't," I said in a hushed whisper. "They couldn't find her and everyone believes Alex got her." My voice choked off. Saying her name aloud was a physical pain. Ever since Carly and I had repaired our relationship we'd always been able to find the other. And now she is gone.

His hand stilled. "Are you sure?" He asked in a choked voice. There was pain and anger in his tone and a touch of fear. We both knew nothing good could happen to Carly in captivity.

I nodded my head against him. "They've almost finished cleaning the battle grounds and she is nowhere to be seen. Including among the dead and wounded." I sighed sadly and tucked my face into the crook of his neck.

Jack swore softly, and his hand balled to a fist on my cheek. "I told her to leave, that stubborn infuriating little woman!" His voice held no venom despite his words, only sadness. I wanted to squeeze that sadness from him, but I held back. I figured squeezing would just hurt him again.

I wrapped my arm tighter across him. "What happened Jack?" I asked, I needed to know. I had to understand what went wrong, I needed to know why there was so much sadness there.

He sighed heavily. "It's a bit of a long story, so bear with me love." He turned his head and gave me a soft kiss. Then he chuckled, "Are you even supposed to be in here?" He asked me. He gave me a look that said, 'are you going to be in trouble'?

I glared, "They don't dare tell me to leave." My face must've given away my hurt and betrayal at John and Doc because Jack stroked my cheek and kissed me again. "I am not leaving Jack, and if you think you will tell me too... I'll... I'll... I'll..." I glared at him struggling for words. "I'll break one of your toes!"

It was the only place that didn't seem to be very hurt and would be extra damaged if I touched it, but I could make a point.

"Viscous," he said with a smirk, not at all taking me seriously. "We all wanted to protect you, love, you can't blame them completely," he said in a soft and soothing voice.

I snarled at him, "Oh I blame you and Carly plenty! You all left me here. They had to sedate me Jack! Multiple times, to say I handled things badly falls into understatement of the year. I would punch you for that, except you're already in a lot of pain!" I closed my eyes again, I was still so angry at everyone.

"I'm sorry, Love. But even if I had to do it again, I would choose the same. Better to have you here and maximize the chance we all survived, than for you to be out there pretty much guaranteed to die." I felt him kiss my cheek and sigh.

I growled. He was right of course but I didn't have to admit that. "Just tell me what happened," I said. I was running out of patience for people telling me I was right to stay behind. I didn't care at this point, I just wanted to be mad at them.

Jack sighed again. "When the door appeared it just seemed off. It was like I could feel it the whole distance between me and it, and when their forces started to appear I understood why. The door was easily ten times the size of any door we've ever seen and they were spilling like ants from a hill.

"It was a terrifying and awe-inspiring sight to behold. There were at least a fifty thousand cross there. And then when they finally stopped coming through and we thought that was the worst of it, a male we recognized came across followed by a female."

He sighed again, and squeezed my hand. "It was Alex and Mary, Kel. They were together on that field." There was a strangeness to his tone.

Jack had never gotten as close to Mary as he had Carly. But Mary and I had been close once, and because of her importance in my life she had been important to her. But the way that her betrayal had hurt Carly and I, it had hurt him most to see us upset.

He was angered when she left, and disappointed. But he was more distressed at the pain and hurt that Carly and I experienced. Our bond had been close, and similar to the way it felt when Jack and Carly vanished on the battlefield we had broken when she left.

"I know," I said. "I was listening when you told John, I owe you for trying to hide that from me." I squeezed his hand hard, trying to convey all my anger and hurt that he had tried to keep me from knowing.

He gave a wry chuckle. "I should've known that you would listen and John wouldn't say otherwise," he sighed again. "When Carly saw Mary, she kind of went out of touch for a while. She just went, umm empty? That's not right but it's close." He paused searching for a better word.

"No, empty is close enough. Anyway, I let her just deal while I called John and then I went and got her back on the goal. Mary was a shock but not a game changer. We still needed to try and capture Alex.

"So I got Carly snapped out of it, and we took off across the field. It was sloo going because we had to be sure not to be seen. And we were now avoiding two sets of roaming eyes. But finally we made it and got to a hidden spot to observe.

"We were too far away to hear what they said when they spoke, neither looked happy though and both seemed to be searching for something. I truly think they were searching for you. They kept pacing and scanning and looking at our lines, like they expected someone to appear.

"Then a signal was given, and that's when the battle went crazy. Nothing seemed to be going to plan, excluding the mass numbers we hadn't anticipated it just fell apart. We saw some cross break away and avoid the opal release. And things started to become hand to hand, it was pure madness.

"We knew we could do nothing for the battle on the field, so we went back to focusing on Alex. At some point Mary had disappeared, we honestly thought she had just gone back through the door." He shook his head. "She hadn't, and we learned that when we left our hiding place to confront Alex.

"I stepped out first and yelled, catching his attention. He had a look of such deep hatred I should've just withered on the spot. I told him I was there to capture or kill him and I didn't care which except that killing sounded more fun.

"He had laughed at me, and ran right for me. We started fighting and I lost track of everything except him, and then I got a blow to the guts that sent me reeling backwards. Carly came out then and I realized our mistake, as soon as Carly was unhidden I saw Mary.

"She had been waiting, and only looked a little surprised to see Carly. That's why I think they were searching for you. She raised a weapon of some kind at Carly, and I told Carly to run and get away. I was so intent on that, I missed the slice Alex gave me.

"I fell from my knees where I had been backwards, and I could feel blood start to soak my clothing and I was staring at the sky. Alex appeared over me, and he told me he would leave me here to die slowly and think about what would happen to you when he found you again.

"He promised he would make you suffer. And then he was gone, and I couldn't hear or see anything. I was on fire, and the pain across my abdomen was boiling lava. Eventually I blacked out, and I woke up here. Every time I tried to get answers or leave I was knocked out again, and then I woke to find you here." His voice sounded weary and depressed.

"Carly had turned when I yelled so she wasn't immediately hit with whatever Mary had, but she must've tried to fight them. Or she got caught running away, but I doubt that, she doesn't listen well and doesn't like to run away."

I was crying again, and sniffled into Jack's neck. "Promise me we will find her Jack?" I asked him. "We have to find her," I said softly. "He's a monster Jack, and I can't hardly stand the thought of him having her. I..." I broke off, unable to finish my thought.

His head turned, "Look at me Kel," he commanded, I opened my eyes and stared at his blue green depths. "Whatever it takes, we will find her! And we will make them all pay for taking her, and if anything happens to her we will make them regret it!" His tone was fierce vengeance and anger.

We stayed like that staring at each other, each thinking on the promise to find Carly, until we drifted to sleep. It was a peaceful sleep, though always in the back of my mind I worried for Carly.

Jack's recovery was slow, and took months. We were both impatient to start our search but he needed to be at full health. No news came from the Phae, no disappearances were recorded. It was all suspiciously quiet, and gave another sense of urgency for Jack to recover.

We planned and plotted and made arrangements, and finally five months after Carly had been taken and Jack injured he was healed enough to leave and we could begin our search. It was now November, and I prayed Carly had survived so long.

EPILOGUE

I screamed and yanked the chains on the wall again. They were attached to cuffs on my wrists, but like the cuffs the chain and anchors in the wall were unmovable. I didn't know long I had been here. I had woken in a cell cuffs on my wrists, a threadbare white gown on and a tray of food nearby.

I had been so hungry that before I could think more about the situation I had scarfed down the food. It was a small fare, a piece of bread and some lumpy porridge-like substance. I didn't think too hard about that, I needed to eat.

When I had finished the sad meal I had tried calling for someone, anyone to come tell me where I was. There had been no answer, and so I had started to scream and yank on the chains attached to the wall.

It felt like hours had passed since I had woken here, my wrists were now raw and bloody and my throat ached. I realized I hadn't been given water with the small fare of food. I stopped and finally took note of my settings.

It was a small cell, maybe ten by ten, and even then my chains only allowed for me to move half way from the far wall towards the door. There was a lump of straw and some blankets in one corner, I had woken up on that, and a large pot in another.

My stomach turned as I realized what the pot was there for, there was no bathroom in this cell. There was also no window, or way to tell time. It could be the middle of the night or day right now, and I had no idea which.

I screamed again for good measure, I hoped it was the middle of the night and I was keeping my captors awake. I walked back to the pile of straw and tried to get comfortable.

I should sleep, maybe when I woke I could get someone to tell me what had happened and where I was.

I dreamed of the battle, I saw Jack go down and I ran to help him. He had yelled at me to leave and pointed at something. When I turned I had seen Mary pointing something at me, just missing her shot.

I heard Alex yell in triumph and saw Jack fall back bleeding from what looked like a stomach wound. I screamed, forgetting Mary and tried to get to Jack. But something cold and wet hit the back of my neck and I fell on my face. The world went fuzzy and then dark.

"Wake up!" A loud gruff voice startled me from sleep. "They want to see you now, stand up!"

I opened my eyes, the voice belonged to a tall male. He had long greasy white blonde hair and a scarred face. It might have been a ruggedly handsome face if he hadn't been sneering at me.

He had dark purple, almost black eyes and a pointed nose. His cheek bones were sharp and matched the sharp jaw lines. His mouth was full red lips that should've smiled more, I could tell the lines around his eyes and mouth were from frowns and not smiles. He had a slim lithe body, and looked like he could be a runner. And I hated every inch of him.

I spat at him and rolled over, facing the wall. There was a tug and sharp pain and I was on my feet, his hand fisted in my hair down to the skull. I clenched my jaw; the pain was excruciating but I wouldn't let him see that.

"I said to stand up," He snarled from behind.

He shoved me and I put my hands up so my face didn't meet the stone wall. As if the wall was covered in the fastest setting super glue as soon as my hands touched I couldn't pull them free. I tried yanking back with everything I had, I even braced my feet on the wall and tried to free myself that way. I only wound up with a deep ache in my shoulders and the sound of the male's laugh in my ears.

"You humans really are pathetic little creatures," he said with amusement.

His hands appeared at my wrists and with a touch the chains disconnected from the cuffs falling to the floor. And before I could register it my hands were free of the wall and he had pulled them behind me where the cuffs then felt linked together.

"I told you they want to see you, human. Let's go." He barked as I realized what had happened.

A hand on my cuffs was used to propel me forward, and I was forced out of the cell and down a stone hall. We took so many turns and twists I was lost, and suspected this was on purpose. They wouldn't want me to know where to go should I escape brute behind me. I didn't know his name.

I was yanked to a stop in front of two large wooden doors and growled. "That was unnecessary, I obviously wouldn't have walked into the doors!" I snapped, my wrists ached and it felt like they might be bleeding again.

I felt a blow on the back of my head, and my forehead connected with one of the doors. Stars exploded in front of my eyes, and my vision swam. My ears were ringing as I was again shoved forward by the cuffs. I kept shaking my head slowly trying to clear it.

I pulled to a stop, and was forced to my knees. I growled again and continued to shake my head. Slowly my vision was returning, as it did, I wished it hadn't.

I was on the stone floor of a large audience room before a raised a dais. On the dais were two chairs occupied by a male and female. I recognized them both, it was Alex and Mary. My gut churned, I felt like I might be sick and leaned forward.

I pressed my forehead to the floor; I had been captured and this enemy didn't play by our rules. I would be lucky to survive today, or perhaps unlucky to survive. I closed my eyes and swallowed back more bile as it raised to coat my throat.

There was another yank on my hair and I was pulled back up to kneeling, my head held so tightly I could only look at the dais and the figures in front me. Alex was smiling, it was a cold cruel and malicious smile. Mary sneered at me, like I was a bug to be squashed. I spit in her direction. Alex chuckled as the male behind let go of my hair and kicked me, sending me sprawling closer to the dais. Then he was back his fist in my hair and forced me to look at them. Mary was smirking now.

"You must be Carly!" Alex said cheerfully, as if he were excited to meet me. "I've heard a lot about you Carly, I admit I was disappointed it was you and not Kel there." His face curled into a look of a fury before he forced another smile. "Though I supposed that opal powder wouldn't have been good for her either," he said a snarl curling one lip. "Nasty trick that, I imagine it was Kel's idea too."

I caught a look of anger and hatred on Mary's face as Alex talked about the opal powder. She was a traitor through and through then, angry we had defeated the enemy.

I smirked at Alex, "it was indeed. She's a pretty smart girl." I put every ounce of defiance in my look as I could muster. I wouldn't let him see anything more than that, I wouldn't give him the satisfaction.

Alex's nostrils flared, "Don't test me Carly, or did Kel tell you nothing of me?" He raised an eyebrow. "Oh she didn't!" He clapped his hands like that was fantastic news. "You'll get to experience it all first-hand then."

He stood and walked off the dais. I was yanked to my feet and he halted in front of me. "She'll come looking for you." Alex said softly. "But until then, you and I will have some fun together." He ran one finger down my cheek, looked at the brute behind me and said, "you know where to take her Garrick." He turned and left then, Mary following without another look at me.

"You're a traitor Mary, and I will make you sorry you ever betrayed us!" I screamed after them. My voice cracking from my raw throat. Mary didn't even turn to look at me as they left.